THE HIDDEN SPRING

Tabitha Summerfield had already selected her husband: William Kirkwood, son of a newly rich brewer. But her father had other ideas, and he little suspected how dangerous it would be to thwart the wishes of a young woman who would stop at nothing to achieve her own ends.

When Edgar Summerfield died in horrible agony Tabitha was at first frightened by the enormity of what she had done. But her crime remained undetected, and the next time someone stood between her and her desires, it seemed so much easier...

THE HIDDEN SPRING

The Hidden Spring

by
Elizabeth Ann Hill

9010020030

MAGNA PRINT BOOKS
Long Preston, North Yorkshire,
England.

British Library Cataloguing in Publication Data.

Hill, Elizabeth Ann
   The hidden spring.
   I. Title
   823'.914(F)

   ISBN 1-85057-455-3
   ISBN 1-85057-456-1 Pbk

First Published in Great Britain by Souvenir Press Ltd. 1987.

Published in Large Print 1988 by arrangement with Souvenir Press Ltd. London.

Printed and bound in Great Britain by
Redwood Burn Limited, Trowbridge, Wiltshire.

'She's more than a rose, she's a garden,' William once said. 'All freshness and perfume and colour.'

He forgot that nettles and brambles and poisonous weeds may grow among the flowers, and in all their years together he never guessed that his 'garden' was watered by a hidden spring, a lively little fountain-head of wickedness.

CHAPTER 1

From the way the sunlight slanted through the leaves above her, Tabitha guessed that it was somewhere near four o'clock. She stretched and sighed, drowsy with the warmth of summer and satisfaction. These lovely afternoons always passed too quickly and normally she would have been content to stay for an hour longer. Today, however, she was stirred to move early by the prospect of a very special treat. A party was a rare event for Tabitha, and this particular occasion held a possible far-reaching importance to her life which made it a very pressing matter indeed.

Slowly she rolled over to lean across the man sleeping beside her in the hollow their coupling bodies had made amongst the long grass.

He was nearly twice Tabitha's age; a man of thirty years to her sixteen. The difference in their social status was clear in the contrast of his rough-woven shirt and faded corduroy trousers with the expensive yellow silk of her dress. Hard work and weather had toughened and browned him in stark comparison to the

9

girl's creamy and much-protected skin, while his chest and forearms bore a springy growth of black hair.

Tabitha loved that. His very coarseness was exciting to her; the calloused hands, the strong, plain features and, most of all, the sustained jolting energy which made him such a rewarding partner. Papa would be insanely angry, she thought gleefully, if he knew what she had been doing these past few months, with whom, and how much she had enjoyed it.

Tabitha Summerfield had spent many a pleasurable afternoon with Daniel Coates, the wheelwright, and she looked forward to many more. Daniel was a Devonshire man. He had come here to Cornwall with his family when Tabitha was only twelve years old, yet even then she had noticed him with more than childlike interest. Naturally she would wed someone within, or close to, her own class, but she saw no reason why marriage should preclude a little dalliance, providing one had a manageable husband.

Sadly though, such partners were not easy to find, as Tabitha was sharply aware. In this year of 1871, a woman's life was firmly controlled. She existed in narrow confines of behaviour, supervised first by Papa and then by the man she married. Tabitha resented this discipline which stifled thought and ability, thwarted every craving, denied her any freedom and labelled her subordinate. She had long since decided that her happiness would depend upon capturing a kindly spouse, hence the importance of this evening's social gathering.

The man still slept and she studied him appreciatively for a moment. A fine healthy animal and source of boundless enjoyment, she thought fondly. He was married, of course, with four children, but that was unimportant. In fact it was a safeguard, for he was one of Papa's tenants, with a nice tied cottage and decent wages that he would not wish to lose. Daniel would never say or do anything indiscreet.

Taking a tuft of the curling hair on his chest, she wrapped it round her finger and pulled. He gave a start, opened one eye, and then grinned to find her bending over him.

'I hope you've a good reason for waking me, madam. Is there something you need? State your pleasure and I'll do my humble best.'

'Tireless and ever willing,' purred Tabitha. 'What a splendid man you are.'

'The work is rewarding,' he murmured, his gaze moving thoughtfully over the girl's features.

11

The face he saw above him was certainly well-favoured. The nose was small and straight; the mouth had a slight upward tilt at the corners and so, too, did the eyes. They were almost leaf-green, alive with the quick intelligence which lay behind them. A mass of chestnut hair, curling gently at the ends, had slipped its white ribbon in the fray and now tumbled half-way down her back. Everyone declared it a pretty face—and so it was—but a careful observer might also have perceived there certain small signs of evil.

The eyebrows were strong and dark, smoothly following the line of the browbone—except at the inner corners, where they formed a pair of tufted peaks, each little hair growing upwards like a tiny spike against the delicate skin. And the nostrils were carved with a slight natural flair that suggested at once good breeding and quietly animal quality. These minor points, however, normally went unnoticed by those who viewed the face as a whole and credited this fresh, dainty little creature with all the regulation sweetness of womanhood.

Daniel Coates, however, had no illusions about Tabitha, being so well acquainted and not given to the sentimental fancy that issued woman a halo to wear with her chains. Her closest kin understood less of her nature than

12

he did, and yet there were still certain things that even he could not have guessed. Just now, as she passed a teasing hand over his thigh, he thought he knew what she wanted, but he was wrong.

Tabitha drew a finger slowly through the fur that coated his chest, descending to his stomach where it thinned out and tapered to a trickle of hair leading down his belly to disappear beneath the band of his corduroy trousers. She noticed the hopeful stirring there below and turned with a knowing smile to see the expectation in his face.

It was a very slow smile. At first the lines of the mouth drew gently up to a point of the utmost sweetness, a disarming and dimpled smile designed for public use. But now it passed beyond this point to become a wide and hungry grin revealing small neat teeth, gleaming white both top and bottom. It spoke of more than mischief. It said that she was bad.

Daniel knew what that grin usually promised and he wriggled with joy as she slipped a hand under his waistband.

'There is one small favour I would ask of you,' she murmured.

'What? Come on, lass, don't tease me.'

She regarded him pensively for a moment,

13

passing the tip of a very pink tongue between her teeth.

'I want you...' she began, with eyelids slyly lowered.

The man waited happily.

'...to fasten my dress for me,' she ended, springing to her feet. 'I have to go now.'

Daniel stifled a howl of rage.

'Why? 'Tis no more than four.'

'I have nearly a mile to walk home and I need plenty of time to get dressed; I'm going out this evening.'

He sat up, watching her sullenly.

'What is so important that you can't spare me a few more minutes?'

'A birthday celebration,' she said brightly. 'Mr William Kirkwood is twenty-five today. There is to be a grand dinner at Copperhill, with dancing afterwards. My brother and I have been invited to attend. I'm sure there will be at least a hundred guests and I wish to look my best.'

Daniel snorted, getting to his feet and resentfully fastening the buttons and hooks of her dress.

'Oh aye, you must be the finest of the fine ladies. I suppose 'tis a man you're out to impress? Rich gents are more demanding than the likes of me.'

'Don't sulk,' said Tabitha coolly. 'You have a wife of your own, Daniel, and these meetings don't give you a claim upon me.'

'I know that well enough,' he said, slipping in the last button. 'Who is it you're so eager to please?'

'Why, William, of course.' Tabitha turned around, beaming. 'I'm going to marry him.'

Daniel looked incredulous. 'But his family's in trade. Mr Kirkwood is a brewer.'

'An exceedingly rich brewer,' qualified Tabitha.

'Does that mean your father's given his permission?'

'Well, not exactly. In fact he doesn't yet know. Nor does William, for that matter. But I've made my decision and am quite determined.'

'And I'm thinking he'll not be good enough to please your proud Papa.'

'I think I can persuade him.'

'Don't waste your time, lass,' he said, stooping to pick up his cap. 'Squire'll never allow it. You and I know how a man's place in the world is fixed. I am deemed better than a tinker or a farm labourer, while a banker's clerk thinks himself far above me, and so it goes on up to the point where even money won't make you good enough. Your father is a gentleman

15

of the sort who resent and resist the 'upstarts' who come from trade—no matter how wealthy. He'll not consent to have you marry one.'

'In that case we'll have to elope,' said Tabitha lightly.

'Then you'll not see Roskarnon again while your father lives, for he'll never take you back. Mr Summerfield is not a forgiving man. If I were you...'

'It's not your place to advise me, Daniel. I'm sure I can manage Papa. Please remember that I am his daughter, while you are merely his employee.'

'Oh, that's right, miss.' He tugged his forelock in mock deference. 'I know that, miss. But not fully paid for all that I do. How would it be if I asked your father for a stud fee? What would happen then, do you think?'

'You'd be homeless.'

Daniel swore softly through clenched teeth and turned away, shaking his head. She was little more than a child, and yet it never paid to quarrel with her, armed as she was with the power of the privileged.

'Now don't be ill-tempered.' She pulled her shawl from the bush where it hung and draped it round her shoulders. 'I'm sorry I was sharp. Did I tell you that I've asked Papa to have your roof repaired and suggested a little more schooling for your sons? I told him they were both very quick to learn and eager to study the scriptures for themselves. Papa seemed to approve and I think he will arrange it for you.'

The man seemed mollified at that. Tabitha's friendship, after all, could be helpful in many little ways.

'Will you be here tomorrow?' she asked.

'If you want.'

'Of course I do. I enjoy our little romps, Daniel, and I believe you, also, find them diverting.'

He stepped towards her with a chuckle. 'I can put the proof in your hands, lass, if you'll only...'

'And so you shall—tomorrow.' She winked at him, turned and sauntered off without a backward glance, unaware that this had, in fact, been her last afternoon with Daniel Coates. Tabitha had not planned it that way, but he was soon to be forgotten in a rush of events and more weighty concerns.

As she made her way homeward, Tabitha's thoughts turned soberly upon the question of marriage. A husband was master, provider, ultimate authority in the home, controller of her possessions and her person, empowered to beat her if he chose and keep her continually pregnant until early death or the change of life

17

put an end to it. Such, at least, had been her Mama's lot, for she had bound herself to a sour and rigorous disciplinarian on the day she married Edgar Summerfield.

Well, that was Mama's mistake and the observant Tabitha had learned from it. She felt little sympathy for her mother, dead these past four years. The woman was foolishly soft and trusting, too quick to admire the commanding self-confidence and social position on the young Edgar. She had taken no warning from the fact that he almost never smiled.

Tabitha was a different breed of woman altogether and had no intention of ending up like her mother. Calculating, self-willed and joyfully shameless, she had quickly perceived the enormous importance of acquiring a kindly and pliable husband; someone indulgent and trusting, to afford her the freedom she wanted. In return for this she would cherish the dear creature, just so long as he did not get in her way, and everyone would be happy.

Tabitha did not believe that suffering was good for the soul. She had no time for the tiresome morality which frowned upon pleasure, especially the sexual kind, and she found it well nigh intolerable to be short of money. The clothes and the outings she wanted would require a man with a bottomless pocket.

None of these desires could be deemed unusual in a young girl, but Tabitha differed from the norm in one vital respect: she would not accept disappointment, nor was she content to make do with daydreams. By one wily means or another, she nearly always got what she wanted.

In William Kirkwood she saw a gentle young man, possessed of enormous wealth and already somewhat smitten with her. For weeks he had worshipped from afar and Tabitha felt it time to offer him some real encouragement. By the end of this evening she planned to have him captive, but her confidence was slightly dimmed by the shadow of Papa's awkwardness.

It was, as Daniel had said, all a question of snobbery. William's father, one of the great brewers, now retired, had far more money than Edgar Summerfield. But while other well-established families were beginning to marry into industrial wealth, Edgar remained entrenched in class segregation and refused to move with the times.

Elopement was a romantic idea, but even if the upright, honest William agreed to such a plan, she would still pay a heavy price for open defiance. She could easily guess how William's parents would react to such a thing. They were fervent social climbers and Tabitha would quite

19

lose her value to them if Edgar disowned her. Mrs Kirkwood, in particular, could not abide scandal. All things considered, Tabitha would much prefer to marry William with Papa's blessing.

* * * *

The Summerfield family were not of Cornish stock, but came originally from a brood of yeoman farmers in Essex—although Edgar preferred to forget about that. This lush estate had been bestowed upon them in appreciation for their efforts against Cromwell in the Civil War. They would have liked a title to go with it, but that, for some reason, was never forthcoming.

Roskarnon was a Jacobean house of sandy-coloured stone, a place of turrets, bays and ornamental gables. There were many cavernous, echoing rooms, sparsely provided with hard furniture, faded tapestries and ancestral portraits. These rooms had barely changed since the Summerfields first acquired Roskarnon in 1661, for the family never used them. They chose instead to live in the west wing, where the apartments were smaller and less draughty.

Edgar, preferring plainness in all things, had

gone against fashion in banishing most ornaments and frills. He could do little, however, about the decorative friezes and fancy woodwork that were so much a part of the house. Patterns were etched in the doors and panelling; oak leaves and acorns writhed up the banisters and a carven fox sat upon the corner post at every bend in the staircase. He allowed the ornate marble fireplaces with their scrolls, bunches of grapes and shell designs, but was slow to embrace new inventions—hence the continued use of candles, oil-lamps and hip-baths.

A city dweller would have said that Roskarnon was isolated, for the nearest large community was a market town by the name of St Lowen, some ten miles distant. He would hardly have counted the small village, the three hamlets and the sprinkling of cottages, scattered wide and linked by narrow tracks. Except on festival days, there was never a crowd to be seen, and yet the people were there—farmers and labourers, blacksmith, carpenter and wheelwright, hurdle-maker, thatcher and miller—all unobtrusively present and quietly busy.

The house faced out across a broad, tidal creek at a spot just two miles from the sea. The great curve of the river served to hide the estuary from view and Roskarnon itself was sheltered from the buffeting of heavy weather. At high tide the creek was a glassy stretch of water reflecting shades of dark and paler green from its wooded banks, and the marshy shallows were the haunt of wading birds.

At the front, the driveway travelled some hundred yards beneath arches of elm and beech until it came to the main gates. A wild garden of about four acres encircled the back and sides of the house, and beyond this lay the farms, woods and stretches of moorland which formed the rest of the estate.

Tabitha had always been a solitary child, having just one elder brother with absorbing interests of his own. Despite this, she had never been discontented and she regarded her home with a deep pride. Most of her happiest hours had been spent in these woods and gardens, always alone—until her recent introduction to more adult forms of recreation with Daniel Coates.

Tabitha sighed nostalgically as she made her way homeward. So many memories. She would be more than content to live out the rest of her days here, if such could be arranged.

Passing through the kitchen garden, she came upon one of Roskarnon's strangest characters: the resident herb-woman, fortune-teller, pedlar of charms, curses and home-grown wisdom. Her name was Gaddy Scanes, the last of a family whose womenfolk were always notorious for their absence from church, and she was one of Tabitha's favourite acquaintances. Gaddy's official function on the estate was that of midwife—a patchy source of employment at the best of times, hence all the other lucrative services. Without a doubt, she was well versed in what she called 'wortcunning' and would sometimes impart a little knowledge to those she found congenial.

Tabitha was just such a person and the old woman occasionally entertained her with titbits of herbal lore.

Among the many services Gaddy offered was the useful trick of 'reversing' pregnancy, as she slyly put it. Tabitha, in her provident way, had ascertained that before embarking upon her adventure with Daniel Coates. Although the necessity had not arisen, she was glad of a little insurance against bad luck.

As Tabitha stopped, the old woman was bending to gather handfuls of a short, spidery herb with pointed leaves, laying them neatly in a basket already half-filled with several other species.

'What are you picking, Gaddy?'

The woman straightened up and looked

round. She was very small—shorter than Tabitha—brown and lined, sharp-featured and brisk in her movements, with a scuttling gait and eager, blackbird eyes. Sixty-three years old (a considerable age in times when life was gruelling for country women), she was proof of her art and her own cures, a living advertisement, Gaddy claimed proudly.

' 'Tis a little something for to make a poultice, missy. One of the shepherds got an ulcer come up on his leg, see. 'Tis nothing s'terrible. Easily set to rights.'

Tabitha smiled. 'I think if I were ill, Gaddy, I would rather be tended by you than by Doctor Prale, but I'm afraid Papa would think it unseemly.'

Gaddy made a grimace of amusement. 'Your Papa finds me good enough for common folks, but not for himself or his family. Well, 'tis no great tragedy to me that he pays out good money to an old fool of a doctor, who's halfway addled and powerless to help him.' She paused and sniffed thoughtfully. 'Not that I could cure him meself,' she allowed with a small shrug. 'He gets pains in his chest, I'm told. There's precious little Doctor Prale can do about that, nothing nobody can do, once it starts. Still, he'll be with us for a few years yet, 'less his temper takes him off. I've seen that happen, too. Best to keep him sweet, missy, if you're fond of him.'

'That is never easy, Gaddy, and I'm very much afraid that trouble is brewing even now. Papa has seldom been willing to allow any of us our own decisions, and I have an important one to discuss with him today.'

'Important decisions, is it?' Gaddy chuckled. 'What could be so pressing to a little lass?'

'The selection of a husband.'

'Ah.' Gaddy nodded and picked up her basket. 'Well, well.' She cocked her head to one side and looked up at Tabitha with interest. 'Do you have someone in mind, then?'

'Mr William Kirkwood from Copperhill.'

The round black eyes widened a little and Gaddy pursed her lips thoughtfully. 'Yes, I believe you may meet with a problem there, missy. Want him badly, do you?'

'He's my choice.'

'From what I know of him, I don't think he's the kind of man who would please your Papa. Too gentle by half—and though Mr Kirkwood seems like a grand enough person to me, I've a feeling your Papa will think himself grander and he's not a man to stoop, as he would see it.'

'You're very perceptive, aren't you, Gaddy?'

'I've wit enough to see what's obvious, missy, and your Papa's views are common knowledge. 'Tis the way of better folks, my dear, to speak in front of servants and the like as if we're not there at all or haven't the sense to understand.'

'Well,' sighed Tabitha, 'you can see, then, that I may have to put up a struggle.'

The old woman reached out and patted her hand. 'I'll say a charm for you,' she whispered. 'It all helps.'

'You'd better make it a strong one.'

'Leave it to me, missy. And if you need a bit of help with the young gent—to entice him, as it were—I have the very recipe.'

'Thank you, Gaddy. I'll remember.'

She watched with amusement as the old woman went on her way. When it came to charms and love potions, Tabitha was as sceptical as any. Every problem, she believed, must have a practical solution. One simply had to use one's wits.

CHAPTER 2

Edgar had been feeling exceptionally grim that afternoon. The reasons were chiefly his offspring: firstly the fact that he had only two when families of eight to a dozen were more usual; secondly because he was disappointed in his son.

Mrs Summerfield had never been robust, but had made a promising start with pregnancies in two consecutive years, producing first Christopher and then Tabitha. After that, however, she had managed nothing but the odd miscarriage, thereby shirking her part of the marital bargain. Edgar felt badly let down. Constant tension had destroyed his wife's health and shortened her life, but when at last she died he was already too embittered to consider remarriage.

His son Christopher, now seventeen, had not turned out in the way that Edgar felt he should. The boy was soft, a dreamer. He showed no interest in fishing, hunting or shooting and his father despised him for it. Neither did Christopher seem to understand or care about the running of Roskarnon. His only consuming passion was astronomy, for which reason Edgar scornfully dubbed him 'Little Copernicus'.

In a few months' time Christopher would be off to university, there to continue the classical education that would fit him for nothing in particular. Edgar was most worried about the fate of Roskarnon after his death, convinced that his son would promptly lose it. Always in sole charge himself, Edgar had no liking for managers. A true man, he would say, needed neither help nor advice from anyone, yet he feared that Christopher, if left to his own devices, would neglect his responsibilities and allow the estate to deteriorate.

For several years past, Edgar's income had been slowly dwindling. Outbreaks of cattle and sheep disease had left some of his farmers unable to pay their rents. Good tenants were more and more difficult to find and he was resentfully aware that prosperity now fell increasingly to the bankers and manufacturers he so despised. The Summerfields' way of life became just a little more frugal each year, and he felt that mismanagement by his son would quickly lead to final ruin.

Edgar had scented the coming of a great change, one with which Christopher could never cope. The upheaval would descend upon him and sweep him aside before he was even aware of it. In recent years Summerfield had seen several landowners ruined by eccentricity they could no longer afford, by complacency and their inability to face what he like to call the 'pestilential tide of clerks and industry'. Edgar felt that he was battling upstream against this flood and privately he knew he was losing, however defiantly.

For this reason he had recently made a radical decision about his will. He was not exactly happy with the arrangement, but felt it to be the best he could hope for with such a poor choice of heirs. There was also an element of spite involved. It was a way to punish his son.

Edgar's brooding upon the invasion of upstarts had also served to remind him of the Kirkwood family and the fact that he had, in a moment of foolish indulgence, given Christopher and Tabitha leave to attend William's birthday celebration.

Contemplation of all this had left Edgar in a volatile mood that day, and this was why a small domestic upset turned into a major uproar which encompassed every member of the household.

The triggering event was quite trivial in itself.

One of the parlourmaids, a dumpy adolescent named Peggy, broke the carriage clock. Over-worked and late in her day's routine, she had blundered in haste through her dusting—until a careless touch of her elbow nudged the clock off the end of the mantlepiece.

It was not a valuable clock, nor did it keep good time, Edgar did not even like it very much; yet this minor breakage was enough to provoke a bellowing outburst.

He fumed about carelessness, sloth and in-gratitude, trumpeting reminders of his bene-ficence at the cowering girl.

Was he not uncommonly generous in pay-ing her an annual three pounds more than a parlourmaid might normally expect?

Peggy tearfully agreed that he was.

And had he not given her a cosy little attic bedroom all to herself? Was she not earmarked for promotion to Tabitha's personal maid in a few months' time?

The sobbing Peggy acknowledged all these privileges and deplored her own clumsiness in the hope of placating Mr Summerfield.

Edgar's tantrums were a regular feature of life at Roskarnon and, although alarming, were generally short-lived. On this occasion, how-ever, his bawling and roaring went on for nearly twenty minutes and finally brought an anxious housekeeper to enquire into the cause.

'Can I be of any help, sir?'

'I doubt it,' snarled Edgar, 'unless it lies within your power to make a competent servant of this blundering creature.'

The woman's eyes turned toward the unfortunate Peggy, who was weeping noisily, and then to the pile of shattered springs and wheels in the fireplace.

'Oh dear...Perhaps I can...' She bent as if to gather up the debris.

'Let it be,' Edgar snapped. 'It's beyond repair.'

The housekeeper straightened up and sighed heavily. She produced a handkerchief and handed it to the quivering maid. 'Hush, Peggy. Crying won't mend it.'

'I didn't mean to break anything,' moaned Peggy, blowing her nose. 'I hope it wasn't very expensive?' She peered piteously at Edgar. 'I'll work for nothing, sir, till I've made up the cost.'

'Indeed you will.'

The girl bit her lip. 'Mr Summerfield, sir, how long will it take to repay?' she ventured nervously.

Edgar said nothing, but his look suggested that it might well take all her life. The housekeeper's mouth tightened a little, for she had seen him inflict similiar mental torment upon his wife from time to time.

A large, fat tear rolled from Peggy's left eye. Mr Summerfield's silence was ominous and she feared she had mortgaged the rest of her working days to pay for the broken treasure.

'Come here, child.' The housekeeper put an arm around her shoulders and then looked Edgar in the eye.

'I believe it was the one Mrs Summerfield bought at a charity auction, sir, wasn't it? A matter of a few pounds, as I recall.'

Edgar glared at her. 'The value is beside the point. The issue is one of principle. Disregard for the property of others is a serious moral failing.'

'It was an accident, sir, and the girl is willing to pay. She can do no more,' the woman said stoutly. 'Chastisement is one thing, bullying is quite another and certainly undeserved in this case.'

Opposition from a servant was more than Edgar could bear.

'Oh, but there is something more she can do. She can pack her bags, madam,' he spat. 'And since you are in sympathy, you may do the same.'

The woman was plainly startled. An employee of long standing, sure of her security, the notion of dismissal turned her face first white with disbelief, then red with indignation.

'Sir, I have been with this family since you were a child. There has never been anything but trust and respect...'

'Until now,' finished Edgar. 'You have fallen from grace, Mrs Bray, a mistake that an ageing servant can ill afford.'

To his great enjoyment, a look of fear flickered across the housekeeper's face. Yes, she was getting old now, had spent most of her life at Roskarnon. Before her stood the man she had first encountered over forty years ago, when he was just a sullen child. Such a long time, so much loyalty and service. He could not possibly bring himself to sack her—could he?

'I realise, Mr Summerfield, that you are upset by this incident. For my part, I simply feel that Peggy has been adequately reprimanded. I don't seek to excuse her clumsiness, but...'

'What about your own impertinence?'

'It was not intended as such.'

Edgar sniffed. 'Nevertheless, Mrs Bray, I choose to construe it that way.'

The woman was silent, her features tense with the effort to hide her fear and maintain her dignity.

'And I am therefore dismissing the pair of you.'

Peggy gave a stifled howl of dismay, while the housekeeper's expression shifted into one of contempt. She knew full well that Mr Summerfield never retracted anything once he had said it. He might have private regrets later, but Edgar would never be seen to back down, no matter what the cost. So, like the condemned on the gallows, without hope of reprieve, she took the opportunity to fire a parting shot.

'Yes,' she said softly, 'I should have expected this from you sooner or later. For a dozen years I watched you terrorise your wife, till finally she escaped to her grave. But you've had less success with your children, haven't you, sir? Neither one will ever fit your mould, although Lord knows you've tried to force them into it. How that must chafe a man who believes his wishes are the most important thing on God's earth. You get no response from your son and daughter, so you make scapegoats of those with no defence or means to hit back. It's not the broken clock which has angered you, but the boy who falls short of what you consider ideal.'

For a moment she thought Edgar would knock her down. His face turned an ugly red, the veins in his temple pulsing with rage.

'That is utter, malicious rubbish.'

'Oh no.' She shook her head with calm certainty. There's no doubt in my mind, Mr Summerfield. I know it for a fact—and so does the whole house, come to that. You conduct your confrontations very loudly, sir. How can there be secrets, when...?'

'...when every idle ear and eye is pressed to a keyhole, and every tongue passing on fanciful gossip. So the whole house knows, does it? Every drudge and menial prattles about the private concerns of my family. If that is so, Mrs Bray, I had better do something about it, don't you think? Replacements, after all, are two-a-penny. I have long suspected, in any case, a certain amount of pilfering in the kitchen, and several of the maids have unsuitable followers. Yes indeed, I believe some fresh faces are called for.'

The housekeeper's mouth dropped open in horror as his meaning became clear—not least because of her own part in this disaster.

'What...? You cannot mean to...'

'Dismiss all of you,' supplied Edgar sweetly, 'and right away.'

'Sir, this is most unjust. I accept the blame for my...' she swallowed hard, both the lump in her throat and all of her pride. '...my insolence, but you cannot punish the entire staff.'

'I most certainly can,' countered Edgar. 'You

35

all have one hour to pack.'

The housekeeper's face registered disgust. 'Will you not even tell them yourself?'

'That, Mrs Bray, will be your last duty.'

★ ★ ★ ★

Tabitha, entering the house through the french windows of the music room, went straight upstairs to change. It was almost half past four but she was too excited to bother with afternoon tea. She would leave for Copperhill at seven-thirty, and since it would take an hour and a half to dress her hair in the style she had chosen, there was little time to lose. Her new dress, especially made for this occasion, was laid out upon her bed in readiness, together with the satin dancing slippers she would wear. Reaching for the bell-cord, Tabitha gave it a gentle tug, fully expecting Peggy to answer.

Five minutes passed, however, and no one came. Tabitha frowned slightly and rang again —two brisk jerks this time.

Still no one came.

She gave a sigh of annoyance and went out along the landing in search of the tardy maid. Roskarnon's house-hold staff numbered a dozen people, but she encountered not a soul on the first or the ground floor. Nobody responded when she called and the rooms below stairs were deserted. With a growing sense of unease, Tabitha went upstairs again, this time to the very top floor where the servants had their sleeping quarters.

Four of the rooms stood empty already, their doors thrown wide and all sign of personal belongings gone. From the far end of the corridor, however, came sounds of bustle as drawers and cupboards were flung open, cleared out and banged shut. There were voices, some of them angry, and the noise of muffled sobbing.

Tabitha hurried to see what was wrong and, pushing back a half-open door, came face to face with two angry kitchen maids.

'Lisbeth, what on earth are you doing up here at this time of day? Elsie, why are you packing your things? What has happened?'

The red-haired Lisbeth, flushed with temper, snorted and slammed down the lid of her box as she hurled the last of her clothes inside.

'We're leaving, miss, as we've been ordered to do. Never mind that there's no good reason nor nothin' we've done to deserve it. Your father's had one of his nasty, vicious moods today and he's sacked us, every last one. He's a brute, Miss Tabitha. He's a wicked, hateful man.'

'Hush, Lisbeth! You mustn't say such things to me.'

'Why not?' muttered Elsie sullenly. 'We've nothing to lose and 'tis no more than the truth.'

'I'm sure there must be some mistake. Papa would never dismiss the entire staff in such a way. I know that he is quick-tempered, but he is not irrational.'

'No?' queried Lisbeth, hands on hips. 'Ask Mrs Bray what it's all about, then. She's next door with Peggy. We didn't do nothin' wrong,' she repeated angrily as Tabitha turned to leave. 'I've worked hard here these past eight years. May the good Lord damn him!'

Tabitha, with a twist of anxiety, went to the next room, to hear the full sorry tale from Peggy and the housekeeper.

'I'll speak to Papa, Mrs Bray,' she said when the woman finished explaining. 'He is impetuous when angry and perhaps, once he has calmed himself, he may...'

'Child, in all the years I've know him, I cannot recall an occasion when your father withdrew a threat, admitted an error or made an apology to anyone.' She smiled sadly, adding: 'I will miss you and Master Christopher.'

'Please don't despair, Mrs Bray. I will see Papa. I will appeal for you.'

Peggy gazed up at her with tearful eyes. 'I

don't know who will do your hair for you now, miss, I'm sure,' she sniffed.

No indeed, thought Tabitha, becoming alarmed, nor do I.

On her way out she met with the stout and belligerent person of the cook, dressed in her black coat and hat, struggling along the passage with two bags and a small trunk.

'Well, Miss Tabitha, have you heard what he's done?' she exclaimed. 'Sent us all packing on account of nothing at all. He fancies we gossip about him, Mrs Bray says. 'Tis hard to say if it's madness, guilty conscience or both. 'T'would be small wonder if we did talk about him, for there's cause enough, the way he carries on. I hope his temper kills him—as it probably will—and 'tis certain sure he'll burn in hell when he goes.'

Tabitha, in complete, if secret, agreement, saw no point in reprimanding Cook for this outburst. Despite her words to Mrs Bray, she entertained no real hopes that Edgar would change his mind and, as if in admission of this, she asked:

'Has my father paid you all the wages due to you? I believe there should be an extra sum to compensate for lack of notice.'

'Oh aye, Mrs Bray saw to that. But what now, miss, eh? I can go to my brother in St

Lowen for a while, and Peggy has her parents at the farm. But what about those little maids? Where are they supposed to go? And Mrs Bray? She's got no one and her savings won't last long.' She shook her head and carried on her way. 'Curse him,' she muttered, 'he gave us no warning and no second chance.'

Tabitha barely heard those last words, for a fear was swiftly taking shape in her mind. Vague at first, it now became specific, giving rise to trepidation as she hastened downstairs to find her father. She was careful not to show this, however, on entering his study. Composure was a most essential defence when dealing with Papa.

* * * *

As always, Edgar's outburst had left him dourly calm. Someone invariably had to suffer when his temper was up, for there was no other way to relieve it. A small whisper of common sense reproached him now for that last grand flourish of unreason, but he stifled it grimly. Pride would never allow him to eat his words, but he recognised, secretly, that he had lost a good house-hold staff and now faced the trying business of hiring more.

Still scowling, he went to the bookcase in his

study, seeking something to suit his mood. He was leafing through *Titus Andronicus* when his daughter came in.

'Papa?'

Edgar jumped slightly and frowned at her.

'You should knock, Tabitha. You startled me.'

'I'm sorry, Papa. It was not intentional.'

She was standing in the doorway, hands clasped demurely before her. An affectionate man would have doted upon such a pretty creature, but Edgar saw only a child of the wrong sex. He had wanted sons, lots of them, boys to mould into close copies of himself.

'Well, what do you want? Can't you see you're disturbing me?' His heavy jaw quivered and the thick mouth tightened a little with annoyance. Edgar still wore dundreary whiskers and looked considerably more than his forty-seven years, due mostly to a cantankerous soul and advancing disease of the arteries.

'What has happened, Papa? Mrs Bray tells me you have dismissed all the servants.'

'All but the stablemen and grounds staff.'

'May I ask why?'

'For insolence, clumsy incompetence and numerous other forms of misconduct.'

'But was it wise? How...?'

'Wise?' Edgar snapped. 'Who are you, miss

to question the wisdom of my actions?'

Tabitha did not flinch, nor did she lower her eyes in shame and fear as her mother would have done. The bright gaze was unfaltering and Edgar felt suddenly uncomfortable. Tabitha was the only person he had ever known who seemed impervious to his rages. Servants cowered, friends protested, his wife had wept and Christopher would fidget in silent, red-faced discomfort, but Tabitha seldom obliged him with any reaction at all. Whatever currents of wish and will ran within the depths of her being, the surface was always calm. Edgar found this disturbing. He never knew quite how to cope with it.

'I was simply going to ask how we will manage without staff, until replacements are found. Could you not have given them a month's notice?'

'It is my wish that they leave immediately and that is the end of the matter. I will not discuss it further. And I suspect, Tabitha, that you are less concerned with the efficient running of this household than the loss of your menial 'friends'. You spend far too much time in the kitchen, chattering with the maids and distracting Cook from her work. This is not the first time I have had to remind you of your position.'

'But I don't have any real friends, Papa, and since Mama is not here to teach me the principles of running a house-hold, I must learn as best I can.'

'Too much familiarity undermines one's authority, Tabitha. And it would seem that certain morsels of gossip have found their way into the servants' hall, that our family problems are a source of interest and amusement to all. One cannot help but wonder from whom they heard these tales.'

'Not from me, Papa, I assure you.'

Summerfield's eyes glinted under the fleshy folds of his lids.

'So, you maintain that you seek the company of servants in a quest for useful knowledge. Most commendable. And has it been fruitful, Tabitha? Have you, for instance, acquired some knowledge of the culinary arts? Has Cook revealed the mysteries of the larder? The secrets of sauce and pastry, roast and grill?'

Tabitha hesitated. 'Why yes, Papa. I have watched her many times. I believe I know how to prepare a few simple dishes.'

'I'm very glad to hear it, daughter. And no doubt you'll be eager to demonstrate these skills to your admiring father. So, you shall have the opportunity this evening. You may cook dinner for us.'

43

Oh yes, it was a very neat trap. Papa was given to mean little fits of caprice. He always believed that the odd dose of humiliation was beneficial.

'But it's William Kirkwood's birthday. Christopher and I are going to Copperhill this evening. Don't you remember?'

'That is now impossible.'

Her fear confirmed, Tabitha's face registered the merest flicker of dismay.

'He will be expecting us. Christopher has gone to St Lowen to buy a birthday gift...'

'Your brother may attend the affair if he wishes, but I insist that you stay at home. You will send a short note of apology.'

'But you know how much I have looked forward to this evening.'

Edgar stationed himself by the fireplace and assumed his pose of implacable father, hands clasped behind him.

'Your first duty is to your family. Selfishness is unattractive in a woman.'

'I seldom go to a social event, Papa, and a party is a very special treat. How ironic that you should choose this particular day to dismiss all the servants.'

'A woeful coincidence,' agreed Edgar, smirking.

'You have never liked me, have you, Papa?'

Tabitha's tone was calm enough, but the green eyes had acquired a brilliant, hard shine.

'Don't be foolish, child. I feed, clothe and house you, do I not? In return you owe me respect and total obedience— a reasonable bargain, I feel.'

'The same could be said of the servants, Papa, Am I to be a scapegoat, too?'

'I hope you are not accusing me of spite, Tabitha. It gives me no pleasure to see you disappointed.'

'Then let me go to Copperhill, if only for an hour or two...'

Edgar sighed. 'I would be lacking as a parent if I failed to acquaint you with the realities of life, my dear. You must learn to cope with set-backs, to bear responsibilities, to control your personal desires and put the welfare of others before your own. A woman's role is one of self-sacrifice and it behoves you to accept that fact with good grace.'

'Duty again, Papa?'

'Yes indeed. When I married your mother she was wilful, frivolous and undisciplined...'

'Really? I cannot imagine such a thing. Mama was broken by the time I was born.'

'It was my task to correct her and if necessary I will repeat the process with you.'

Tabitha's chin lifted with that slight suggestion of defiance that angered him most. Where he hoped for submission he saw arrogance and it made him want to strike her. His study fingers flexed and curled into fists behind his back.

Mrs Summerfield had often felt the weight of his hand. She had responded with swift obedience to a slap, but never had he used the same treatment on Tabitha, for he sensed in his daughter a turn of character which touched him with unease.

She lacked the shy gentleness and humility he expected in a woman. He could not recall a single occasion when he had seen her cry. Worse still, he detected a quiet, precocious confidence, and sometimes a flash of dark humour, which troubled him greatly. She would need the supervision of a stern husband, someone to take her in hand; and it happened that Edgar believed he had found the very man, for he had seen a way to control his daughter's life and safeguard his heritage at the same time.

'Your mother was not "broken", as you so dramatically put it.'

'Brought to heel?' suggested Tabitha.

'She was taught the proper demeanour of a wife and it's patently clear to me that you are in need of similar instruction.'

Tabitha seemed unimpressed.

'I have therefore been giving serious thought to your future. That is to say, I have been pondering the choice of a husband for you.'

The look of boredom vanished from her face and the green gaze fastened intently upon him.

'I thought that would catch your interest.' He motioned her towards an armchair. 'Sit down, Tabitha. I have one or two things to tell you and this would seem an appropriate time.'

The girl sat, waiting while he cleared his throat and straightened his waistcoat in the manner that usually went with the announcement of some far-reaching decision. Tabitha suspected that she would not like what Papa had to say.

'I suppose you're aware,' began Edgar, gazing distantly over the top of her head, 'that your brother has not lived up to my expectations. In fact he has shown himself to be irresponsible and ill-equipped to take over the handling of this estate when I am gone. I have sought repeatedly to instil some common sense, but all to no avail. I no longer have any real hopes of him.'

On that score, Tabitha was inclined to share Papa's opinion.

'Long-held tradition decrees that an eldest—or only—son may expect to inherit virtually the whole of his family's property,' continued

Edgar, now studying the carpet. 'Your unfortunate father, however, is afflicted with a useless dreamer for a male heir and deprived of any alternative but a daughter.'

'It must be very trying for you,' murmured Tabitha drily.

'To come to the point, then. I do not intend to leave the estate in the hands of a careless incompetent who will let it slip from his grasp while he is busily gazing skywards. Regardless, therefore, of tradition, I have amended my will, bequeathing a half-share to you.'

Tabitha was rarely startled by anything, but at this her mouth popped open in surprise. As a daughter, she had never expected much from her own family's estate, but looked toward William's wealth for compensation. A claim to part of Roskarnon had always seemed like a dream beyond reach.

'It pains me to feel that this is necessary,' grumbled Edgar, 'that I cannot confidently trust in my son as other men can trust in theirs. The decision was a hard one and has cost me a great deal of pride, but it seems the only sensible course.'

'I'm astonished, Papa,' said Tabitha, not untruthfully, 'and touched to think that you have such faith in me.'

She spoke in tones of humility and awe, but

already the sharp mind was calculating the implications of Papa's gesture and a ravening excitement began to unfold within her soul.

'I haven't the slightest faith in you, Tabitha,' Edgar snapped. 'None whatever. I haven't finished yet, so you had best listen carefully.'

Ah yes, but of course. There were conditions. The girl's mouth twisted almost imperceptibly at the corner, and the thrill died back into cynical understanding.

'If caution forbids me to leave the whole estate to Christopher, I certainly could not entrust any portion of it to a female. However, the law very wisely provides that a woman's property shall pass into the care and possession of her husband at the time of marriage. With this in mind, I have selected a young man of fine qualities and impeccable family background to become your fiancé. I may not have a worthy son, but by God I will have an admirable son-in-law.'

I should have guessed, thought Tabitha with cold disappointment.

It was typical of Papa to lay his own plans for her future, high-handedly deciding whom she should marry. And whoever the young man might be, he was clearly not William Kirkwood. Edgar only spoke highly of men in whom he saw a reflection of himself. She would have no freedom, no access to her money with another budding tyrant clutching the purse-strings. All the same, the idea of being named as equal beneficiary in Papa's will advised a cautious response. Half the estate! Dear Lord, what a prize! Why, indeed, should Christopher have it all when she cared for it so much more?

'I think I understand, Papa. May I ask the name of the person you have chosen for me?'

'Young James, Colonel Robson's boy. He's conscientious and highly-principled, nothing flippant or foolish about him, and he knows the importance of duty, standards. He has admired you for some time, and the Colonel certainly approves the idea of a match.'

My, we have been busy, haven't we? thought Tabitha behind her politely bland expression. There's plainly been much discussion, although no one saw fit to consult me.

'You remember James, don't you?'

Tabitha remembered him all too well, recalling one particular image from a dinner party with the Robsons. James and the Colonel, both of them lean, solemn and long-nosed, facing each other across the table like a pair of herons. It had been a dreary evening. She imagined that James was somewhere in his late twenties, but his bearing was that of a man far older. He was also appallingly religious.

'I remember him very well, Papa.'

'I think he's an excellent choice,' continued Edgar smugly. 'I went to school with his father, you know. They're a fine family, good old stock who've been established in the county even longer than we have. You won't catch the Robsons mixing and marrying with a lot of ambitious upstarts.'

So much for the Kirkwoods and their kind, reflected Tabitha, realising just how right Daniel Coates had been when he said that Edgar would never countenance the idea of William as a son-in-law.

There were indeed many families like the Kirkwoods. Newly wealthy, they sought to set themselves up as country gentlefolk, but it was far from simple to buy acceptance from die-hards like Edgar. They could build great houses, hunt, shoot, send their sons to public school, keep splendid stables and carriages, concern themselves with innumerable charities, and still he despised them.

Since the Restoration, his own forebears had all been bishops, military men and country squires like himself. Edgar was a man trying grimly to hold on to an order that was inexorably melting away.

'Am I to understand that Mr Robson has made an offer of marriage, Papa? Nothing has been said to me.'

'Indeed he has. We reached agreement in no time at all.'

Dear Lord, thought Tabitha, I'm being disposed of like a bartered bride from some primitive tribe.

'And did you strike a good bargain, Papa? How many goats am I going to cost him?'

'Don't be facetious, girl! James had the good sense to seek my approval before approaching you. He admires you most earnestly and I am sufficiently confident to have already made the necessary alteration to my will. The only possible source of difficulty, Tabitha, is you. I trust I shall find you obedient and ready to accept your father's judgement in this matter? I shall take it much amiss if you are unco-operative.'

Tabitha knew a threat when she heard one and was briefly at a loss for a wise response. Although Papa could not actually force her to marry James, he would certainly make her life a misery if she failed to do so, and for sheer spite he would deny her the chance to court anyone else. For years she had managed quietly to circumvent Papa's authority, but this was one order which could not be slyly sidestepped. It was evident that her father looked upon the marriage as a foregone conclusion. At last she took refuge in feminine bewilderment.

'You must understand, Papa, that this is all very confusing for me and...'

'Not at all. It's perfectly simple. I expect you to marry Mr Robson, and within the year. He will not wait while you shilly-shally. He has asked permission to call upon you and I have granted it. He must be received graciously and given every encouragement. I know of no one else so suitable, and I shall cease to worry about the future knowing that you and Christopher have the benefit of his guidance. You may be sure of a very grand wedding, my dear, something far more lavish than this little event at the Kirkwoods'. You belong in better company than theirs. Think about it while you cook for us tonight. Plan your trousseau, if it amuses you.'

Tabitha's eyes glittered with renewed anger at the mention of William's party. She had looked forward to it so very much.

'I'm afraid my cooking may prove disappointing to you, Papa. I have never before attempted...'

'Don't be such a ninny, Tabitha. It cannot be very difficult. In any case, I will make allowances for inexperience and I'm sure the cook has done much of the work in advance. I'm glad to find you taking an interest in things domestic. It's very timely. I cannot wait to see what you have learned.'

No, Papa would not relent. He never did. So that was that, she supposed dismally. She had so often pictured herself standing with William at the altar, embarking on a life of freedom and enjoyment. Now the groom's face was that of James Robson and the promise was one of gloomy subervience. Unless...

An echo of the cook's parting words floated into her mind:

'I hope his temper kills him as it probably will...'

The idea was born with a sudden simple clarity, like a whispered hint from a sympathetic goblin. In a flash she saw the way to achieve her every wish at a single stroke. And how deliciously pleasing that Papa himself had suggested the means. Tabitha was always a user of circumstances, and here was the silver lining, the hidden advantage, she thought, weighing the possibilities of Edgar's declining health and his taste for spicy, pickled foods. What joy it would be to rid herself of Papa once and for all, and how fitting that he should pay for his meanness.

She regarded him thoughtfully for a brief space, and finally her face lifted in a little smile.

'Very well, Papa. I will show you what I have learned.'

★ ★ ★ ★

On leaving Edgar's study, she met Mrs Bray and the kitchen maids making a defiant exit by way of the front door. They had clearly expected no reprieve and Tabitha regretted that she had no good news for them.

'I'm sorry, Mrs Bray,' she said. 'Papa's mind is quite made up. He will not relent. I hope you will quickly find positions elsewhere.'

'So do I,' said Lisbeth glumly. 'It looks bad, miss, to be thrown out, bag and baggage, like this, and I'm sure he'll not give any one of us a good character if asked.'

Tabitha nodded thoughtfully. 'Well, Lisbeth, I know that I am quite young and not the mistress of the house, but should a reference be required for a future situation, you may tell your prospective employers to consult me. I will help if I can. My father's—disposition—is well known.'

'Oh, thank you, miss.'

'You're a good child,' said Mrs Bray. 'Young Peggy was looking forward to being your personal maid.'

'Has she left yet?'

'Yes, miss. The Master gave us an hour to get out and she was frightened to stay any longer. How will you manage this evening, miss?'

Papa has forbidden my visit to Copperhill, if that is what you mean, so I shan't need anyone to help me dress.'

'Oh, the wicked...' began Elsie.

'It doesn't matter,' sighed Tabitha. Then, with strategic guile, she added: 'I think it best, in any case, that he should not be left alone. This trouble has upset him. He does not seem well.'

'He's lucky that you care for him, Miss Tabitha. Goodbye, my dear.'

'Goodbye, Mrs Bray.'

CHAPTER 3

Upstairs, in the sunny little room which had always been her own, Tabitha stood silently regarding the cream coloured moiré dress laid out upon her bed. Blessed with an inborn sense of what suited her best, she had chosen the pattern, fabrics and trimmings most carefully. The style was comparatively sparing on the bustle draperies to give an effect of fragile innocence. Tabitha knew the value of her youth and had no wish to copy the full-blown magnificence of older women. William was a shy and gentle soul, he would appreciate simplicity.

Tabitha stared for some time at the precious frock. The disappointment was deep and bitter but she felt no inclination to cry. Tears were as foreign to Tabitha as they had been familiar to her mother. She would always remember Mama as a poor, shrinking creature with red-rimmed eyes, dabbing piteously at her damp nose with a crumpled handkerchief. The meek, thought Tabitha wryly, shall inherit scorn and ill-treatment

Her gaze wandered thoughtfully from the dress to the window and the garden beyond. It lingered intently upon a shadowy pathway between the trees and her mouth curved gently in a smile of dark and secret pleasure. Weeping and pleading would solve nothing. No indeed. It was better to be strong, and Tabitha had already decided what she would do. There was great risk involved, of course, but of a calculated kind—and oh, so much to be gained if all went well. Life, she believed, dealt roughly with the timorous, while the bold claimed all its prizes.

Quietly she slipped out onto the landing and padded along the gallery above the main hall. From there she descended a short flight of steps which led to the library.

Tabitha was alone so much that she had a great deal of time for reading. Edgar assumed that Tabitha's taste, like that of her mother and most other women, would favour sentimental poetry and romances. In fact she was more likely to choose a tale of mystery or the supernatural when she wanted an hour's amusement. Stranger still, she had an appetite for learning which led her again and again to the textbooks.

Had he known this, her father would have found it ludicrous. He would dismiss with derision the idea that his daughter was clever. Intelligence was not a quality that Edgar valued, or even recognised, in women. Believing them essentially empty-headed, he graded them in terms of obedience and fertility, nothing more. To be fair, Papa was not alone in this view. 'Blue-stockings' found little favour anywhere and Tabitha was seldom foolish enough to air her knowledge, nor would she risk her popularity by correcting any man, however dull-witted.

Roskarnon's library was comprehensive and well-stocked. Methodical as ever, Edgar had arranged it in the most orderly fashion, under subject headings and alphabetically. Tabitha trailed her fingers lightly across the neat rows of spines, past Africa, Archaeology, Astronomy,

Biology—to Botany.

Here she found a chunky volume entitled *Wilmott's British Flora*. She lifted it down from the shelf and turned to the section headed 'South-West England'.

Tabitha already knew this book very well. It was splendidly illustrated and conveyed quite advanced information in a form that any reasonably bright young person could understand.

'Here we are,' murmured Tabitha, smiling. *'Aconitum anglicum'*.

Her finger, tracing its way down the index, had come to rest at the entry she required. 'See page five hundred and ninety-two,' it said. Tabitha quickly found the page and the article she sought.

'*A. anglicum,*' said the heading '(commonly called Monkshood, Wolfsbane, Hecateis...).'

She paused for a moment to savour these folk-names, and then went on reading. There was very little here that Tabitha did not already know. Indeed, she had gleaned from Gaddy Scanes some snippets of extra information which the book, with its scientific bias, did not contain. Nonetheless, she studied the text carefully. She had just wanted to be sure, to review any small, forgotten details.

At last, satisfied, she tucked the book back

in its place and went upstairs to change her clothes. Something old and shabby would be quite good enough for what she had to do next.

Twenty minutes later Tabitha slipped out through a side door and round to the out-buildings. In the gardener's store-shed she helped herself to a knife, a trowel and a pair of heavy canvas gloves.

Now, ready for business, she set off along the cool pathway between the trees, following the downward slope and the sound of running water.

Round and about the garden a number of stone figures occupied various niches and bowers. There were satyrs and fauns, a crumbling Father Time, a unicorn, and a sylph with a water jar. Tabitha's favourite, however, was Pan. It seemed that he watched her with a playful, sidelong glace from his nook amongst the laurels. The curly mouth smiled knowingly, as if he understood her very well. She found him pleasantly wicked and winked as she passed him by, certain that he would appreciate the little prank she had planned for that evening.

Tabitha knew a place where the stream ran slowly, drifting deep and clear over the sandy bottom. It had carved away the banks on either side to make a broad, gentle pool, shielded from bright sunlight by the branches twining overhead. And in this dim, dark green place, there grew a plant with purple flowers.

It stood about three feet high, with leaves that divided like soft, slender fingers and a flower which did indeed remind her of a hood, pulled low as if to hide the nature of what lay beneath. But it was not the flowers she wanted, nor was it the leaves. Calmly she pulled on the canvas gloves, knelt upon the damp ground and began to dig for the root.

CHAPTER 4

A problem arose when Christopher returned from St Lowen. He declared that if his sister had to forgo the evening's gaiety, then so would he. Despite all assurances that she truly did not mind, the boy was adamant and refused to go to Copperhill without her. Like all his actions, it was well-meant, a gesture of sympathy and support, but it caused Tabitha some consternation in view of what she planned to do. It seemed at first that the scheme would have to be abandoned.

On reflection, however, she saw a way round the difficulty, although the risks were now much increased and she would have to implicate her brother in the deed. The matters of Papa's new will and his plans for her future demanded immediate action. With so much in the balance, angry that her hopes for the party were already ruined, she was not prepared to be thwarted a second time. Christopher was her affectionate brother, she knew him well and she would gamble, for such an opportunity might never come again.

Tabitha always liked to dress up for special occasions and the evening meal promised to be quite momentous, so she put on the cream dress before serving dinner that night.

Edgar noticed that she looked unusually festive and he felt moved to comment upon it.

'Why are you wearing your new frock, Tabitha?'

'I thought it would please you, Papa.'

'It was very expensive and not meant to be worn about the house. Don't expect another one if it gets soiled.'

'No, Papa. Did you enjoy the soup?'

Edgar hesitated, always reluctant to praise. 'It was adequate.'

Tabitha beamed and turned to her brother. 'Christopher?'

'I thought it was excellent,' said the young man firmly. 'Perfect, in fact.'

Christopher Summerfield was seventeen. His face, like his character, was open and straight-forward. Wavy brown hair tumbled over a broad forehead, while the eyes and mouth showed a gentle intelligence. For all that his father belittled him, there was nothing malicious or devious about Christopher, and he seldom believed ill of anyone else. His soul was a thing of plain, honest stuff and he never guessed at the splinters of evil that ran like silver threads through Tabitha's nature.

Edgar sniffed. 'Let us hope the standard is maintained throughout the meal. What have we next?'

'Scallops, Papa. They were delivered fresh this morning.'

'And what is the main course to be?'

'Roast beef, Papa. Your favourite, I believe.'

'Indeed, it was dutiful of you to remember.'

Tabitha smiled prettily, collected up the soup plates and went to fetch the scallops. The cook, in truth, had planned on lamb for that evening, but this had not suited Tabitha's purposes. Roast beef, on the other hand, would accommodate them perfectly.

Christopher turned to the old man, wishing he would unbend and show more generous appreciation.

'You must admit, Father, she's made a

splendid effort. See how beautifully she's laid the table. There's even a flower arrangement.'

Edgar was not in the least bit moved. He merely glanced at his son and looked away again without answering.

'Kirkwood's party was important to her,' persisted the boy. 'She has taken the disappointment with good grace.'

'That's just as well,' Edgar said, refilling his wine-glass. 'I will not tolerate sulking.'

Christopher sighed as he regarded the old man across the swaying halos of the candle flames. Father would never change. Mealtimes had always been like this—dismal and strained, everyone weighing their words before they spoke, wary of Edgar presiding irascibly at the head of the table.

'Well, here we are.'

Tabitha seemed quite merry as she entered with the scallop dish. She set it down upon the table and watched while Edgar served out the portions.

He criticised the seasoning of the sauce and grumbled that the scallops were not thoroughly cooked. However, when the beef arrived he found it nicely browned on the outside and pinkly tender within.

When he had finished carving and everyone was amply supplied with roast potatoes and green vegetables, Tabitha reached for a little silver sauceboat and casually offered it to her father.

'Ah, so you remembered the horseradish.'

'I like to be thorough, Papa. I wanted everything to be done properly.'

'That's highly commendable, Tabitha. I'm sure you'll be a very efficient wife when the time comes.'

'Thank you.'

The smell of the roast teased at Edgar's nostrils and he was obviously eager to begin. It had been well past eight when the family sat down to eat and his appetite was considerable. He ladled two generous spoonfuls of sauce onto his plate. In the candlelight its faintly pinkish hue was all but invisible.

Tabitha was watching him as he sat, his knife and fork poised over his plate with its spreading puddle of horseradish. The tension as she waited was almost exquisitely thrilling.

'Anticipation is the best part of everything,' Mama had once said.

Tabitha quite agreed. The thought of springing a trap on Papa was truly exhilarating. As soon as he took the first mouthful she felt a sense of anticlimax and the excitement was replaced by a practical concern that he should eat it all.

As Papa set to work on his dinner, Tabitha helped herself to a piece of bread and made a leisurely start on her own meal.

'This beef is superb,' declared Christopher. 'You deserve congratulations, little sister. Isn't that right, Father?'

Edgar nodded and grunted his approval, although he did think that the sauce was unusually pungent. Just a little too much mustard or vinegar, he wondered? It tingled and pricked at his tastebuds as he continued to eat, one forkful after another, and another...

Tabitha watched him from the corner of her eye and began to keep count.

Edgar's meal was all but gone within ten minutes. It was at this point that he put down his knife and began prodding at his cheek and jaw, puzzled and faintly alarmed at an odd sensation of creeping numbness there.

His son looked up and asked him: 'What's the matter, Father? Have you broken a tooth?'

Edgar shook his head, but the signs of distress were becoming more obvious with every passing second. Suddenly he dropped his fork and pushed his chair back.

Tabitha paused and regarded him with interest for a moment, then went on eating.

A rough, gulping sound began to issue from Papa's throat. He was evidently having some trouble in swallowing.

Christopher jumped to his feet as the old man lurched from the chair, trying to steady himself against the table.

'Father? What's wrong?'

Edgar was unable to answer. His eyes were watering. He felt dizzy and sick. Aware that his vision was somehow impaired, he started to grope his way towards the door. He blundered against the corner of the sideboard and would have fallen if his son had not caught him.

As he supported the gasping old man, Christopher turned angrily to his sister.

'Tabitha, why are you just sitting there? Can't you see...?'

'Of course.' She reached for the butter dish, spread a thin layer upon her bread and took a dainty bite. 'What's the matter, Papa? Is something caught in your throat?' she enquired sweetly. 'Give him a good hard pat on the back, Christopher.'

'Don't be idiotic, Tabitha. We must get the doctor.'

'Why?'

'I believe he's having a heart attack,' hissed the boy, trying to impress her with some sense of urgency.

'Don't be silly.' She turned reproachful eyes on Edgar. 'Really, Papa, you shouldn't eat so fast. It is dangerous to bolt your food, you know.'

Edgar's reply was a desperate gurgle.

'For God's sake, Tabitha,' snapped her brother, 'he's genuinely ill. Now help me to get him upstairs and into bed.'

'Very well,' she sighed, seeming much put upon. 'Isn't he a fusspot, Papa?' she crooned. 'Such a to-do. But I shan't mind if you would prefer to leave the rest of your meal.'

It took them ten minutes to negotiate the two flights of stairs up to Edgar's room. It was a struggle, but at last they managed to lower his hefty bulk onto the bed.

'You'll have to undress him by yourself,' announced Tabitha primly. 'I couldn't possibly remove a man's clothing.'

'All right, but go and rouse one of the lads and send him for Doctor Prale. I'm certain it's a heart seizure.'

'Nonsense,' said Tabitha lightly. 'There's no call to trouble poor old Prale.'

'Don't argue, just do as you are told,' snapped Christopher.

'All right, all right.' She turned, still in no great hurry, to carry out the errand—but then paused, briefly, and whispered:

'But I'll wager a guinea it's just Papa's dinner which has disagreed with him.'

68

Christopher glanced up sharply, open-mouthed at the note of gleeful significance in her voice. Tabitha winked at him slyly and the smile upon her face was enough to fill him with an awful apprehension.

'And doesn't it serve him right?' she chanted gaily, as she skipped outside and quickly shut the door behind her.

'Dear God,' muttered the boy, 'what has she...?'

Edgar's hands clutched at him convulsively, mutely begging help from the son he despised. Christopher turned his attention to the choking, retching figure on the bed and tried to quieten Edgar as he loosened his collar and clothes. There was he knew, little to be done until he found out just what his father had eaten.

When Christopher went back to the dining-room a quarter of an hour later, he found his sister placidly munching an apple. He failed to notice at the time, but the sauceboat and its contents, along with Papa's plate and cutlery, had already disappeared.

'I'm afraid there's no dessert,' Tabitha informed him mischievously. 'I didn't think Papa would want one. There is plenty of cheese, of course, if you're still hungry.'

Beside himself with panic, the boy pulled her

69

to her feet and slapped her. He was trembling as he gestured helplessly in the direction of Edgar's room.

'You're quite right, Tabitha. It's plainly no heart attack. I've never seen anything like this. Now, I want to know exactly what you gave him and by what means.'

Tabitha eyed him peevishly for a moment, stroking her inflamed cheek.

'You're a brute and I shan't tell you.'

'You'd better, my girl.'

She peeped archly at him from beneath her eyelashes and chewed at her bottom lip with small white teeth.

'Guess.'

'Please don't treat this as a game.'

'But that's just what it is. Can't you see the joke? Oh, come on. It's not so very difficult.'

'Do you want me to hit you again?'

Tabitha sighed. 'You've no sense of humour, have you? Very well, then. The sauce, of course—I added something extra.' She giggl-ed, twisting a lock of hair playfully around her finger. 'I doubt he'll ever ask me to cook for him again.'

'But what was it? For pity's sake...'

'I shan't tell you if you shout at me.'

Christopher made an effort to control his mounting fright.

'Please Tabitha,' he said slowly, 'This is not a matter for levity. It's extremely serious.'

The girl gave a pert little smile and tossed her head.

'What a worrier you are. He'll be all right. It was only a root from the garden to make him feel sick. After all, Papa trapped me into saying that I could cook a little and then he used that as a reason to keep me at home this evening. I knew he meant to deride my efforts, however hard I tried, so I thought it would be good, plain justice if the meal made him ill. It seemed a grand joke to slip a dose of emetic into his food, but when I went to the medicine cupboard there was nothing I could use. And then I remembered this root...'

'What kind of root?'

Tabitha shrugged. 'I don't know the name, but it's such a pretty plant. It has lovely purple flowers. One of the village children pointed it out to me when I was small. She said it made people feel sick and gave them stomach pains. Well, it seemed ideal, so I used it.' She frowned, pretending surprise. 'Strangely enough, though, the root turned a reddish colour when I started grating it up, so I didn't dare put in too much in case Papa noticed. It was such a small amount, Christopher—hardly anything, really—it can't have done him any harm.'

71

'There are substances, Tabitha of which a minute quantity can do terrible damage. Where, may I ask, does this pretty plant grow?'

'Down beside the pool where we used to catch sticklebacks. You must have seen it many times.'

Something connected in Christopher's mind. Purple flowers and a root which reddened when cut. He seemed to recall something from the darker side of folklore. It had to do with potions, ointments, superstition...

Appalled, he sat down in Edgar's chair and passed a hand despairingly over his eyes. 'Dear God, I think I know what it is.'

Tabitha's eyes sparkled with merriment and a sly pride at her own extensive knowledge of that plant. She could tell him its Latin name and all its common names. She could enlighten him upon its habitat and its pedigree as a death-dealer. She could list its effects stage by stage and hazard a fair guess at Papa's life expectancy.

Christopher gazed up at his sister's laughing face and swallowed hard. The gravity of her action seemed to escape her still and he tried angrily to make her see it.

'In heaven's name, Tabitha, are you mad? You've poisoned him! You little idiot. Do you understand that? He may very well die.'

72

Tabitha was quite sure that he would. He had to. She would get no second chance if he recovered.

'Oh, don't exaggerate!'

'Will you stop laughing and take heed!' Christopher slammed his open palm upon the table with a crash that made Tabitha jump and wiped the smile from her face.

'All right, I suppose it was irresponsible,' she allowed cautiously. 'I must say, I hadn't expected quite such dramatic results. I do hope I didn't pick the wrong thing by mistake. That is a possibility, of course. There are so many plants with purple flowers, aren't there, and they often look alike...'

'Dramatic!' exclaimed Christopher. 'It's a nightmare. How could you have been so stupid?'

'It just seemed appropriate. You know, poetic justice and all that. If it's any comfort to you, Papa will probably give me an awful hiding tomorrow, so you might at least let me enjoy the joke while I can.'

Her tone had become defensive, that of a child caught out in an act of mischief, and it never occurred to Christopher that this could be anything other than a prank by a silly young girl. It seemed altogether too juvenile, too inept and brazen for deliberate murder.

When man underestimates woman, reflected Tabitha, he gives her a useful advantage. Furthermore, long experience had taught her that a half-truth was often more convincing than an outright lie, harder to disprove and easier to sustain.

'You may very well escape that hiding, Tabitha, because I don't think he'll live to inflict it. And what about me? What if I had taken some of that sauce?'

'Nonsense,' quavered Tabitha, her lip beginning to tremble. 'You know you hate horseraddish, just as you know I would never do anything to harm you. I wanted you to share the joke, not fall victim yourself. I realise you stayed at home out of sympathy for me and I hoped my little escapade would make you laugh.'

The boy stared at her pityingly. 'Oh, God. Tabitha, my dear, empty-headed girl, you've done a terrible thing.'

Tabitha thought this the appropriate moment to start showing fear.

'Oh, Christopher, I won't get into trouble, will I? He will be all right, won't he? I've sent one of the lads for Dr Prale, but it's such a long ride into St Lowen—nearly an hour each way. Isn't there something we can do in the meantime?'

The boy stared blankly back at her. Shocked and confused, he realised hopelessly that he had not the first idea of what to do next. Finally, in desperation, he scurried off to the library to consult *The Complete Household Physician.*

'He would be helpless in a crisis,' Papa had once said.

How true, thought Tabitha smugly. And how fortunate.

For the next fifty minutes, Christopher scuttled ineffectually up and down with towels and basins. There were, as his sister had said, no emetics or purgatives of any kind in the medicine cupboard and Edgar could not have swallowed them in any case. It did not cross Christopher's mind that she might have removed them herself.

Tabitha, meanwhile, sobbed piteously at the foot of the stairs. She wrung her hands, begged forgiveness, generally got in the way and took care to be of no practical use whatever. She was wondering how much longer it was going to take, when suddenly she heard her brother's voice bark an order from the landing outside Papa's room.

'Tabitha! Come here!'

Warily she went upstairs and encountered Christopher at the top. He looked dreadful, for the healthy roundness of his face had given way to a gaunt pallor and his eyes were dark-shadowed, brilliant with anger. He seized his sister by the arm, half-dragged her across the landing and shoved her into Edgar's bedroom.

'I want you to see what you've done, you confounded little fool.'

The figure on the bed was utterly still, the eyes and mouth half-closed. This curious dead thing was all that remained of the family despot. Papa's overbearing presence had gone and Tabitha was intrigued that such a transformation could be achieved so easily.

'...Convulsions followed by asphyxia or failure of the heart,' the book had said. She had read it carefully and knew, in a cool, theoretical way, just what she was doing and what to expect. Only now, with the final result laid upon the bed before her, did she fully grasp the enormity of the peril in which she had placed herself. For a moment she was genuinely frightened, but the prospect of personal freedom and half the Roskarnon estate kept an edge on her wits.

'Well, are you content?'

She glanced sideways at her brother. 'Oh, Christopher,' she whispered shrinkingly, 'what am I going to do? Will they lock me up?'

The boy stared numbly at his sister's tearful face. At first he could hardly think coherently at all, but slowly, one by one, the implications began to present themselves.

How could he possibly have his little sister consigned to the rigours of the law over a foolish trick which had gone tragically wrong? And was it so simple anyway? The more he thought about it, the more complications he saw. Without doubt, Christopher was experiencing a certain guilt himself, for was he not faintly glad that the old man was gone? Had he not felt a small shiver of excitement in the instant when Father stopped breathing? Was there not a momentary sensation of lightness?

For years Edgar had treated him with outright contempt, and Christopher now acknowledged a twist of loathing for the old man which made him reluctant to condemn Tabitha.

And what about the family name? Instinctively he sought to safeguard the pride and respect hitherto enjoyed by the Summerfield clan. He thought nervously of scandal, about those vulgar 'confessions' and verses that were sold for the public to read. He imagined the pointing and the staring, the details of their private lives recounted in court for the amusement of the riff-raff—especially since Father had been a magistrate himself. His prestigious old family would not have a shred of dignity left. Would it not be degrading if they all ended up in a 'Penny Dreadful'? At the very least he would be expelled from the Amateur Astronomers' Club. Equally disgraceful and doubly horrific was the possibility that Tabitha's sanity might be called into question. Whichever way he looked at it, Christopher knew that any exposure of this incident was going to be very unpleasant indeed.

'Christopher, I'm frightened,' wailed Tabitha. 'What are we going to do?'

They stood face to face at the foot of the bed, the object of their dilemma sprawled obliviously in the background. Christopher was silent for a while.

'The doctor should be here in about half an hour,' he said finally. 'We'll have to say that we think it was his heart, that he's complained of pains once or twice today. Doctor Prale has been predicting a bad attack for years. He was always warning him about his temper. I suspect he'll find some satisfaction in being proved right, and no one could deny that Father had a rare old tantrum this afternoon.'

'What if he doesn't believe us?' whimpered Tabitha.

'You'd best pray that he will. Be thankful, Tabitha, that Father died before the doctor's arrival. No one who witnessed the last half hour of his life could believe this to be a simple heart seizure. Even I know enough to be certain that such attacks do not produce convulsions and violent delusions, or cause the victim to drool and grind his teeth like a madman.'

Tabitha did not feel that prayers were really necessary. Edgar's heart and breathing had indeed failed him at the end. That much was perfectly true. Her own contribution to the process could be simply overlooked.

Christopher turned as he opened the door and glanced anxiously round the room, for Papa had been copiously sick.

'I'm going downstairs. I feel the need for a very large brandy. You'd best clean this room and put everything in order, sister dear. A distasteful chore, I know, but you've earned it.'

'Yes, Christopher,' sniffed Tabitha meekly. But as the door closed behind him her expression shifted into lines of triumphant mirth, and she softly whistled a jaunty little tune as she set about arranging her father in a tidier posture upon the bed.

CHAPTER 5

There were few who lamented Edgar's passing and most regarded the fatal attack as a natural result of his quick temper. It was not the first time a man had died in a fit of fury. An excitable nature, they said, could be most injurious to the health. Tabitha listened gravely and agreed that she was certainly lucky to have such a placid disposition.

She accepted condolences with dignity and everyone said that she was a very brave little thing. It must have been a shock, they agreed, for two young people—both of them minors— to find themselves suddenly alone, with only a squad of bankers, trustees and family lawyers to guide them.

The funeral attracted a number of banished relatives who were never seen at Roskarnon while Edgar was alive. He had frightened some and offended others, thus ensuring that they would not come calling, even at Christmas. Tabitha noted their presence and guessed, with some amusement, that they had come not to grieve but to gloat.

Among them was Papa's most spirited opponent, a woman of great girth and commanding mien. She was Aunt Clementina Dalby, Mama's sister. She had so often denounced Edgar as a bully that he finally banned her from visiting Mrs Summerfield, thus depriving poor Mama of her last means of defence. For some months after that, Aunt Clemmie had laid siege to the house, calling daily and demanding to see her sister, but all to no avail.

It was plain to everyone that she greatly enjoyed the funeral, snorting contempt when the vicar spoke too generously of Edgar, and hurling her clod of earth triumphantly onto the coffin. Tabitha found Aunt Clemmie vastly entertaining and was thoroughly pleased to see her.

On that cool, cloudy day, as the service ended and the graveside gathering began to disperse, a young man stepped shyly up to Tabitha and laid a hand on her arm. He was pale and freckled, his hair and eyelashes a kind of ginger-blond which rendered him slightly pretty.

'Miss Summerfield, please accept my sympathies.'

She turned around and smiled wanly up at him through the black lace of her veil.

'Why, thank you, Mr Kirkwood. It has all

been a very great shock, of course.'

'If there is any help I can give, please be sure to ask. I would like very much...' Here he faltered slightly and blushed.'...to be your—friend.'

Tabitha supposed that he felt it indecorous to suggest anything more in the circumstances.

'That is most kind,' she said warmly. 'And I'm sure that we're going to be very special friends. I hope, when we have all recovered from this blow, that we may see more of you at Roskarnon.'

It was enough, she knew, to keep him dangling for months, his ardour fermenting all the while.

'Give my regards to your Mama and Papa,' she added artfully. 'You're very lucky, you know, to have both parents with you still. I have my brother, of course, but I do feel lonely at times, for all that. He'll be off to Oxford in September and I shan't know what to do without him.'

William gave her hand a comforting squeeze.

'You know where to find me,' he whispered.

As Tabitha was leaving the churchyard she was stopped by another young gentleman—thin and bespectacled this time, with a nose like a paper-knife.

'I wish to convey my profoundest regrets,

Tabitha. Your father was a fine man and will be sadly missed.'

She glanced up at him and half smiled, but declined to stop. 'Thank you, Mr Robson,' she murmured distantly.

'I shall, of course, be on hand to assist you—and your brother—in any matters of business that may arise, and as soon as you feel strong enough we can discuss our arrangements for the future. I understand, naturally, that a period of recovery is required and I shall respect that need,' intoned James, striding manfully along beside her.

I'm going to enjoy this, thought Tabitha.

She halted suddenly and turned sharply to face him with wide, questioning eyes. 'What on earth do you mean, sir?' Her voice carried just the right touch of indignation. 'Matters of business? I hardly think my family finances concern you. Our arrangements for the future? I'm sorry, Mr Robson, I am at a loss. I do not understand.'

For a moment he seemed disconcerted.

'But, surely you... That is to say, your father and I had decided...' His words trailed away under Tabitha's green stare.

'Yes?'

'Well, our engagement. I thought...'

Tabitha's eyebrows lifted sharply.

'Engagement? What in heaven's name are you talking about?'

'The understanding between us, Miss Summerfield,' he said stiffly.

'Don't be preposterous, sir. You have never even taken tea with me. There has been neither courtship nor proposal. If this is a joke, it is in poor taste.'

Robson seemed nonplussed. 'Last week your father made it clear to me that I might begin to call upon you, with a view to marriage. I assumed that he did so with your full knowledge and consent.'

It was Tabitha's turn to look bewildered. 'Indeed not. No mention was ever made to me of such plans and I cannot help but feel that you are somehow mistaken...'

'There is no mistake.'

'Sir,' she said sternly, 'I know my father was something of a despot, but I doubt that even he would seek to dispose of his daughter through an arranged marriage. He may have voiced to you his own feelings on the matter, but he was not speaking on my behalf, I assure you. I knew nothing about it.'

'Oh.' James, in a state of abashment quite unfamiliar to him, shuffled his feet awkwardly.

'Furthermore, I'm bound to say that I find it neither flattering nor appealing to have a suitor approach my father behind my back, without any word to me, as if I were some sort of commodity. There are certain niceties, such as courtship, which should always be observed; a lady likes to be consulted in these matters, she likes to be the first to know.'

He cleared his throat and fiddled with the starched collar of his shirt. Reprimand from a woman was hard to take, but he was not entirely discouraged. Female resistance, he believed, was a poor thing and easily overcome by a really determined man.

'No affront was intended, Miss Summerfield. You may take it, instead, as a measure of my esteem for your father that I consulted him first. Like any good parent, he was greatly concerned for the future of his children and I had no wish to cause him any displeasure. I merely sought to outline my good intentions.'

'You must have discussed them very fully, Mr Robson, if you got to the point of suggesting marriage. However...' Tabitha treated him to a polite smile. Magnanimous now, she softened her tone. '...it is clear to me that your motives were good and I thank you for the compliment bestowed upon me.'

'May I assume, then...?'

'You must excuse me, Mr Robson. Funerals are so upsetting and I have guests to attend.'

With that, she was gone in a swish of black crêpe, leaving James to stare after her in puzzlement.

★ ★ ★ ★

Christopher could not help noticing that his sister recovered from the tragedy far more rapidly than he did. Despite all the sound and logical reasons for it, he knew that his connivance made him party to the incident, and he still harboured feelings of shame at the joy which had momentarily engulfed him when Edgar breathed his last.

Tabitha was undoubtedly much more resilient. She had not fallen victim to fits of brooding and melancholy; in fact there were moments when he was almost appalled at her composure as she entertained sympathetic visitors over cherry cake and cups of tea.

The very sameness of the daily routine was unnerving to him, for it underlined his inner turmoil. It seemed incredible that life could carry on as normal after what had happened. He felt that something calamitous should follow and Tabitha guessed that he was expecting some kind of thunderbolt.

It was on its way.

If Christopher's conscience required a penalty, it received one on the day the will was read. It was hardly absolution, but it did make him feel somewhat better. He had been deprived of half his expected inheritance—an embarrassing statement of Edgar's lack of faith in him. Christopher felt suitably punished and he hoped that Father's largesse to Tabitha would sting her into fresh remorse.

Tabitha claimed huge astonishment at this development and afterwards she allowed him to find her weeping tears of contrition.

On reflection, she had half feared that Papa might have qualified the bequest with some proviso in the will, making it officially dependent upon her marriage to James Robson. Such, however, was not the case. The wording was simply that her share should be held in trust until she either married or attained the age of twenty-one. It was careless of him, Tabitha thought, or perhaps a matter of simple complacency. Papa was too well accustomed to being obeyed and had not really counted on quite such an early death. He had doubtless expected to supervise the wedding and enjoy many years in the company of son-in-law James.

Tabitha thought it all a most delicious joke, although for the next few days she seemed subdued and crushed beneath a great burden of guilt. Christopher would never have guessed at the fierce joy which possessed her, or that her spirit danced a jig behind the downcast eyes.

Tabitha's apparent repentance, however, was not enough to lift her brother's gloom, and as the weeks passed he viewed his forthcoming move to university with some relief. It would be a tonic, he thought, to remove himself from the atmosphere and the memories of Roskarnon.

Naturally, certain arrangements would have to be made before he left, and one of these was the problem of finding someone to 'look after' Tabitha. It was true that she had a houseful of servants, many of them well known and trusted—for he had reinstated some of those whom Edgar had sacked, including the housekeeper and young Peggy. All the same, he thought it fitting to provide some sort of guardian for his sister and he was wise enough to consult her on the matter beforehand.

'Aunt Clemmie,' she said without hesitation. 'Can I please have Aunt Clemmie? She's such good company.'

Christopher paused to consider. It sounded like a good idea, for Clementina was a very capable woman and a sharp administrator, as useful as any estate manager. She would make an excellent guardian and he felt that the family lawyers would be amenable to the idea.

'You're sure that's what you want?'

'Oh, yes!' Tabitha clapped her hands delightedly. 'That would be lovely.'

'Very well, then. I'll write to her this afternoon and let us hope she'll be willing to come.'

'Oh, I'm certain that she will. Aunt Clemmie doesn't like living alone, and she's very fond of me.'

★ ★ ★ ★

So it was that two days later a small procession trundled up the drive. First of all came a carriage, with Aunt Clementina lodged enormously in the back seat, while a great cargo of trunks, pot plants and furniture was stacked upon the two carts following behind.

Tabitha greeted her aunt with immense pleasure, but it was some time before Clementina was ready to come indoors for tea. Instead, she stationed herself at the front entrance to supervise the unloading of her belongings, waving her folded parasol as she issued the carters with orders and instructions.

Christopher had found it passing strange that his sister should favour such an overpowering woman. And yet, he supposed, history was full of odd partnerships and Tabitha was nothing if not capricious.

When at last Aunt Clemmie's possessions were all arranged to her satisfaction, and the carriers had made their escape, she settled down to tea with her niece.

'Dear Aunt,' Tabitha chirped, 'I'm so very pleased you've come. Christopher thought I should have someone to keep an eye on me and take care of things while he's away. I must say, I was a little anxious at the propect of staying here alone.'

'Yes, dear, well that's only natural. A young girl cannot be expected to cope with the running of a large house. It's sensible of Christopher to make proper arrangements. He will have no cause to worry while you are in my care.'

'Of course not, Aunt.'

'I know how to manage money, you see. A woman who has never married cannot afford to subside into helplessness. I have never had to rely upon anyone for support or advice and I shall do my best to equip you with similar competence.'

'Oh dear,' murmured Tabitha, pouring the tea. 'Papa would have frowned on that, I'm afraid.'

Clementina's face darkened at the mention

of Edgar. She took a snapping bite at her currant bun and chewed ferociously.

'Oh yes, he'd have happily turned you into a poor, whimpering rabbit, just like your mother. I'm quite sure he'd have married you off to another such man as himself, leaving you no freedom, no dignity, not even a mind of your own. I'm not ashamed to say that I'm very glad he died before he could ruin your life. My poor sister was such a happy, high-spirited girl before she married him—and look what became of her.'

'Don't worry, Aunt. I wouldn't let that happen to me.' A spark of humour appeared in Tabitha's eyes. 'Would you like a biscuit?'

Clemmie took two.

'Yes, I must admit that you have certain qualities of character which your Mama did not possess.'

'Qualities?'

Clementina nodded. 'You are clever and therefore resourceful. And I suspect that you are not too highly principled.'

Tabitha managed to look wounded, but Aunt Clemmie chuckled and two deep dimples appeared in her pink, floppy cheeks.

'Now don't think I'm being critical. I've always said that it doesn't pay to be too virtuous. But sometimes, Tabitha, I sense a phantom pair of horns peeping through that lovely hair. It's one of the reasons I'm fond of you—just so long as you know where to draw the line.'

Tabitha's little white teeth gleamed in a smile of pure delight. 'Dear Aunt Clemmie, you're so droll. We're going to have a splendid time together, aren't we?'

In her loathing for Edgar, Clementina had often wished him dead, with a vague proviso that this should come about by natural causes or some happy accident. And whilst she approved a streak of mischief in a healthy young girl, she would have been appalled to learn that Tabitha could contrive to grant that wish.

A short while later, Christopher came downstairs to greet his aunt.

'I must say, you really have become a fine young man,' she said, inspecting him proudly. 'You've a much better physique than your father. Edgar was always rather squat.'

'Thank you, Aunt Clem. And are you quite well?'

'Yes and no, dear. I've suffered with my back for several years now. I had a fall, you know—tripped half-way down the stairs on my thirty-seventh birthday. Of course, spinal injuries always leave a weakness.'

'I'm sorry to hear that, Aunt.' The boy sat

down and accepted a cup of tea from his sister.

'Oh, there are worse things,' shrugged Clementina. 'So you'll be on your way to Oxford soon?' she added, beaming. 'Are you looking forward to it?'

'Yes, I think it will do me good.'

'I'm sure it will. If you'll forgive my saying so, you look dreadfully pale and melancholy.'

'Christopher hasn't quite recovered yet from losing Papa,' explained Tabitha. 'He was with him when he died and it still plays on his mind.'

'Good heavens,' snorted Clemmie impatiently, 'you mustn't allow yourself to mope over that. It's not healthy for a young man with his whole life in front of him. I'm surprised at you, Christopher. Protracted grief can make a person ill, you know, and I cannot imagine why you should miss a man like your father.'

'I won't pretend that I miss him, Aunt, but it was an unpleasant shock to see him die so...suddenly.'

Tabitha responded with her prettiest smile. 'Yes, dear, but Aunt Clemmie's quite right. Life must go on.'

'Sensible child,' said Clementina. 'Really, Christopher, I think a spell in Oxford is just what you need. New friends, new interests. You'll have your mind fully occupied and there won't be time for brooding. When do you leave, anyway?'

'Next Wednesday, if all goes well.'

'Splendid. You know you can rely on me to pay the bills and guard your interests while you are away, so you needn't give the estate another thought. I shall do my very best for you.'

'Thank you, Aunt. I've no doubt you'll do a fine job and I hope you'll be happy here.'

'But of course I will, my dear. After all, I have Tabitha to keep me amused.'

★ ★ ★ ★

On a day in early September, Christopher left for Oxford. Aunt Clemmie had tried to organise his packing and would have sent him off with a mountain of luggage if he had not been firm with her. In the end he managed to pare it down until only two trunks remained. In these were stowed a supply of clothing, some of his personal treasures and all his astronomy books.

Clementina sniffed a little sadly as she and Tabitha followed him out to the front door, where the carriage was waiting.

'You just look after yourself, young man. And mind what you eat.'

She clasped him in one of her crushing hugs

and, as he patted his aunt's back, Christopher's gaze strayed across her chubby shoulder and came to rest upon Tabitha.

Her face, as ever, was alert and sweet. The tilted eyes were fixed upon him, wide and intensely bright—but just for an instant he thought he saw shades of mockery dancing there. And although her smile was merely pleasant, he briefly fancied there was laughter; muffled, faraway laughter, rolling through Tabitha's being as water flows through a cave. Somehow, Christopher doubted that she would miss him. He received a strange impression that she was glad, indeed eager, to see him go, as if she had plans and was anxious to set about them.

The feeling, however, was a fleeting one. It disappeared as swiftly as it had come and Christopher dismissed it as foolishness, for his spirits were high on this fine morning with so much excitement ahead of him.

Detaching himself from Clemmie's grasp, he said simply: 'Do be good now, Tabitha. Promise me.'

'Why, Christopher, I shall be a positive saint. I vow not to do anyting wicked for at least a week. Aunt Clemmie will keep an eye on me—won't you, dear?'

'Assuredly,' said Clementina.

'There, you see? Now off you go and don't give me another thought.'

'I shall expect a letter every week,' said Clementina, as he climbed up beside the driver. 'And woe betide you if you forget.'

'I will write every Sunday, Aunt Clem. You may depend upon it.'

She waved tearfully as they rolled away down the drive, and watched until the carriage clattered through the gates, out into the lane.

'Well, that's that, I suppose. I do hope he's taken enough warm clothing.'

'Come on, Aunt, let's go indoors. He's big enough to look after himself—and you've still got me. Christopher says I'm the one who needs supervision, the guidance of an older woman, if you like. I missed Mama very much, you know. But now that you're here everything is all right, isn't it? You can help me choose my dresses and show me how to amuse a gentleman.'

Clemmie chuckled as she looked at the eager, upturned face.

'Why, Tabitha, I'm an old maid, my dear. Whatever makes you think I know the ways and wiles of catching men?'

Tabitha squeezed her hand. 'Oh, come now. I'm sure you do.'

'In theory if not in practice, eh?'

The girl bubbled with laughter. 'That's right, and I'm nearly seventeen, you know. It's time I started thinking about a husband.'

'Well the first lesson is this,' said Clementina, suddenly severe. 'Be very cautious and practical in your choice. A woman's property passes to her husband when she marries, leaving her utterly dependent upon him, so avoid wasters—and dictators like your father. Marry someone you can govern, and thereby keep control of what is rightfully yours.'

Tabitha, needless to say, had already reached that decision for herself, but she looked suitably attentive and nodded gravely.

'Very well, Aunt. You shall help me select a nice, manageable husband. And if ever he's troublesome we'll quash him, won't we?'

Clementina began to shake with laughter. 'Really, Tabitha, are you quite sure you need any advice from me? Perhaps I should reserve my support for the man you marry, whoever he may be.'

CHAPTER 6

Mrs Edith Carkett was undeniably a very capable dressmaker, in fact the best in St Lowen. She was never short of customers and could proudly claim to have garbed the town's most affluent ladies. Thus far, however, she had only once been favoured with an order from Miss Tabitha Summerfield. That, of course, had been for the cream moiré frock.

Although, for her own reasons, Tabitha had never cared to wear that dress again, it was plain that she was well satisfied with Mrs Carkett's efforts, for she arrived on the dressmaker's doorstep one morning, accompanied by Miss Clementina Dalby.

The child was to have a complete new wardrobe, explained Clementina. Three months in mourning black were quite enough, she declared. A perfectly decent interval had passed and youth should not be burdened with dreariness. Tabitha's taste, she said, was admirable and would need no supervision, but Clementina would be keeping an eye on cost, and total expenditure was not to exceed one hundred pounds.

Thereafter, many mornings were spent in St Lowen, poring over fabrics and patterns. Tabitha's choice of colours was very consistent —predictable, in fact. Shopkeepers angling for her custom soon made a point of stocking wide varieties of mauves and purples, spring and emerald greens. They kept bolts of satin and velvet in dusky blue and indigo, especially for Miss Summerfield.

Many more afternoons were passed with Mrs Carkett. Critically, Tabitha would study her image in the glass while the seamstress turned her this way and that, pinning and tucking, always precisely to Tabitha's instructions. Unlike many of Mrs Carkett's young ladies, Miss Summerfield would not accept advice. She always knew exactly what she wanted.

New outfits began to arrive regularly at Roskarnon, together with countless accessories. There were high-heeled ankle boots in soft kid with patent leather toe-caps. There were velvet slippers and silk stockings, tiny hats with plumes and ribbons. There were parasols, purses and fans, corsets and lacy knee-length drawers.

'I think you have enough now, dear, don't you?' said Clemmie finally. 'Heaven knows when you'll find occasion to wear all these things.'

'Well, we must make opportunities, mustn't we, Aunt? Perhaps I might invite some guests to take tea with me one afternoon? After all, one invitation usually begets another.'

'I hope you don't mean to include that pompous young Robson fellow who's been calling so persistently. He seems to feel that he has some sort of claim on you, my dear. There's a distinct air of ownership in his manner. Not a pleasant type, I'd say.'

'Papa always spoke very well of him.'

'Which perfectly illustrates my point.' Clementina frowned at her niece. 'You don't like him, do you, Tabitha?'

The girl shrugged. 'Not especially,' she said mildly.

'Then I shall put a stop to his visits. He's much too presumptuous for my liking. Edgar was the same way when courting my poor sister.'

'If you think it best, Aunt. I don't mind.'

'Very well. Now then, who will you ask to tea, Tabitha? You seem to have so few acquaintances.'

'Papa didn't allow me any close friends,' explained Tabitha sadly. 'He seldom considered anyone suitable company.' She paused for a moment, apparently considering possibilities, and then her face brightened as with the dawning of an idea. 'Perhaps I might ask that nice Mr Kirkwood. You remember him, don't you, Aunt? William Kirkwood. He was very kind after Papa died, and no one could accuse him of being forward. In fact, I think he is shy.'

'Ah yes, I believe I recall the one. Inoffensive young fellow—with a great many freckles. His father's a brewer, isn't he?'

'Yes Aunt, but I don't think that matters, do you?'

'Not a bit. I'm sure he makes excellent beer. I must say, I quite enjoy the occasional glass of stout with a roast joint. By all means, ask him if you wish.'

Tabitha jumped to her feet and pecked Clementina fondly on the cheek.

'I shall write him a note straight away.'

Aunt Clemmie smiled as Tabitha flitted up the stairs to her room. How nice to see the child happy. If only fortune had treated her mother as kindly.

Upstairs, Tabitha spent a quarter of an hour carefully wording the invitation. She was confident that William would accept, although he might not realise that he was to be the only guest. For certain, he would have been astounded to know that Tabitha had him earmarked to be a bridegroom the following autumn.

Although Edgar and successive governesses had always forced her to use her right hand, this went very much against the grain. Freed now from their influence, she had returned to her natural left-handed inclination and the hesitant, laboured scrawl of her childhood became an elegant, flourishing script, embellished with many swirls like the tendrils of a climbing plant. Tabitha was really quite proud of it as she briskly blotted the note and read it through for the last time. It would do very well, she thought happily, folding and tucking it into an envelope.

She thought she would ask Cook to bake one of her lovely peach and chocolate gateaux for the tea party. William was especially fond of sticky cake.

* * * *

Friday afternoon found Tabitha sitting before her dressing table mirror, critically inspecting her appearance. Her dress was dark green plaid with a broad inset of white lace in the bodice and a crisply pleated jabot. The effect was both smart and youthful, she thought approvingly, patting the smooth upward sweep of her hair at the sides and flicking the bouncy little curls in front.

As the clock struck four-thirty, she was searching through her jewellery box for something to finish it all off. She decided on a brooch to be pinned in the lace at her throat—a little silver spider with emerald eyes. Spiders, after all, were said to be lucky and she had a preference for the wearing of silver rather than gold. She always said it reminded her of moonlight—and what could be more romantic?

She was on her way downstairs when William arrived. He was surprised but not displeased to find there were no other visitors, for it meant he would have Miss Summerfield virtually to himself. He had to endure Clementina's scrutiny for five minutes or so, but by the time the tea arrived she was beaming at him over the top of her spectacles and regaling him with little jokes.

William was twenty-five. He had four younger brothers and a sister, none of whom resembled him at all. He was modest by nature, considerate and shy. No matter what his station in life, Edgar could never have liked him, for William was anything but masterful where women were concerned.

However, Papa would have been perplexed to learn that, despite his gentleness, young

Kirkwood was surprisingly adept in matters financial. Like Christopher, he possessed a quiet intelligence, but William's cleverness was directed to practical ends.

Without doubt, he seemed to meet all of Tabitha's requirements, and she was already thinking of a honeymoon in Italy as they chatted politely over tea and gateau.

'I'm sorry that I missed your party, William, but as you know, misfortune intervened.'

'It must have been a dreadful experience for you, to lose your father in such an abrupt and distressing fashion.'

'Humph,' snorted Clementina. 'It was just like Edgar to die at such a time. He always was spiteful.'

William looked startled.

'Yes, William, it was most upsetting.' Tabitha smiled sadly. 'But please tell us about your birthday.'

'Oh, well, it was a grand evening, of course —but don't be too disappointed. As it happens, my family are planning quite a round of dinners and receptions at Copperhill during the coming holiday, beginning with a ball on Christmas Eve. We should be delighted if you —and Miss Dalby—would come. My mother loves to entertain guests and it all promises to be quite splendid.'

He sounded faintly amused and Tabitha could guess why. William's mother was socially ambitious and would spare no expense to impress. Already glutted with cash and all things material, she now sought the rarer elements of status and was ever intent on establishing connections with 'better people'.

Copperhill had been especially designed for the Kirkwoods by a famous architect. Its walls, bays and colonnade shone snowy white amidst the velvet green of perfect lawns, clipped hedges and geometrically formal gardens. If set beside this immaculate symbol of wealth, Roskarnon's mellow grace and wild garden would seem slightly shabby, but infinitely more inviting.

Mrs Kirkwood made frequent expeditions to London and the continent to buy clothes, and her hoard of jewellery was widely envied. She felt it necessary to keep a landau and pair, a brougham and a victoria, for outings and errands of varying importance.

Her husband hunted, shot and fished to amuse himself and maintain the proper style, while Mrs Kirkwood supported many charities and entertained. She scoured the county for the 'right sort' of guests, cultivating the notable and the fashionable, pouncing upon the occasional specimen of nobility to install at her table. And yet, alas, she could never escape the knowledge that all her grandeur was founded on bottles of halfpenny beer. None of the extravagance brought her much pleasure, for she was humourless by nature and believed that 'bettering oneself' was a most serious business.

Tabitha had long been covetous of the Kirkwood fortune. Even Clementina, with her considerable private means, remarked that their income must be prodigious. And unlike her father, young Miss Summerfield cared not a jot if it came from halfpenny beer or eel pies. All money was equal in Tabitha's eyes.

'Oh, William, how lovely! Of course we'll come—won't we, Aunt?'

Clementina beamed and patted him fondly on the knee.

'It's very thoughtful of you to ask us, young man, and we're pleased to accept. It will brighten what might have been a rather dull Christmas for us.'

'Will Christopher be home from university?'

'Undoubtedly.'

'Then he must come, too,' said Kirkwood firmly, and his soul gave a leap at the warmth in Tabitha's voice and the affectionate gaze she turned upon him.

'Oh, William, I'm sure we're going to be the closest of friends.'

* * * *

Tabitha was right, of course. Having neatly given their relationship its first gentle push, she made certain it would have every chance to flourish. Sure enough, William's visits became more and more frequent. By spring he was calling five times a week.

He took her out on picnics and boat rides down the river. He gathered posies of wild flowers for her, talked much about sunsets, and gave her a book of love poems. Hampered by shyness, he was never able to pour out his feelings in pretty words of his own, but adoration was writ large on his face and Tabitha knew that all was going well.

Clemmie smiled upon this splendid match and Tabitha considered that the best possible endorsement. The Kirkwood family thought her enchanting and pushed the young couple together at every opportunity. In fact there was approval on every side. Predictably, the courtship swiftly gathered momentum and went hurtling down the road to an early proposal. Tabitha naturally accepted, hinting coyly that a long engagement would be most trying, for she could hardly wait to become Mrs Kirkwood. And so the date was set for September 20th.

CHAPTER 7

It was a very grand wedding and made everyone extremely happy. Clementina was especially delighted, for she thought most highly of William. His family, she agreed privately with Tabitha, were mirthless and dull, but William was the one sweet apple on the Kirkwood tree.

Ruth and Ambrose Kirkwood wallowed in the splendour of it all. Clementina found this faintly irritating and considered William's mother foolishly overdressed. Apricot satin, she thought, was unbecoming to such a withered little woman. Ruth's skin had a brownish hue and looked as if it might crackle to the touch, while her mouth was a short, clamped line and the eyes bespoke a soul full of censure. By contrast, Ambrose Kirkwood was ponderous and puffy, a bloated old man whose cough and mumble made heavy work of his wedding speech. Nonetheless, Clemmie felt that Tabitha had made an excellent choice in William Kirkwood. For preference he should have been a rich orphan, but in a less-than-perfect world one had to tolerate in-laws.

For his part, William was engulfed in bliss as he gazed upon his glowing little bride and heard the Reverend Devoy pronounce them man and wife. He could not know that he was destined for a life of subtle subjugation, for the yoke she place upon him was a honeyed, silken thing of which he was scarcely aware. From the very day of their engagement she had cast about him the first sticky threads of dominance, quietly ensuring that she always got her own way. When it came to decisions, William seldom drew a winning hand, for Tabitha was far too sharp a player. With tears and sweet manoeuvrings, she tripped and tied him every step of the way. His wishes were always over-ridden if they clashed with hers, his authority always undermined—but so gently, so prettily, that he never recognised this coercion for what is was.

In the late afternoon the wedding guests began to leave and the couple set out on the first stage of their journey to Italy, where they planned to spend the next four weeks. Tabitha's luggage comprised several large trunks whose contents included a number of beautiful silk nightgowns. Now that they were married, she felt that the double bed would provide her with an even more potent source of power. She meant to keep William ecstatically contented, to enliven his days with promise and sweeten his nights with fulfilment. An adoring husband was a manageable husband and Tabitha looked on this benevolent form of control as a bonus to her own enjoyment.

Here, however, she had miscalculated for the first time. For although he worshipped her, William was not a sensual man. His love had more to do with poetry than physical passion. It revolved around beauty, perfection, virtue and ideals. He was romantic in the truest sense of the word and had never guessed at the carnality of Tabitha's nature. He believed in the delicacy of women and meant to spare his little wife any excessive, lewd demands.

William might have abstained altogether, but for the fact that he wanted a family. And of course, he thought, women needed babies, did they not? Tabitha, he assured himself, would love to have babies, lots of them. It would compensate his darling for all the indignity, would it not?

That, at least, was the misguided belief that he took to the bedroom on his wedding night.

★ ★ ★ ★

Three days later, on a sunny terrace overlooking Lake Maggiore, Tabitha smiled fondly at her husband across the breakfast table and was careful to hide her sense of pique. Covertly, though, she eyed him with impatience, still vexed at the memory of William apologetically claiming his marital rights. The only thing for which he needed to apologise, she thought crossly, was the half-hearted mildness of it all.

Three nights, three encounters, each one brief, tepid and very disappointing—an exercise in begetting children with the minimum expenditure of time and effort. And when she had tried to prolong the episode, to encourage him and inject a little pleasure, he had been shocked, explaining patiently and with much embarrassment that it wasn't quite 'nice' to take so much interest.

'But, dearest,' she had said, 'I want you to enjoy yourself.'

Thereupon he had gasped, apologised yet again and promised not to bother her too often.

For his part, William was bewildered and disconcerted by the whole experience. He recalled with alarm the previous night, when he had been startled from sleep by a small hand sliding deftly beneath his nightshirt to take an encouraging grasp on his manhood. He had stammered a gentle rebuke there in the darkness and told her she must never do such a thing again.

'But I thought it would please you, my love,' came the hurt reply. 'Your happiness is very important to me.'

William was both touched and upset by this. Of course his poor little sweetheart meant well, nobly sacrificing her dainty sensitivities for him—but he felt he had somehow corrupted innocence and tainted purity. Finally, swamped in guilt, he had silently turned over and gone to sleep.

Now, as she sipped her coffee in the morning sunlight, Tabitha began to realise that her marriage was unlikely to have any real sensual dimension. She would have to look upon William as a very special friend rather than a lover. It was, she reflected, something of a pity, for he was otherwise a splendid catch—so pliable, generous and rich.

This little villa, of course, was a solid token of the latter. Close to Baveno, it perched upon a wooded hillside looking down upon the rusty-coloured tiled roofs, the spires and creamy-buff walls of the village below. Ruth and Ambrose had bought it for them as a wedding present after hearing Tabitha lightly mention Italy's beautiful lakes. With sunbleached walls, balconies and ornate railings, it stood like a big

112

iced cake amid brightly flowering terraced gardens, cypresses, olive and lemon trees.

Tabitha sighed as she gazed out over the blue waters of the lake. Drawbacks there might be, but money was never to be despised. It would always compensate for a very great deal, and pleasure could be found elsewhere.

She had no fears that her husband's reticence in bed would make him any less easy to handle, for William's affection was plainly not dependent on sex. Inwardly she made a note to show more modesty in future and let him keep his illusions.

'What are you thinking about?'

'Why, how beautiful it all is. And how lucky I am.' She reached across the table and curled small fingers over his freckled hand. 'It was so kind of your Mama and Papa to buy us this lovely, lovely villa.'

'I'm glad you're pleased with it.' A contented smile settled upon his features and the blue eyes fixed on her with warmth and pride. 'And so if you would like another in Paris, or Scotland —or anywhere you care to name—then you shall have it.'

He was worthy of more than tolerance, Tabitha realised suddenly, with a feeling akin to genuine fondness. It would do no harm to treat a good heart kindly, not only for a means to control, but also because he deserved it.

'What a dear you are,' she said, and meant it despite the lack of ardour which had so disappointed her.

'Well, while we're on the subject of houses,' said William thoughtfully, 'perhaps now is a good time to discuss where we're going to live. My family would like to have us at Copperhill, but I thought you would prefer a home of your own. We can either have one built or else buy something with a history. What do you think?'

'Oh—but William...' Tabitha looked surprised and faintly alarmed. 'I thought we could live at Roskarnon. that is my home. I was born there.'

'Yes, but it's half Christopher's and surely you would rather have your own house than share?'

'Heavens! You make it sound like a mere cottage. Why we could live at opposite ends and hardly ever see each other.'

William looked a little crestfallen.

'I had always planned to provide a new home for you, the very best you could ask...'

'But, dearest,' she coaxed, softly squeezing his hand, 'you know that everything I have now belongs to you. Roskarnon is half yours, is it not? You need have no qualms about living there.'

'I know that. It's only…' He shook his head and shrugged helplessly. 'Is that what you really want?'

'Oh yes, William, truly. I've always loved Roskarnon. I couldn't bear to live anywhere else. You won't make me leave, will you?'

The soft voice and the green eyes were pleading with him. A warm breeze stirred the little curls round her ears and William was instantly vanquished. Happiness, above all, was what he wanted for his darling and Tabitha's next words settled the matter conclusively.

'I suppose I should…' She hesitated slightly, as if pondering a doubt, then: 'Yes, I think I must tell you. There is another reason. I don't mean to be disloyal to my brother, but it's all for the best. You see, Papa felt that Christopher was not—suited—to looking after the estate. He said so many times and I fear that he may have been right.'

She spoke slowly, choosing her words precisely, as if trying to avoid any injustice to her brother, any outright charge that he was incapable of running Roskarnon.

'As you know,' she went on. 'he has a passion for astronomy which quite absorbs his attention and diverts his mind from all else. With the best will in the world, I do not think he will make a diligent manager and, like Papa,

115

I fear to see Roskarnon neglected. I'm very, very fond of Christopher, of course, but I would be much relieved if you were there to take the reins, so to speak. I've not the slightest doubt that Christopher would be glad to shed the responsibility and concentrate on his studies. I believe the two of you get on well enough together and it seems a fine solution for all of us. Unless, for some reason, you dislike Roskarnon and would not enjoy living there?' she added anxiously.

'I have always liked it very much, my dear. And if this will please you, then so shall it be.'

'Oh, William! Thank you!' She jumped up and scampered round behind his chair to fling her arms about his neck. 'You're so good to me.'

'If you are happy, so am I. Now then, what shall we do today?'

'I don't mind,' she purred, kissing his freckled cheek and tickling his ear. 'Whatever you suggest.'

'In that case I shall take you over to visit those little islands out there. I'm told they are very beautiful. If only it were possible, I would buy one for you instead of a house.'

Tabitha giggled and cooed gently in his ear. 'William, I think we'll be very contented together, you and I. What a pity Papa cannot see us now. He'd have been so surprised at the way everything has turned out.'

CHAPTER 8

Although greatly consoled by William's easy-going nature and his tireless generosity, with the passing days Tabitha became increasingly restless. The nights of sleeping beside him and the cool, polite couplings affected her like an appetiser for a main course which never arrived. They left her fidgety throughout the day and her eyes would covertly follow the movements of every passing Italian youth as she walked with her husband in the gardens and streets of Baveno. With the hunger that concentrates the mind upon a single object, she noticed them everywhere—in cafés and restaurants, in shops and alleys and on the little boats from the Fisherman's Isle.

On one particular Sunday, outside the Parish Church in the shadow of the bell tower, she was lucky enough to turn her ankle and stumble against one such brawny young man. She was gratified to see the suggestive admiration in the long-lashed black eyes as he caught her arm, murmuring with intimate concern. He smelt very faintly of sweat and wine, and she glimpsed a shadow of curling hair beneath his shirt as she thanked him, dimpling softly, for his help.

It was nothing serious, she assured the worried William as they walked on. The ankle did not hurt in the slightest and was it not fortunate that someone had been there to catch her?

He agreed that it was, but told her to be wary of such fellows, They were apt to be familiar, he explained, and would often mistake mere civility for encouragement.

Tabitha replied wryly that she did not feel at all unsafe, since her husband's presence was sure to forestall any advances.

William's chest swelled proudly at that. He patted her hand and felt very protective.

All through that evening, Tabitha's mind dwelt appreciatively on the young Italian. Her imagination kept turning back to the colour and form of him. She had always admired swarthy men, and how beautifully made he was, how elegantly supple.

His neat hips and buttocks were still swaggering through her mind when she got up next morning. Tabitha pictured them wistfully as she toyed with her breakfast. If only she could spend a few hours alone with such a man. William, however, with no other business to occupy him, would be at her side throughout the day. Unless...

Once again the goblin whispered. Tomorrow, perhaps? Something in the blackcurrent jam he enjoyed so much? Just a small indisposition to keep him in bed for the day?

Well—why not?

* * * *

The following morning, William blamed the fish he had eaten for breakfast when his stomach began to torment him with sudden rumblings and nausea. A doctor was called and, with many apologies, William was forced to take to his bed for twenty-four hours. Tabitha fussed and cooed until he fell asleep, but her spirits secretly soared at the prospect of a day's liberty.

With growing anticipation, she decided on a walk into Stresa. It was only a couple of miles and she had no wish to take the carriage and have a driver waiting around for her return. Dismissing her maid, she locked herself in one of the unused bedrooms and set about dressing.

There were many who noticed the petite English lady strolling demurely along the promenade in Stresa early that afternoon. She attracted glances of interest and curiosity from passing males, and disapproval from their womenfolk, not simply because she was looking uncommonly pretty in her lacy, clover-coloured dress with the jaunty little straw hat and parasol, but also because she was unescorted.

Those who cared about such things considered it most improper to see a woman walking alone. Such a young woman, too. Hardly more than a girl, in fact. Where, they wondered, was her chaperone?

Tabitha did not give a fig what people were thinking here in this strange little town so far from home, where nobody actually knew her. She nodded politely to gentlemen who raised their hats, but carefully declined to stop and talk to anyone until she came to a bustling little maze of stalls, apparently set up for a market day.

She lingered for some time among the baskets of brightly coloured fruit and vegetables, interested only, it seemed, in their contents. She bought a bag of oranges and then, as she dropped the money into the vendor's hand, noticed with a jolt of expectation the olive-skinned man who was watching her keenly across a display of silk shawls and fancy glassware.

He was aged about thirty, well-groomed and

expensively dressed, but his look was intense, insolently hopeful of an invitation, and Tabitha guessed that he would shed all gentility along with his clothes.

For a fleeting instant, the green eyes crinkled at the corners and dimples played in her cheeks as she gave him a guarded little smile of assent. Then she moved slowly on, drifting past counters bearing fish and wines, stands with shoes and small items of furniture, to stop at last at the flower stall, admiring the bundles of colourful blossoms.

She knew without looking round that the man was standing at her shoulder, just as she knew he was attracted by something far more human than petals and pollen. Busily examining the flowers, Tabitha made no move to turn round until a slim brown hand appeared before her, offering a large white rose.

She spun about and twinkled up at him with a murmur of thanks and feigned surprise. The man grinned. He spoke no English at all, but they read each other's faces well enough and Tabitha's smile broadened with recognition of just what she was seeking.

As she took his arm and they walked away, she gave not a thought to her husband. When William woke briefly at about half-past three, he wondered what his little love was doing. It was such a shame, he thought drowsily, turning over and sinking back into sleep. However would she amuse herself and pass the day all alone?

He could never have imagined that the mauve dress was lying on the floor of an expensive hotel room in Stresa, while its owner twisted and cavorted in breathless joy with a stranger. Nor did he know when he woke again at eight o'clock to find her sitting by his bed like a deeply concerned wife, that she had only returned within the last half-hour, in a carriage hired by the same stranger.

It had been an almost wordless encounter, she recalled later, musing upon her adventure. A dialogue of rustlings and broken, urgent breathing. The man carried the marks of her nails on his back and buttocks, and in return had left her in sated contentment to dwell upon memories of wanton pleasure. Tabitha was well pleased with the stranger, for she loved a man who would bite and admire and tease, a man who was knowing and pleasantly coarse. William, sad to say, was altogether too civil in bed.

The atmosphere of that balmy, stolen afternoon stayed with her and had to sustain her for some time to come. Lust after lunch had always been Tabitha's preference, but her husband required the discreet cover of darkness.

CHAPTER 9

The young Mr and Mrs Kirkwood returned to Roskarnon that year in time to spend Christmas with Aunt Clementina and, as duty demanded, with Tabitha's in-laws.

Her first concern, as the new year drew in, was to make a few alterations to the house. She was naturally obliged to consult Christopher on the matter, but this was merely a token gesture, for she knew full well that he was not really interested and could hardly wait to get back to Oxford and his telescopes. Roskarnon was hers to do with as she pleased

William, of course, was no obstacle at all. Tabitha's appealing enthusiasm went straight to his heart and thence to his pocket. Ever indulgent, he agreed to redecoration, new-fangled gas gadgetry and sundry other concessions to household fashion.

Ancient, draughty apartments, unused in her father's day, were now warmly furnished and carpeted, with a view to holding weekend house parties. Feeling very progressive, she next ordered the installation of two bathrooms. The great dining hall had been redundant for the best part of forty years, since Edgar never cared for social functions of any kind, except his beloved hunting and shooting parties. Tabitha, however, planned on music and dancing and lost no time in turning it into a ballroom.

For herself and her husband she staked a claim on the most spacious of the turret bedrooms. It overlooked the creek and the eastern side of the gardens, receiving the first of the morning sun. William raised no objections as she furnished it with inlaid mahogany, curtains of lace and blue velvet, soft wool rugs and filmy bed valances. Despite tassels, ruffles and a dressing-table draped in white muslin, he knew that Tabitha's taste was comparatively restrained. It certainly stopped well short of the flouncy excesses at Copperhill and so he paid the bills without murmur, for Tabitha was his darling and he would allow her anything.

To keep him contented and out of her way, Tabitha turned one corner of the house into what she called a 'gentleman's retreat'. She had always disliked the smell of tabacco—hence, she introduced a smoking room beside his study and banished him there whenever he wanted to indulge. There was also a well-equipped billiard room for the after-dinner amusement of male guests. It was all very modern and masculine, Tabitha said admiringly. She thought it only right and proper that the head of the house should have his own private domain and she would be very careful not to intrude.

All this refurbishment, of course, required the removal of many existing features, so Tabitha cleared out a great number of unwanted articles and ordered them to be stowed away in the attics. Some things did not fit in with her plans for the décor, others she simply disliked. Among the items discarded were rugs, pictures and small pieces of furniture, together with what Clemmie called 'those disgusting dead things'. By this, she meant Edgar's trophies, his glass cases full of stuffed fish and game birds.

'He was always happiest when tormenting human beings or slaughtering wildlife,' she sniffed. 'I'm surprised he didn't have your mother stuffed and mounted, since, he so loved to preserve his kills. Poor, mouldering things,' she murmured, peering at the pheasant which adorned an alcove in Edgar's study. 'I cannot fathom the mentality which likes to surround itself with animal corpses. Get rid of them, child, for heaven's sake.'

'They're not to my taste, either,' agreed Tabitha. 'I'll have them thrown out. You know, Aunt, this is such a pleasant room and receives the best of the sun in late afternoon. I thought I might use it for entertaining friends to tea. William has a larger study now and I'm sure Christopher won't mind. It will need complete redecoration, of course. I would like to make it more—feminine. Firstly, I'll get rid of all these leather chairs, those awful paintings with their battle scenes—oh, and this,too, I think.'

She crossed to the fireplace and laid a hand thoughtfully upon the barrel of the rifle which hung above the mantel.

'Ah, yes,' murmured Clementina. 'That was Marsden Summerfield's, wasn't it? How unfair that the better of two brothers should be the one to die young.'

'Papa was very proud of him,' Tabitha said. 'He used to tell everyone about Uncle Marsden's exploits, and always ensured that the rifle was kept oiled and polished, in perfect working order. He even used it once or twice himself on hunting weekends. He kept a box of special ammunition for it—I believe it's in that cupboard there. All-in-one cartridges, he called them.'

'Hm,' observed Clementina, peering over the top of her spectacles, 'it's one of those breechloaders they issued to the troops in Abyssinia some years ago.'

'That's right. That's where poor Uncle was killed. His commanding officer said he was very brave and sent Papa the rifle as a memento. Perhaps...' She hesitated, turning doubtful eyes to Clementina. 'Perhaps I should leave it where it is?'

'Oh, heavens,' Clementina shrugged, 'it'll make no difference to Marsden, my dear. And one should never be sentimental about a weapon of war. Remember, Tabitha, that thing has killed people.'

Tabitha nodded. 'You're right, Aunt. Well, it will never do so again. I'll have it stored away upstairs with everything else.'

'Very well, dear. Now, what about this carpet for the drawing-room...?'

Tabitha's expensive round of playing house occupied her for fully eight months, and by September all was finished. The timing was perfect, everyone said, for it was precisely at this point that she found herself carrying William's child.

CHAPTER 10

Christopher abandoned his studies the following April and came home to Roskarnon, bringing with him a wife. He had quietly married her in Oxford after a very subdued courtship, because she could not endure noise or fuss or stress of any sort. The daughter of a history professor, her name was Beverley and she was, in her own opinion, a very sick woman.

At nineteen years of age, she believed herself chronically if indefinably, ill. Despite the fact that doctors could find nothing actually wrong with her, she drooped and sighed beneath a host of fancied ailments, vague pains and constitutional weaknesses.

Waifishly thin, Beverley was a pallid, ethereal blond. There was a translucent, waxy pinkness to the skin around her sorrowful grey eyes and brief nose, which suggested sickness nobly endured and a helplessness in the face of life that would call for constant protection.

As Christopher introduced her to his astonished family, she smiled wanly round at them all and said that the journey from Oxford had been so exhausting that she felt quite faint.

For a moment Clemmie and Tabitha simply stared at the ashen little creature, while the ever-thoughtful William offered her a seat and ordered some tea in the hope of reviving her.

'Well,' said Clementina finally, 'what a surprise. Why did you not write and tell us, Christopher? Was it one of those impulsive, whirlwind romances?'

'Not exactly, but we thought it best to have a quiet wedding, Aunt Clem. Beverley's been ill, you see. Too much excitement could have meant a relapse.'

'But you didn't even tell us you were courting.' Aunt Clemmie peered curiously at Beverley over the top of her spectacles. 'Where did you meet my nephew, child?'

Beverley smiled nervously, aware that she was under inspection, that instant acceptance was too much to hope for.

'In church, Miss Dalby. My father is a professor of history at Oxford. He likes Christopher very much and introduced us after morning service one Sunday. Papa is a widower and deeply involved with his work. He has always been most anxious that I should have a kind husband to look after me.'

Perhaps the good professor felt he had borne his cross for long enough and was glad to pass on the burden to a younger man, reflected Tabitha privately.

'I see,' mused William. 'And how long have you known each other?'

'Four months or thereabouts.'

Tabitha, in her shrewd way, became still more convinced that Beverley's Papa was glad to be rid of her.

'Good Lord, Christopher, that was quick work—and I always thought I was the impetuous one.' She studied Beverley with faint amusement and much curiosity. 'What sort of illness did you suffer, dear? And have you quite recovered?'

'A deficiency of the blood, coupled with nervous debility and a delicate digestion,' said Beverley plaintively. 'I have never enjoyed good health and fear I never shall.'

She gazed pathetically at the green-eyed young woman who was now her sister-in-law, hoping for signs of concern. Tabitha, however, merely raised an eyebrow, murmuring: 'How complicated.'

'There is such a thing, child, as terminal pessimism,' declared Clementina sternly. 'I suspect that we must first rid you of that and good health will surely follow.'

Beverley bit her lip and glanced imploringly at Christopher for support. He sat down beside her and slipped a comforting arm round the narrow little shoulders.

'Aunt Clem,' he told her with a wink, 'is brusque but very wise. You should listen to her. Now don't worry. We'll have you feeling better in no time at all.'

The girl smiled weakly. She had hoped for sympathetic coddling here, but first signs were not encouraging. They were plainly a very robust family, with little experience of invalids, and she sensed herself to be out of keeping here. Her eyes flickered once more towards her sister-in-law and now spotted for the first time that tell-tale bulge of pregnancy.

Tabitha patted it fondly, with a sly grin which caused Beverley to drop her gaze in embarrassment. She knew her husband for a gentle, sensitive soul, and perceived similar virtues in William Kirkwood. But these other two, the womenfolk, were not entirely to her taste.

When the tray arrived, she managed to force down half a cup of tea and a ginger biscuit, sipping and nibbling with no sign of enjoyment whatever. In the same space of time, Tabitha demolished two large pastries and everyone kept pressing the new Mrs Summerfield to do likewise. It was all quite dreadful and at length she begged to be excused, escaping upstairs to lie down until dinner.

She was delicate, Christopher explained. She had been so since childhood and he meant to take care of her, convinced that the peace and country air of Roskarnon would restore her to glowing health.

★ ★ ★ ★

Try as she might, Tabitha could not imagine why her brother had married such a joyless creature. Perceiving no evidence of genuine illness, she sharply concluded that here was one of those vapourish women who spent half their lives reclining in darkened rooms with cologne-soaked handkerchiefs on their brows, cosseted and pitied by all. She had never before given much thought to the idea of a sister-in-law with whom she would have to share Roskarnon, but it now became clear that she had nothing in common with Christopher's wife.

Beverley's conversation centred always around her ailments. She responded with an air of tragic envy to any show of humour and high spirits by those about her, and had the effect of casting a respectful, sickroom hush wherever she went.

Convinced that her illnesses were all terribly real, she looked almost with resentment upon Tabitha's exuberant good health. For herself,

Beverley dreaded the possibility of pregnancy, certain that it would kill her, and was mystified that Mrs Kirkwood ate enormously, grew very rosy and withstood the ordeal quite unperturbed.

Finally, after a short and uneventful labour, Tabitha presented William with a baby girl, whom they later christened Miranda.

Beverley could not understand why Tabitha had not suffered more, and even the midwife secretly reflected that the birth was almost indecently quick and easy for a first child from a woman of small build. Tabitha, it was true, did recover from her confinement with remarkable speed and was up and around in no time, seeming more energetic than ever.

For Christopher, the years spent at Oxford and all the recent changes conspired to dull the memory of Edgar's death, edging it ever further from the realms of reality. Now, as he watched his sister assume the mantle of motherhood, as he saw her leaning over the cradle and crooning to her baby daughter, he found it hard to believe that the nightmare had ever happened at all. It was simply a ghastly accident, he thought; a tragic error of youth which could never be undone but was, thank God, receding swiftly into the past, propelled by the new concerns of adult married life. It

was over, he assured himself gratefully, finished, and nothing like it would ever happen
again.

★ ★ ★ ★

Having obliged William with a much-wanted
child, Tabitha now felt entitled to a little
reward. Some excitement was well overdue, for
she had seen no other men since the Italian in
Stresa, and she was more than ready for an
affair.

Thus it was that she embarked upon a series
of liaisons that were to keep her happily entertained for the better part of three years.

Her lovers during that period numbered four
in all—a lawyer, a music teacher, a gentleman
farmer and a shipwright. There could have
been a great many more, since she was widely
admired, but it must be said to Tabitha's credit
that she was discriminating in her choice. An
attractive appearance was important in a man,
but not to the exclusion of all other qualities.

Each *affaire* would last from three months
to a year and she did her best to preserve her
lovers as friends when it was over. Of course,
this could only succeed so long as a certain
detachment was maintained on both sides. The
emotional type, therefore, was strictly avoided

and so were those whose circumstances made if difficult to arrange a regular meeting place. A sense of humour was a vital requisite; a partner with wit could add much to the entertainment and be relied upon to accept the final parting with good grace.

She always selected married men, thereby ensuring their discretion. She wanted no scandal, no scenes, for none of those men meant anything more than a pleasurable romp and gratification which her husband failed to provide. In every other way she was perfectly contented with her lot, and sufficiently fond of William to keep him blissfully unaware of her infidelity. She saw no reason to hurt him, and caution served also to protect her comfortable situation.

When, after two years, she produced another child, William received it with delight and never doubted for a second that the little boy was his own. In all, it was a splendid arrangement and Tabitha saw no reason why it should not continue indefinitely.

Only Clementina, ever astute and mildly suspicious, paused to speculate about those afternoons when Tabitha slipped away into St Lowen on her own. So many shopping trips? So many fittings with the seamstress? Was her niece really so deeply involved with charities and church bazaars? If, indeed, Tabitha was up to no good, she certainly covered her tracks well. Her declared intentions when she went out were probably true four times out of five—thereby storing up credit for the exceptional fifth.

Whatever conclusions Clemmie reached, she always kept them to herself, for William and Tabitha were plainly happy with their lives. The wheels turned smoothly and interference could prove a bad mistake. There might, in later years, have come a time when Clementina would have felt driven to tackle Tabitha on the subject and issue a quiet warning, but a sudden and lethal illness served to prevent this.

★ ★ ★ ★

Clemmie died of meningitis at the end of March 1877. She was only forty-eight and quite robust, but nevertheless she succumbed within twenty-four hours. It was Tabitha's first experience of genuine grief and it left her profoundly upset, especially since none of the family was allowed to see Clementina before she died, for fear of contagion. For a while even Beverley ceased to whine and complain in the face of such obvious anguish.

This was also a time when Tabitha actually

sought her husband's kindly affection in preference to the current paramour. William did his best to comfort her, but Tabitha's gloom had taken a very firm grip on her and as the weeks wore on he began to fear that the moping would never end. He wondered if she were falling into some sort of decline, if she would ever again be his bright little sweetheart.

As he cast about for a way to help her, William became convinced that change would effect a cure and so he hit upon an idea. Finding her perched despondently on the edge of their bed one morning, he put a consoling arm round her shoulders, took a languid little hand in his, and asked if she would like a trip to London.

'You'll enjoy it,' he said confidently. 'I know you will. A change of scene will make all the difference.'

Tabitha sighed. 'I know you're thinking of my good, dearest, but I'm hardly in a frame of mind for gaiety.'

'That's exactly what I mean to cure,' said William firmly. 'I really think we should go, Tabitha. In fact I insist upon it. As you know, I have a cousin in London who has recently married and this would seen an excellent time to pay a visit.'

'Cousin?' queried Tabitha vaguely.

'Why, Coralie, of course. I've spoken of her many times.'

'Oh—yes, I think I do recall something or other.'

'Well, I believe it's high time the two of you met. She's a very quiet person, but delightfully kind—and blessed with quite extraordinary musical abilities. I'm sure you're going to like her.'

'Oh, William, I don't think...'

'Not another word. I shall send her a telegram straight away. Meanwhile I suggest you galvanise the servants into action and start to organise our packing.' He got to his feet and bent to kiss her fondly on the forehead. 'Come along now, that's my brave girl.'

It was the first time William had ever been sufficiently masterful to stifle his wife's objections and make a unilateral decision. Tabitha, of course, was not on fighting form. Had she been so, he would not have found it so easy.

Too depressed to argue, she listlessly ordered the maids to pack, although not without a secret sense of annoyance. It was stupid of William to drag her off on a tiresome journey and inflict upon her more of his odious relations, she told herself crossly. The weekly dinners at Copperhill with Ruth and Ambrose were quite trial enough. It seemed she would now be expected to endure parlour recitals by the musical cousin. She would have to listen politely, applaud, compliment and suffer encores without yawning. Prepared to humour William for only a week or so, she determined to seize upon any excuse which presented itself to cut short their stay.

CHAPTER 11

Had she but known it, Tabitha was not the only one who viewed the visit without enthusiasm. Coralie had replied to William's telegram with words of welcome, as civility demanded, but in truth she was less than happy about receiving house guests. She had not seen William for six years and was apprehensive about his wife, whom he had proudly described in his letters as 'exquisite'.

Miserably shy and fearful of meeting anyone new, Coralie had been fortunate in finding a husband who shared her preference for privacy and peace. Even here, in the bustling heart of London, they did very little entertaining, both for reasons of temperament and because they simply could not afford it.

From the day she married Mark Emerson, Coralie had become what her mother described as 'irretrievably declassée'. Coralie really could not see that a struggling young doctor was any less worthy of respect than a banker, like her father, or a brewer, like Uncle Ambrose. Mark's only fault was a lack of money, but her mother dismissively proclaimed him a person of no great consequence and pitiful prospects, declaring that Coralie had let down the whole family.

Oh yes, she had been a great tribulation to Mama, for Coralie was a plain Jane, whose five younger sisters had been speedily and advantageously married and were already moving up in the world. A frumpish daughter could only be a vexation to a woman who wanted all her girls to make prestigious and profitable matches.

She was alone when William and Tabitha arrived in the middle of a Thursday afternoon, for Mark had some visits to make and would not return until dinner. William's description of his wife was no exaggeration, she thought nervously as she made them comfortable and ordered tea.

Coralie was always intimidated by attractive people and, later, as she sat at her dressing-table making ready for the evening meal, she pondered her husband's reaction to Tabitha Kirkwood, feeling hopelessly and unfairly out-matched.

The mirror was never kind. There was something derisive in the way its elaborate gilt frame encircled a reflection so drab. The fussy clothes merely emphasised her homely features and angular figure. Throughout her life, Coralie had been scrutinised and criticised from head to foot. Not a flaw or a failing had been overlooked, not a single feature escaped the sting of someone's tongue.

Her mouth was full, but too wide. The eyes were large and anxious, of a weak shade approaching pale green, and the fringe of colourless lashes did nothing to flatter them. A dull frizz of coarse brown curls failed to offset the somewhat stubby nose, and the overall effect was insipid. Mama had often expressed irritation because Coralie's bosom was negligible, her shoulder-blades and collarbone starkly outlined in evening dresses. Heavy meals were forced upon her in the hope of producing some curves, but all to no effect.

Coralie's mother, Amelia, was a sister to Ruth Kirkwood. Having no sons, Amelia sought aggrandisement for herself and her daughters through good marriages. She had not given up easily on Coralie. For many years the hapless girl was propelled from one social gathering to the next, where she hovered shyly in corners and was mostly ignored. Amelia impatiently steered her onto balconies with eligible young men, prodded her into conversation, ordered her to smile, dance and try, for God's sake, to be amusing. Alas, not a single conquest was made.

The campaign was finally abandoned when Coralie reached the age of twenty-four. At that point Amelia had thrown up her hands in disgust, declaring the girl a spinster and hopeless failure. And yet it was at this stage that fortune produced Mark Emerson.

He was thirty when she met him. She had taken a hansom to the house of a not-so-wealthy friend—only to find that the young lady was suffering from a stomach complaint and had called in the doctor. Since the friend was in no mood for visitors, Emerson offered to drive Coralie home. It was only a mile or so out of his way, he said. No trouble at all.

Coralie thought it very civil of him and quite enjoyed his conversation en route.

Evidently her company had pleased him just as much, for a note arrived at Coralie's home the following day—an invitation to the theatre that night. And so it all began.

Amelia said caustically that he was plainly an

opportunist, prepared to overlook homeliness in a wealthy woman. For once, however, Coralie ignored Mama altogether and when at last he suggested marriage she accepted without hesitation.

From the day she became Mrs Emerson, Coralie's happiness soared while her standard of living dropped. Her parents informed her that they had no intention of subsidising a lowly 'shilling' doctor. Having married the man, she would have to make do on his income.

Coralie did not object to this at all and moved into Emerson's modest but comfortable little house without the slightest regret. Neighbours and relations shook their heads to see her thus plunging down the social ladder, but assumed she was grateful to have found any man willing to take her on, poor thing. In one way, they said, she was remarkably lucky, for Mark was certainly a personable young fellow. Hopelessly poor, of course, but attractive, and a woman like Coralie naturally had to compromise and should not expect perfection.

Coralie, however, felt that she had gained the world and believed herself thrice-blessed. Mark had made her happy. He loved her and, for the most part, she trusted him. In the quiet routine of their daily lives she felt safe and relaxed. It was only in public and on rare social occasions that a sense of unease came creeping back, only when pretty women took an interest in her husband.

Women like Tabitha Kirkwood.

That evening, as she sat at her mirror performing a few token beauty rituals, Coralie once more felt the onset of fear. She tried to beat it down, reminding herself that Tabitha was contentedly married and had been so for nearly five years. Surely there was no real cause to worry? This was her home, her haven, and no baneful influence could intrude or touch her here.

At last, as the clock struck seven, she stood up and smoothed the folds of her gown. It was chocolate brown, a shade she often favoured, and the current fashion for the bustle went some way to conceal her thinness. The heavy satin of the skirt was draped in loops across the front, with most of its volume drawn tightly over the hips to form a cascade of ruffles, pleats and flounces down the back. Bows of dark gold ribbon nestled amongst the folds and the neckline was edged in cream lace. It was the most becoming of her gowns and it made her feel a little less defenceless when faced with William's lovely wife.

CHAPTER 12

In truth, Tabitha's initial reaction to Mark Emerson was almost one of indifference. She recognised a certain easy-going charm in him and inwardly acknowledged that he was personable enough in his own way, but Mark was not of the physical type which normally excited her interest. William's restrained attentions had confirmed in her a preference for partners who were swarthy, hirsute and muscular. And although Emerson was somewhat darker than her husband, Tabitha would still have classed him as fair.

His moustache and the springy waves that curved loosely round his ears and forehead were tawny in colour, and the eyes were the gold-brown shade of neat whisky. It was a face both humorous and thoughtful with pleasant, even features. Tabitha read great intelligence there and she found the talk amusing but she was not, at that time, sufficiently interested to ponder his possibilities as a lover.

'How's Aunt Amelia?' asked William as they started on the soup. 'We must find the time to call and visit her before we go back.'

Coralie looked faintly uncomfortable. 'I don't know how she is. I'm afraid I seldom see Mama these days.'

Tabitha, ever so quick on the uptake, needed no more explanation, for she had guessed that there might be tension between Mark and his in-laws over what seemed to her a very odd match.

'Really?' blundered William innocently. 'Why?'

Coralie cast a questioning glance at her husband, but he merely raised an eyebrow, gave a slight smile and shrug, and went on with his meal.

'She's not ill, I hope?'

'No, you see, she...'

'We may as well be candid,' Emerson cut in quietly. 'Amelia doesn't like me or the way I conduct my practice. She feels I should charge more for my services, move into a smart neighbourhood and select an exclusive list of patients. As I stand, I'm not good enough to be her son-in-law. Nor is this house good enough for madam to be seen entering, so she never comes here. Furthermore, she doesn't want my undistinguished presence under her roof and Coralie will not visit her without me.'

There was a brief, awkward silence.

146

'Oh—I'm sorry.' Embarrassed, William cleared his throat.

'Don't apologise, William. You weren't to know. It's unfortunate, I agree. After all, she is still my mama. But I do resent all this silly snobbery. Her attitude to Mark is most unpleasant and I have to confess that I don't really miss her very much.' Coralie sighed ruefully. 'Anyway, enough of that. Let's make some plans for your stay in London. Oh—and I hope you found the room acceptable? We so seldom have guests that I...'

'We're very comfortable,' said Tabitha. 'You've thought of everything.'

Emerson chuckled. 'You're being gracious, Mrs Kirkwood, but it must seem rather spartan after Roskarnon. We could never entertain in grand or formal style. I'm afraid Coralie paid a high price in lost material comfort when she consented to marry me. Mine is not the most lucrative occupation, and although the wolf never comes too close to the door, we can often hear him howling in the distance.'

'You make a comfortable living for us both and that is enough,' said his wife. 'I have a healthy respect for money, but I also know what it is to be rich and miserable. It is certainly poor compensation for loneliness or the loss of a loved one.'

'Yes,' agreed Tabitha quietly, 'I've discovered that of late.'

'Well, while you are with us we'll do our utmost to take your mind off your troubles,' promised Emerson. 'There's plenty in London to keep you occupied and entertained. We'll plan a few outings together, if that would please you. Tell me, do you like the city or is it too noisy for someone country-bred? Wealthy visitors, of course, see only the best of London, never the misery and squalor of the poorer districts. Coralie and I have often evied those who live amidst greenery, peace and fresh air.'

'There is a deal of poverty and ill-health to be found in the country, sir, although I venture to say that Roskarnon's tenants are uncommonly well cared for. I count myself very lucky to have a home in beautiful surroundings, but an occasional change is nonetheless refreshing. William and I spend a few lovely weeks in Italy each winter, although I never care to leave Roskarnon for too long. It's my natural habitat, so to speak. But certainly you must show me all the interesting features of London while I'm here. I confess, to my shame, that I know almost nothing about it.'

'That's settled, then. Plenty of rides and theatre and shopping. We shall all have a splendid time.'

William sounded hearty and well-pleased. Mark, however, had not missed the implication that Tabitha did not wish to stay too long.

As he sipped his wine, he studied her guardedly over the rim of the glass and gained a curious impression that here was a being of an unusual nature. It had nothing to do with her conversation, that polite social chatter which she practised in common with most other women. No—it was when she fell silent that he perceived a strangeness in her, as if she existed within an atmosphere of her own, something far removed from the lamplit dining-room of a house in busy London.

As William and Coralie discussed their kin, it seemed that Tabitha had withdrawn from the company, pensively quiet, her empty plate pushed to one side.

Her natural habitat, she had said. Yes, he thought, still watching her covertly, she reminded him of some exquisite little woodland animal, despite the formal evening dress of dark blue velvet and the shimmer of silver filigree at her ears and throat. It was an odd contrast in a well-bred woman, but he thought he detected some quality that was very sensual and not quite civilised.

Perhaps he had stared for a moment too long, for suddenly she turned her head and the bright eyes fixed upon him with a calm, questioning look, the eyebrows slightly lifted. It was, he realised, a very knowing face and more than a little wicked when caught off-guard. He gave her a smile made sheepish by discomfort, and Tabitha returned it, broadly.

Oh yes, he decided, a goblin's grin. It was not the smile of a gracious lady.

Neither William nor Coralie had observed the look which passed between them. Mrs Emerson's anxiety had all but died as the meal progressed. She had been foolish to worry, she told herself, believing the Kirkwoods to be a devoted couple and her husband too honourable to betray her.

Indeed, at that point, Mark's interest did amount to little more than curiosity, while Tabitha's grin indicated only the recognition of yet another fascinated male.

'William tells me you have two children now —a girl and a boy,' Coralie said, turning to Tabitha. 'Mark and I are hoping for a family soon. A large one.'

William leaned back comfortably in his chair. 'Children,' he declared, waving his glass of port, 'are the very hub of a marriage, the final fulfilment. I admit without apology that I'm enormously proud of them both.'

'Do they show any striking resemblances?' enquired Coralie. 'Mama always likened me to one of her distant aunts—the least loved of them, I suspect.'

'Well, Miranda undoubtedly favours William,' said Tabitha. 'She has his colouring— including the freckles. The little boy, Jonathan, is surprisingly dark. We think it must be a throw-back of some sort, don't we, dearest?'

An enchanting little smile capered disarmingly upon her face as she looked to her husband for agreement.

'Most certainly,' supplied William. 'He has beautiful brown eyes. Stocky little fellow, too. I think he's going to be strong and quite a sportsman.'

Coralie sighed. 'They sound delightful. I do wish you had brought them with you. Won't you miss them?'

Tabitha gingerly sidestepped that question, for she did not miss them at all.

'Well, you see, they have a wonderful nursemaid and governess to keep them amused, so we don't feel overly guilty about taking this holiday. After all, it's not for very long.'

'In that case,' said Emerson, 'we must make the most of your time here. Perhaps, if tomorrow is fine, Coralie could take you to see some of the famous sights and landmarks.'

His wife beamed across the table at Tabitha. 'Of course I will. It will be a treat for me, and I'm so glad to have found a new friend.'

CHAPTER 13

Time moved on through a parade of museums, art galleries and exhibitions, parks and music halls, fairs and historic landmarks. Tabitha was forced to admit that her husband had been right. There were days when she forgot about Aunt Clemmie altogether.

'I enjoy these public amenities far more than a dinner party or a ball,' Coralie confided once, as they wandered through a great indoor aviary at the zoo, where the cages teemed with gaudy, exotic birds. 'I was never a social success and I cannot dance at all well. I would rather attend an opera, see the work of a fine artist or spend an evening here.'

'That is understandable,' said Tabitha. 'A painting is more pleasing to the eye and a parrot more amusing than the average dinner guest.'

'Good heavens!' There was a peal of mirth from Coralie. 'You sound exactly like my husband. Mark can be very forthright and he does not suffer fools gladly.'

'It's hardly surprising,' William said. 'The man works punishing hours and doubtless encounters a lot of very trying people. We've seen little enough of him these past weeks. He seldom has a day to himself.'

'Yes, if the truth be told, he takes on too many patients. He's popular, you see, and the word gets round. Sometimes I wish we could leave London altogether, but...'

'Oh, look!' exclaimed Tabitha suddenly, 'there's a tropical aquarium as well. Let's go in.'

She tugged at William's arm. 'Dearest, are you listening? Shall we visit the aquarium?'

'What? Oh yes, if you like,' he said absently.

'Is there something wrong, William? You seem preoccupied. I could have sworn for a moment that your thoughts were miles away.'

'There's nothing wrong, nothing wrong at all,' he said suddenly beaming, for the thought which had so distracted him had sprung from Coralie's last remark and given him an interesting notion to consider.

★ ★ ★ ★

During the final days of their stay in London a scheme began to shape itself in William's head and rapidly grew into what he thought a very bright idea. All-powerful though a husband might be, he seldom did anything of family importance without first consulting his darling. And so, one night at bedtime, he offered his plan for Tabitha's consideration.

'Dearest,' he said turning out the lamp as he climbed into bed beside her, 'do you not think that Dr Emerson is a fine and conscientious young man?'

'Undoubtedly,' said Tabitha, yawning.

'Well then, I have a suggestion to make which may surprise and I hope, please you.'

Tabitha, fatigued by a day at Cremorne Gardens, gave a barely perceptible sigh and prayed that he was not going to be long-winded.

'The notion came from something you said at dinner on the night we arrived,' he went on. 'I have been thinking it over and have hit upon a splendid scheme.'

'Indeed, William? What was it I said?'

'That Roskarnon's tenants were well cared for.'

'And so they are. Their cottages are sound and dry, their wages higher than most.'

'But what about their health?'

'You have always been a generous landlord, William. You have nothing for which to rebuke yourself.'

He was silent for a moment, then he said: 'The man Coates, Tabitha, the wheelwright—do you know him?'

'Why yes, dear.' Her answer was cautious. 'I believe I do.'

'Did you know also that his wife died some three months ago?'

'Yes. In childbirth, was it not?'

'It would have been their seventh. The woman was still young and strong, yet something evidently went amiss. I don't pretend to understand these matters, but I cannot help feeling that the presence of a doctor might have made all the difference. Tabitha, we have a great many tenants on the estate, each with a family, sometimes of seven or eight children. The men often suffer injuries in their work. Last summer one of the graziers lost his eldest boy with lockjaw and his mother with gangrene. These are the people who work our land and make it profitable. It is our duty to take care of them, for their sakes and our own.'

'I suppose it is,' murmured Tabitha, uninterested.

'Sudden illness can become a nightmare when the nearest medical man is ten miles away in St Lowen. Your own father might have been alive today if help had been closer to hand—although I've no great faith in Doctor Prale. The man is close to his dotage and I don't believe he has ever obtained any modern qualification or kept up with the latest advances. Learned by apprenticeship, I've no doubt.'

'Let's not be unfair, William. He was always warning Papa about his health, and the attack was so sudden, so devastating that I doubt anyone could have saved him.'

'You're very charitable, dearest, but I would hesitate to trust Doctor Prale with my life or those of my family. I think, in the best interest of us all, we should have a younger, more capable man readily available. If a landlord may appoint clergymen, schoolteachers and the like to his estate, then why not a doctor? Why not young Emerson?'

'Well...' Tabitha's voice did carry a note of surprise there in the darkness. 'It's a very advanced idea, my love. Have you asked him how he feels about it?'

'Not yet. I wanted your reaction first, Tabitha. For my part, I am quite convinced that Mark would be an excellent choice, if he can only be persuaded to accept.'

'Do you mean to suggest that he and Coralie

should live at Roskarnon with us?' Her tone had become wary, for she had no wish to share her home with yet another female; Beverley was annoyance enough.

'Not at all. And I don't suppose Emerson would accept such an arrangement in any case. The man is rightly proud of his independence. What I had in mind was to sell them one of the houses on the estate—most probably Curlew Quay. The place has been empty since the ferryman died, which of course is a great waste. If Mark and Coralie were to sell this house, it would fetch more than enough to pay for Curlew Quay, for I've no wish to profit from the transaction. Furthermore, I think they would find it less expensive to live in the country, and both have expressed a desire to do so.'

'Indeed, William, I can see that you have reasoned it all through most carefully.'

'And how does it appeal to you?'

Unprepared for this development, Tabitha tried to collect her thoughts and decide whether she objected.

'But he already has a practice here and he may not want to abandon it.'

'True enough, but cities have their fair share of physicians and nobody in London need travel ten miles to find one, as we must do. Anyway, we can do no more than ask him. I must say, I like the idea of having Coralie to live at Roskarnon. She's had a lonely life, you know. Not much happiness until now.'

'Well, you know I have every confidence in your judgement...'

'You agree, then?' prompted William eagerly. 'Shall we put it to them tomorrow? Naturally they'll need time to think it over, and if they accept it will take some months for Mark to settle his affairs.'

There was a short silence while Tabitha examined the plan from all angles. On the whole she saw no real grounds for protest. It was, as he had said, a very practical arrangement and one could hardly take exception to that. She had also to admit that selling Curlew Quay was not a bad idea. The place had stood empty for some years and would probably fall into decay if left so for much longer.

William felt her give a slight shrug. 'By all means. As far as I'm concerned they'll be very welcome, but you must also consult Christopher, you know. I'm aware that he leaves nearly all the decisions to you, but we must observe the courtesy of asking him.'

'As a matter of fact,' confided William in a whisper, 'I telegraphed him on Tuesday and he has already agreed—prompted by Beverley, I suspect.'

'Oh, but of course. She could keep a doctor busy all by herself. We must see that she is not allowed to monopolise him.'

'It's my hope that he can talk some sense into the silly creature. Sometimes I'm torn between pity and exasperation. I know she firmly believes herself to be an invalid and that Christopher's interest in her was short-lived. I suppose she does feel lonely and neglected. On the other hand, it taxes my patience to see a perfectly healthy young woman spending her life in morbid uselessness.'

Tabitha chuckled. 'If Mark can make a fit and happy woman out of Beverley, he'll be more than a doctor. That would require a magician.'

'Speaking of which,' pondered William, 'I suppose the presence of a qualified physician on the estate would be a blow to poor old Gaddy and her remedies.'

'Yes, I fear it would. The local people have always relied upon her. She would be very upset.'

'I know,' said Wiliam, 'and I'm sorry, but it can't be helped. They would be better off without Gaddy's dubious potions. She's fortunate that these are enlightened times. Two centuries ago they'd have burnt her at the stake.'

'You shouldn't scoff, William. I've heard it

said that she's very knowledgeable and her cures remarkably effective. I've known Gaddy since I was tiny and, believe me, she's no simpleton.'

'Oh, to be sure,' teased William. 'Did you know she put a curse on the miller because he thumbed his nose at her last Christmas? You'll note that nothing has befallen him so far?'

'William, you know I'm not superstitious. I don't believe that ill-wishing has any effect at all, but I wouldn't dismiss Gaddy's methods altogether. There may be some nuggets of useful knowledge and sound common sense amidst the hocus-pocus. I like to give credit where it's due.'

'You're very generous, my dear,' said William sagely, 'although perhaps a little naïve. I hate to speak of such things, but it has been said that she occasionally performs a certain sevice for young ladies in trouble—although I cannot swear that it's true.'

Tabitha smiled in the darkness.

'Really, William, what an appalling idea. You should never listen to gossip.'

'Perhaps not, but I've no faith in weeds and roots and country cure-alls. It's science we need today and it's my earnest hope that Mark will take up our offer. He would make a lot of changes at Roskarnon.'

CHAPTER 14

It took Doctor Emerson little more than a fort-night to make a decision on William's offer. Coralie was hotly in favour of the idea and Mark had to admit that he, too, found it attractive.

Selling his practice and making all the necessary arrangements took rather longer. It was close to the end of March 1878 when the Emersons finally arrived by train at St Lowen, having left London with very little regret. When William and one of the stablemen arriv-ed at the station to meet them, they found the couple waiting on the platform, surrounded by a stack of trunks and other portable belongings. A few items of favourite furniture, including Coralie's piano, were on their way by road.

It was already late evening and the Emersons wanted nothing more than a hot meal and a good night's sleep. Both had been arranged, William assured them. Tabitha had seen to it that their new home was cleaned and prepared from top to bottom. She had also detailed the cook and maid to ensure that dinner was waiting at Curlew Quay.

After many tiring hours on the train and a bumpy carriage ride from St Lowen, Coralie was much relieved to see the vague outline of a single-storey lodge-house looming up a few yards ahead. The glow from the lantern in the porch revealed that it was built with thick blocks of sand-coloured stone, and the lighted windows were of the pointed arch style, with leaded panes of diamond shape.

Inside, she found that the walls were either whitened or panelled, and the furnishings were mostly of dark, grainy wood. Before the hearth stood a pair of easy chairs, their plump cushions patterned in fawn tapestry. A fire was already leaping in the grate.

Just before midnight, Mark and Coralie thankfully made ready for bed, having eaten well and sent the borrowed servants back to the main house. Many of their possessions had already been discreetly unpacked and put away, while in the bedroom the wash-stand offered soap, towels and a jug of hot water. Beyond a doubt, Tabitha had ordered every welcoming little comfort they could wish for.

Mark opened a window to let in the mild spring air, for he could never sleep in a stuffy room. The journey from London had tired him more than a hard day's work and he was much in need of a long, comfortable night.

The bed, he thought, looked very promising. There in the corner it stood, plump and fresh, gleaming with white linen beneath its dusky blue quilt. It was, he recalled, one of Tabitha's favourite colours, that bottomless, night time blue which covered him as he climbed in and lay beside his wife.

'It's a lovely little house, isn't it?' Coralie's voice quietly happy.

'Splendid,' came the drowsy reply.

'William says it was once the lodge for the ferryman, the old man who used to row people back and forth across the creek. He died only a few weeks before Tabitha's Papa. It's such a cosy little place. I'm glad we decided to come.'

'Yes,' he murmured vaguely, 'I think we were wise to take the opportunity.'

'The silence is quite overpowering, isn't it? No rattle of carriage wheels and hooves; no one shouting in the street outside. I wonder if I'll ever become used to it.'

'Of course you will. Anyway, it isn't true silence. The sounds have changed, that's all.'

He was right. Listening, Coralie caught the creak and flutter of leafy branches and the light hushing of the wind that moved them. And from somewhere close by, soft but clear, came the dipping, bubbling call of a bird.

'That's a curlew, I think,' she whispered. She paused for a second, remembering something. 'Somebody once told me that it's ill-omened to hear them at night.'

'What superstitious rubbish,' were his last muffled words as he fell asleep.

'No, I don't believe in such things either. I'm going to be happy here. I'm sure of it.'

Once again, as she drifted into sleep, Coralie heard the curlew's looping cry, but this time it simply brought a smile at the foolishness of old wives' tales. Nothing malefic could ever feel at home in such a lovely place.

★ ★ ★ ★

Early next morning, while Coralie busied herself in arranging Curlew Quay to her liking, Mark set off for Roskarnon. The Emersons were due at the house for dinner that night—a formal welcoming party—but he had a few practical matters to discuss with William in the meantime.

As he turned and paused to take a good look at his new home, he told himself that the lodge was well-named, for it stood beside an old stone quay at the creek's edge and a flight of steps led down to a shingle beach, where a rowing boat lay high and dry. They were fortunate indeed, he thought. This was a beautiful place to live.

Keen to see more of his new surroundings, he ignored the carriage track that led straight to Roskarnon, and chose instead a path which wandered away to his right and disappeared up a thickly wooded slope.

For a while the path went straight uphill, then turned at a right angle to cut across the slope that stretched away above and below him, roofed over with dense foliage. This, he thought, was plainly an alternative way to the house.

An hour later, however, fatigued and slightly worried, he realised that woodlands could be very deceptive and admitted to himself that he had very little idea of where he might be. Plodding onwards, he was starting to curse his foolishness when the track suddenly took another turn and made a steep descent towards a broad, slow-moving stream. Across the water stretched a narrow footbridge and there he saw a shabby little figure, whom he took to be a village girl, sitting on the edge.

Her simple cotton dress was faded and well-worn, and the wide brim of an old straw sun hat concealed her features. She seemed to be intent upon something in the water below.

A fat, speckled trout hovered in the current beneath the bridge, steadied by the gentle stirring of its tail. Her arms folded and resting upon the lower railing, Tabitha watched it with a faint smile. Papa, she was thinking, would have given his soul to land such a fish, a glorious trophy to stuff and display in one of those glass cases which were now banished to the attic.

Emerson went down the slippery track at a half-trot and called out to the figure on the bridge.

'Young lady, can you tell be where this path goes? I'm trying to get to Roskarnon, but...'

Startled, Tabitha's glance jerked sharply up to focus on the man hurrying towards her.

Emerson stopped in surprise.

'Good Lord—Tabitha! What's this, fancy dress?'

She smiled, composure restored. 'Silks and stays belong in the drawing-room, sir. They're a hindrance in the woods.'

He seated himself beside her. 'You're quite right, of course. You'll have to forgive a city man for lacking country sense.'

'I'm sure you'll acquire some in no time at all.' She tossed a scattering of pebbles into the water, whereupon the fish vanished downstream with a flick of its tail. 'I hope you are

166

comfortable at the lodge?'

'Very. Coralie is already in love with her new home.'

'I'm glad you like it, though I fear it's rather small. There are one or two other empty cottages and houses on the estate, but we thought it the nicest—and the most convenient. If you had taken the carriage track you would have reached Roskarnon in fifteen minutes.'

Emerson gave a rueful grin. 'I know. I suppose you realise I was lost. It was idiotic of me.'

Tabitha chuckled. 'Many a past guest has found himself in the same predicament. Almost half of Roskarnon is wooded and criss-crossed with narrow paths which are most confusing to a stranger.'

'And what about you? Ladies usually confine themselves to short strolls around the rose garden, do they not?'

'I know this estate very well, sir, every little path and glade. This in particular was one of my childhood haunts. I have happy memories of these woods and this stream. I come here now and again to sit for a while and—reminisce.'

'I would never have taken you for a sentimental person.'

Tabitha tipped her head to one side in that

engaging little way of hers, smiled at him and shrugged.

'Do you never seek to re-live the enjoyment of a special day, Mark? Would you not agree that pleasure is increased by anticipation beforehand and reflection afterwards?'

Something in her tone made him wonder just what kind of memories she was savouring.

'Certainly. I hope you found worthy and innocent ways to amuse yourself? Or were you a wayward and mischievous child?'

Tabitha laughed. It was the same unladylike grin he had seen across the dinner table that evening in London. There was something rapacious about it and once again he had the impression that all was neither righteous nor pure within Tabitha Kirkwood.

'I was always clean, always polite and never forgot to say my prayers. What more could you ask?'

He studied her thoughtfully for a moment and could not prevent the answering grin which spread across his own face.

'That's very laudable, but somehow I doubt that you're truly religious, Tabitha. You're not of the pious kind and I don't think obedience or self-denial would come easily to you.'

Well, well, reflected Tabitha, at least he's perceptive. She had, indeed, no time for a stern, patriarchal doctrine imported from a distant, arid country, intruding on these green woods and fields where it had no right to be. Tabitha, as surely sprung from Mother Earth as any tree, had always resented this invader.

She cocked an eyebrow in surprise and observed him with some curiosity. Men who recognised the truth of her nature beneath the camouflage of gentility were usually those who shared her instincts. And perhaps it was the atmosphere of these woods, the scene of so many bygone licentious romps, that made her look upon him in a different light. After all the intense, dark paramours of the past few years, she suddenly paused to ask herself if an eager, inventive lover might be found in the person of this autumn-coloured man.

He was slimly but solidly built, and she wondered if he would bring to bed with him the same vitality he invested in his work. The possibilities were intriguing, but she doubted that a woman like Coralie could bring out the best in him.

'I attend church every Sunday, sir, as befits my position on this estate. One must set an example to one's tenants—not to mention the children. I know Jonathan and Miranda find the weekly sermon tedious, but some things must be endured.'

'Oh, to be sure.' He nodded and half-smiled. 'Discipline is said to forge a fine character.'

'Of course it does,' agreed Tabitha. 'My Papa was always very strict with me and it never did me any harm. In many ways I'm much the better for it. One learns how to cope with all sorts of difficulties.'

'I'm sure you're a very capable lady, Tabitha.'

'I try to be competent and—thorough—in everything I do.'

'I have noticed that. I must thank you for preparing the lodge in such a welcoming manner. We were both exhausted and your kindness was much appreciated.'

'It was a pleasure. We want you to be happy here. Anyway,' she said, getting to her feet, 'I take it you were on your way to see my husband, so we'd best go now if you are to catch him. William is seldom at home between eleven and four. Business, you see.'

Emerson stood up, slapping the dust and moss from the seat of his trousers.

'I hope your clothing has suffered no serious damage, Mark.' She indicated some snagged threads on the sleeve of his jacket. 'I see you encountered some brambles along the way.'

'There's not much harm done, but I concede

that your apparel is more wisely chosen, Tabitha. And if I may say so, it looks very well on you. As a medical man, I abhor corsetry.'

'Fashion is often absurd,' agreed Tabitha. 'It has regard for neither health nor comfort.' Then she added softly: 'How nice to meet someone who shares my dislike of foolish restraints. I shed them whenever possible—don't you?'

There it was. The first encouragement. The hint, veiled in humour, was dropped to see if he would take it up, but Emerson merely nodded his approval with a faint smile and she could not be sure that he understood.

'Anyway,' Tabitha went on brightly, 'I think we had better hurry.'

She continued along the pathway on the other side of the bridge. It was only wide enough for single file and, as he walked behind her, Emerson could not help but study the figure swinging briskly along in front. He saw that when freed from the hobbling strictures of tight, bustled skirts her natural walk was an easy, female swagger that carried her rapidly and sure-footedly on her way. The fashionable ladies of London were often tediously vapourish and delicate, but Tabitha fairly glowed with sensual health.

When, after a while, the trees thinned out,

he found the beginnings of cultivated hedges and shrubbery as the land passed almost imperceptibly from wild countryside into wild garden, and the turrets of the house came into view some half mile ahead.

'Well, there it is.' Tabitha stopped to pick a bunch of spring flowers from beside the path. 'Please don't wait for me. We'll have more time to talk at dinner tonight.'

'I'll look forward to that.'

Emerson did not know that she watched him appraisingly as he walked the last quarter mile to Roskarnon, just as she had watched the Italian lads in Baveno.

CHAPTER 15

On the following Sunday, the Reverend Hugh Devoy noted from his pulpit the presence of two new faces in the Kirkwood pew. A Dr and Mrs Emerson from London, it was rumoured, related in some way on William's side. They looked a pleasant couple, the clergyman decided. Certainly there was nothing disturbing about either of them, which was more than could be said for the younger Mrs Kirkwood.

There they all sat in a motionless row. Next to the newcomers was Christopher with Beverley beside him. She had already assured the Reverend Devoy that she admired him very much and was comforted to know that he would officiate at her funeral—an event, she hinted plaintively, which could not be far away. His glance swept on past Ruth, straight-backed and grim-faced, with Ambrose lolling fatly at her side, to the ginger, freckled Miranda and her chunky little brother, so strangely unlike the other Kirkwoods. Lastly there was William, showing his usual polite interest. And Tabitha.

The minister could never pinpoint the exact reason why she so disconcerted him. Always immaculately dressed, she gave generously when the plate came round and never failed to congratulate him on his sermon when she left. And yet he always sensed mockery behind the carefully attentive features, insolence in the steady green stare. More than that, he recognised an earthy quality which said that Mrs Kirkwood was better suited to some moonlit pagan frolic than a Sunday service.

Later, as he stood in the porch while the congregation filed out, he heard her discussing just such a gathering with young Emerson. The subject was the regular spring event known as Ember Night.

173

Of course, it was, in reality, quite a harmless little festival, mused the Reverend. Just a silly, superstitious tradition to amuse the local girls— but heathen in its origins for all that.

'What, may I ask, is Ember Night?' queried Mark.

'I suppose you would call it a fortune-telling game,' Tabitha said. 'It has been held on the estate every year for longer than anyone can say—probably since the days before the house was built. The purpose of the gathering may have changed a little in the course of time, but it certainly goes back a long way. In any case, it's a cherished custom at Roskarnon.'

'Where is it held?'

'There's a clearing over on the northern side of the estate. We have a big bonfire there, with dancing and a few refreshments. All the tenants come with their families, all the villagers and people from the hamlets. It's quite an occasion, and though our country traditions may seem curious at first, I think you'll find it entertaining.'

'Then we'd love to come. Coralie cannot abide formal parties, but I'm sure she would enjoy something of this kind.'

What a nice young woman Mrs Emerson is, thought the clergyman. His glance flicked across to where she stood talking at the lych-

174

gate with Beverley. They seemed to have struck up a friendship, he noticed approvingly, as he shook hands with the last of his congregation and turned to go inside.

He was glad for Beverley's sake, since no one else seemed to care about her. Even the girl's father paid her only a fleeting visit once a year.

Beverley had taken an instant liking to Mark's wife. Since coming to Roskarnon she had felt increasingly isolated, for Christopher's attention and his energies were given mostly to astronomy. He was kind in an absent sort of way, but she knew he did not really listen or understand about her illnesses, and Tabitha was never sympathetic, so all in all she was left to suffer alone.

The patient Coralie had seemed like a gift from the gods. Good-natured and tolerant, she listened gravely as Beverley unleashed a flood of anguished complaints and worries.

'I detest this close, heavy weather,' she sighed as they walked toward the carriages. 'It makes my head spin. I don't think my sense of balance is quite what it should be. Sometimes, when I'm lying flat in bed, I feel as though I'm tumbling over and over. It's horridly frightening and no one seems to care. I tried explaining to Tabitha one morning at breakfast, and do you know what she said?

''Have your ears syringed.'' Truly, Coralie, I think it was a spiteful thing to say. I'm sure she was implying that I don't wash.'

Coralie smiled faintly. 'Don't take it to heart, my dear. I expect she meant well.'

'She did not. She never does. William seems to think she is an angel, but I know better. Tabitha can be very unkind. When Christopher told me he had a sister, I thought she would be a friend and a comfort to me, but every time I try to start a conversation with Tabitha she remembers some pressing errand and leaves the room. I'm sure it's deliberate, Coralie. I cannot imagine what I've done to make her dislike me so. She happily devotes several afternoons each week to charitable causes and visits to the poor of the parish, but...'

'Well, there you are, then. That is hardly selfish or insensitive of her, is it?'

'Charity begins at home,' quoted Beverley peevishly. 'She will not spare me so much as half an hour and she knows how I need company. Christopher has no time for me at all. He shuts himself away in that turret room till all hours with those silly telescopes and charts.'

The pink-rimmed eyes regarded Coralie wistfully.

'I do wish I were strong and healthy like you, with a nice protective husband. You're very lucky, you know.'

'Yes, I do know.'

Beverley blinked unhappily and her nose quivered a little, as if on the verge of a sob. It was on account of this particular twitch that Tabitha privately likened her to an albino rabbit.

'I hope you are not cramped at the lodge,' she said, briefly mindful of someone else's welfare. 'I really couldn't endure to live anywhere small. It's a fear of confined spaces and...'

'We're very comfortable and contented,' interrupted Coralie. 'And whenever you feel lonely you're welcome to call and visit me,' she added.

'Oh, may I? How lovely!' Beverley's smile was almost radiant with pleasure and surprise. Impulsively she took Coralie's hands and clasped them warmly between her own. 'I will, I most certainly will.'

Christopher was waiting for her as they reached the carriage. She turned to deliver an affectionate peck on Mrs Emerson's cheek and then he helped her clamber in.

'Tell the driver not to go too fast,' she instructed anxiously.

'I've already done so.'

'It upsets my stomach.'

'I know, dearest, and we'll go just as slowly as you please.'

'Hmph. I know how you begrudge every moment spent away from your precious telescopes. Last week we galloped home at breakneck speed and...'

'Now you're exaggerating, my love. However...' Christopher cast a guilty glance at Coralie and reddened a little as he met with raised eyebrows. '...I don't mean to be neglectful, and if you would like a picnic and a boatride this afternoon, I'll arrange it.'

'Christopher, it's Sunday! We must show respect for the Sabbath. Anyway, I'm tired. I just want to go home and lie down.'

Christopher glanced at Coralie again, and this time his expression said: 'There—you see? What's the use?'

She shrugged and waved as the driver whistled to the horses and the carriage rolled away.

Trying and unreasonable though she was, Beverley did arouse a certain sympathy in Coralie Emerson. She knew what loneliness felt like, and plainly Beverley believed in all her ailments. The fact that she created her own suffering was another matter. Coralie saw no harm in extending a little comfort to a silly young woman.

* * * *

Ten days later, in her shaded bedroom at Roskarnon, Beverley watched Mark Emerson roll down his sleeves and put on his jacket, hoping this time for an interesting verdict.

'You are not gravely ill, Beverley. You are not even mildly unwell. I can offer you neither sympathy nor medication. I suggest that you get up, go for a brisk walk in the fresh air, then find something useful to do.'

'Oh! What a cruel thing to say!' She stared helplessly at him through tearful eyes. 'You're supposed to help me, give me some medicine, make me better.'

Mark sighed. 'Humour you, in other words.'

'No! I'm very ill. I feel dreadul. Why are you being so horrid?'

'I am merely being honest. Pampering will do you no good. Be reasonable, Beverley. I've examined you for just about every malady known to man and I can find nothing wrong.'

'I know how I feel!' came the indignant retort.

Emmerson nodded. 'Disappointed, by the look of it. Childishly so.'

Beverley's mouth formed a pursed 'O' of outrage.

'This is the third time you've called me here

in a week,' he reminded her. 'I have found you fit each time—except for a morbid disposition and there's little I can do about that.'

'You could give me something for my nerves, and something to help me sleep.'

'You already have a vast stock of weird and wonderful preparations.'

'They don't work. Please...' She stared pitifully at him, a wan little figure lost in a large bed. '...can't you think of anything?'

Her gaze flickered and dropped under Mark's steady stare.

'I'm sorry, Beverley. I suppose this will sound trite, and I know it isn't what you want to hear, but if you could find something other than your health in which to take an interest...'

Beverley blinked at him, apparently mystified. 'And what, pray, do you recommend?' she asked pettishly.

'Perhaps you should have some children. I'm sure Christopher would like that. It might even bring him out of seclusion a little more often.'

'How can you suggest such a thing when you know I'm not strong enough?' she flared. 'I won't even contemplate it!'

'It was just a thought,' he said, picking up his bag.

'Not a very helpful one.'

He grinned as he paused at the door and

glanced back at her. 'Perhaps the best cure for you is to rouse your temper now and again. Go to the mirror, Beverley. Look at yourself. Your face is almost rosy.'

The moment his words sank in, she collapsed back against the pillows with renewed melancholy.

'You're very unkind,' she sniffed.

Emerson merely shrugged and went on his way.

She stared resentfully at the door as it closed behind him. No medicine, no sympathy. He was not Beverley's idea of a good doctor.

The consultation had quite upset her and now she was doubly in need of something calming and restorative. Wearily, Beverley got up and went to the cupboard in the corner. She opened the door and peered in, her eyes roving hopefully over a great array of bottles, ointment jars and pillboxes. A stale, drugshop smell wafted out to greet her, a bouquet of old prescriptions and patent potions, many of which were opium based. Sour chemical odours mingled with whiffs of peppermint. There were chalky and clear solutions in assorted colours, pots of congealed creams and traces of spilt powders.

But nothing new. She sighed wistfully, recalling the feeling of promise that once accompanied every fresh product. They had always let her down, of course, and it seemed that finally there was nothing left to try.

If only there were some way to render them more effective. Perhaps if two—or even three— were taken in conjuction...

Thoughtfully, Beverley reached into the cupboard and extracted a number of bottles whose contents were aimed at broadly similar complaints. She carried them across to a table by the window and arranged them neatly in a row. She then collected an empty glass and a water-jug from her bedside, placed them with the bottles and pulled up a chair.

With a sense of adventure she began mixing and sampling the various combinations. So absorbed did she become in these experiments that her miseries were quite forgotten for the rest of the day—which only went to prove that Dr Emerson had been absolutely right, although this little insight bypassed Beverley completely.

None of the potions worked, of course, but they had at any rate afforded her an afternoon of innocent entertainment. She thought she might do the same again at some time. In fact she would probably have to, since Emerson was so unobliging. Beverley decided that he was a most disagreeable person, but at least she had found a good friend in his wife.

★ ★ ★ ★

'Oh, dear Lord, here she comes again. Thank God I'm going out.'

Glancing from the parlour window, Mark had sighted Beverley hurrying down the path towards the lodge.

'She's lonely,' Coralie said. 'I wish you'd be a little less impatient with her.'

'She's a pest. I see too many instances of real suffering to waste my time on spoilt, idiotic women like her. She's always asking me for new medicines and she whines when I refuse to give her any. God knows, she already swallows enough of those patent cure-alls to kill a weaker person. Far from being fragile, I'd say she's nigh indestructible.'

'Nevertheless, try not to be short with her. She doesn't understand why you're always so abrupt.'

Emerson sighed and folded his wife in a comfortable hug.

'Oh Coralie, I wish I had your capacity for kindness. I suppose a man of my calling should show more tolerance.'

'I'm a lucky woman and that makes me generous. Anyway, a medical degree does not

183

guarantee a saintly disposition and I doubt I could be happy living with a pillar of virtue.'

'So I'm allowed a few endearing faults?'

'Quite a few.'

Coralie beamed up at him, fastening his waistcoat and the cuffs of his shirt. At home he seldom dressed the way of a gentleman, in stiffly buttoned jacket and tie. He looked, and was, a busy man, his sleeves always rolled to the elbows, his collar open more often than not.

He had been the turning point in Coralie's life, the great unbelievable gift of fortune. Sometimes at night, if she woke in the small hours, she would quietly light the lamp and sit up for a while, just to watch him sleeping and savour the feeling of privilege that came from sharing his bed. He never guessed how often she had studied him, tracing his features while he slept, the movements of the slim, capable hands as he ate, and the thick tawny hair curling and wisping at the nape of his neck as he bent his head over a book. No one else had ever given her so much affection or respect, and Coralie adored him.

At Beverley's knock he turned to scoop up his bag and jacket, planting a sympathetic kiss on his wife's forehead.

'I wish you joy of her. Now it's time I was off. I hope to be back by late afternoon.'

He flung wide the front door to find Beverley hovering on the step.

'Good morning, Beverley!' His voice was boomingly hearty and she gave a nervous start. 'You're looking more robust than ever, I see. Have you, by any chance, taken my advice to beget a fine, bouncing infant? What an excellent, motherly figure you have. I trust you will use it to the full and frequent advantage in the years to come, as you build up a large, healthy family. To think I shall have the privilege of delivering them all!'

She emitted a small squeak of shock, pressing a protective hand to her heart, and skipped smartly to one side as he strode past her.

'Well...! How disgracefully vulgar and personal!'

She watched indignantly as he climbed into the gig and whistled to the pony.

'Is he often so dreadfully coarse?'

Mrs Emerson struggled to subdue a burst of laughter.

'Come in, Beverley, and take no notice. His work leaves no room for gentility, so you mustn't expect it of him.'

With a last affronted glance at the doctor's gig disappearing through the trees, she followed Coralie inside and sank feebly into a chair.'

'All the same, it was thoughtless of him. My

185

palpitations have started again. It always happens when I'm upset.'

'Never mind. Make yourself comfortable and I'll fetch you some tea.'

Beverley sniffed sadly. 'Thank you, dear. Not too strong, now. I can only digest a weak brew, if you recall.'

'Of course. I won't be long.'

'You know,' began Beverley, catching her by the sleeve, 'it isn't proper...' She hesitated briefly, as if embarrassed by what she had to say. 'Coralie, it is not fitting that you should wait upon me as if you were a maid. Don't you think you should have some servants? Or at least a girl to do the cleaning? It is not seemly for a lady to do everything herself, especially one of your background and upbringing. Truly, I don't know how you manage. Do you not find it exhausting? People would think it most odd if they knew.'

'I don't care what anyone thinks, and my tasks are really not as arduous as all that. This is only a small house and there are just the two of us. Furthermore, I never touch anything in the little room where Mark sees his patients. In years to come, when we have children and a larger home, I shall doubtless need some help, but at present it is no hardship at all, believe me.'

'Well, I still don't think it's right for you to perform the work of menials.' Beverley paused for a moment, plainly groping for a way to broach an awkward subject. Then, leaning confidentially forward, she whispered: 'Is it a matter of money, dear? If so...'

'Not at all. I simply don't want or need a maid. Wherever would we put her, anyway? There's no spare room.'

'Well, if you're quite sure. I must say, I would be frightened to spend so many hours alone here every day—and sometimes nights as well.'

'Frightened of what? Of whom? Truly, my dear, you have a troublesome imagination.'

'One never knows,' said Beverley darkly.

'I'm prepared to take my chances,' twinkled Coralie.

'And as for money, the fact is that Mark has been doing surprisingly well. We had a few misgivings when William first suggested this move, but everything has worked out quite comfortably.'

'Oh, well, good. I'm very pleased, of course. And where was he going just now in such a rush?'

'He has two or three calls to make this morning, nothing very much. Mind you, he sometimes goes out before breakfast and I don't see

187

him again until nearly bedtime.'

Beverley gave a peevish little snort. 'Hmmph, Christopher rarely honours me with his company at all. He disappears upstairs for hours on end and he's not even doing useful work, just playing with those silly charts and things like an overgrown schoolboy. It seems he has now decided to write a book on his observations, and the Lord only knows how long that will take. He shuts himself away up there from mid-morning till past midnight. sometimes he doesn't even come out for proper meals. If it weren't for William and his good sense, I swear the estate would go to rack and ruin. Christopher is so irresponsible. However, I admit I would rather lose him to his studies than to some other woman and at least he shows no tendency to wander. Truly, dear, it's the only consolation I have—except for your friendship.'

★ ★ ★ ★

In Beverley's estimation, Coralie's life at Roskarnon could hardly be looked upon as easy, and yet the Emersons counted it a vast improvement on the noisy, dirty atmosphere of London. Far from missing the city with all its amusements and facilities, they found the country and its denizens a source of endless interest.

Mark in particular had taken time during his travels about the estate to pause and observe the nature of the local flora. Here, growing wild, were the sources of many powerful drugs.

To the knowledgeable eye the countryside offered a host of useful herbs, some beneficial and others deservedly ill-famed. It was like an apothecary's shop—or a witch's kitchen—depending on the nature of one's intent. Enough simples and bad weed to cure, or kill, half the county, he reflected. Many were shrouded in superstition and fear, their malefic properties often concealed in bright flowers, enticing fruit or a treacherous resemblance to some innocent, edible species. By contrast there were other plants that formed the basis of old and trusted household remedies which he would hesitate to condemn or dismiss.

The local people had relied heavily on such cures—as dispensed by Gaddy Scanes—for most of their lives. He took it as a pleasing sign of acceptance that so many of them had already come to him for treatment. At first he had been amused to discover that they often paid his small fees in kind, with a chicken or a rabbit, a slab of cheese, a basket of eggs, pots of honey or favours done. The Kirkwoods' circle of relatives and well-to-do acquaintances had further extended his list of patients and he was happily surprised to find himself a little more solvent than he had been in London. They kept him comfortably busy, without the relentless pressure he had suffered in the city. It was undoubtedly a gentler way of life—although not without its dramas.

On one particular day, a small boy arrived at Curlew Quay and handed him a dramatic message from the head gamekeeper's wife. Her husband, it said, was 'beaten black and blue, with half his bones broke and blood all over him.' He was dying for sure, she declared, but wanted the doctor anyway.

The road to the keeper's home took Emerson through several miles of thin woodland, and on the way he passed a small procession of four gypsy caravans, driven by dour and shabby men, each with an equally sombre woman and a number of children on board. Suspicious, weary-looking people, they watched him sourly as they trundled by, exchanging muttered comments in some peculiar patois that was only part English. He gave them no more than a passing glance, his mind upon his business and the contents of that ominous note.

It all turned out to be a gross exaggeration. He found the man bearing the indisputable marks of a lively fist fight, but well enough to be downing pints of ale and cursing loudly on his assailants.

'Gypsies, they were,' he rumbled, as the doctor felt around for broken bones, discovering just one cracked rib and a few pulled muscles. 'Irish, too, with scores of ragged children and half-starved dogs. Trespassing, thieving...'

'Ah,' murmured Emerson, 'yes, I saw them on the road. What exactly happened?' He turned the man's face to the light and whistled softly to see the left eye swollen shut, circled dark blue and purple.

'Well, you know, don't you, Doctor, that it's Ember Night in less than two weeks' time? So up I goes to the clearing to cut down any scrub that's grown over—and what do I find but this rabble making itself at home. So I do my job and tell 'em to move out.' He lifted his mug of ale and took a long draught. There was, Emerson noticed, a livid ring of human teethmarks on the brawny forearm, and the keeper's knuckles were coloured to match his eye. 'Anyway, they say they aren't ready to go. They'll be heading north and on to Ireland after that, but not for a day or two.'

'Hmm. Go on,' prompted Mark, deciding that the scalp would need a few stitches.

'You're leaving right now, I says, and

191

nat'rally, since I've got the shotgun to hand, I wave it around a bit.'

'Naturally. And then?'

'Well, you'd hardly expect it, would you sir, that a little sprite, a nipper not ten years old, would grab your arm and sink his teeth in? Well, that's what happened. I've had dog bites that were less painful, and while I was trying to shake him off, two of the men set on me together.'

'I see. I can picture the rest.'

'Good-for-nothing gypsies,' grumbled the keeper.

'Well, it looks as if they've packed up and gone after all.'

'Oh, aye. They know I'd be back up there tomorrow with half the village. 'Tis important, you know, Ember Night. 'Tis a big event. That clearing's never used for anything else. That's the party ground. You'll be coming, won't you, Doctor?'

'Yes, My wife, too. We're looking forward to it.'

'That's good, that's good.' The keeper waved his ale about approvingly, slopping a deal of it onto the floor. He was beginning to slur. 'She'll have a grand time.'

'I'm sure she will.'

★ ★ ★ ★

A telegram arrived at Curlew Quay on April 28th—two days before Ember Night. It was sent by one of Coralie's sisters to say that Amelia was gravely ill. It also hinted that, having broken her mother's heart, Coralie might at least present herself respectfully at Amelia's deathbed.

'I suppose I'd better go,' she said anxiously.

Her disgruntled husband tossed the telegram into the fire and scowled as he watched it burn.

'Why? It's probably just one of her chills again.'

'But I can't be sure of that and I'd never forgive myself if I ignored this note and it turned out that she really was dying.'

'That's what she's counting on. Your mother is an extremely tough woman. She's also domineering and she won't easily accept that you've slipped your leash and turned your back on her. We've been here less than a month, Coralie. She managed well enough without you when we lived in London, but as soon as we move down here she's tugging the chain to see if you'll come running. If you go to her now, I'll wager there will be another peremptory little summons every few months.'

'I can't help it, Mark. When all's said and

done, she's still my Mama and I'll have to go. If I find she's not seriously ill I promise this will be the first and last time.'

'Oh, all right. If you must.' He shrugged impatiently. 'She certainly has an uncanny way of choosing her moments.'

'Ember Night, you mean? Yes, I'm sorry about that. I was quite looking forward to it. But that doesn't mean that you must miss it, too. Tabitha's made such preparations. She's been quite taken up with it all for nearly a week. I want you to go and enjoy yourself—and I shall tell her to ensure that you do!'

CHAPTER 16

Ember Night arrived with fine spring weather and the party began just after eight.

'A few refreshments,' Tabitha had said.

Mark's eyebrows lifted in amusement at the mountainous feast laid out upon draped trestle tables beneath the trees. There was roasted ox and suckling pig, trout and salmon, pies, cakes and cream, plum puddings and spiced apple dumplings, cockles and winkles, flans and pancakes, cider, ale and brandy punch.

There was nothing, of course, to please a fancy palate. Designed for country appetites, it was all traditional fare and most of it Roskarnon's own produce.

In the centre of the broad clearing a great cone-shaped stack of logs and brushwood had just been lit, and the flames were climbing skywards in the dusk. From infants to the ancient, every soul for ten miles about had turned up, all in Sunday best.

Even Beverley had decided to brave the night air and was seen nibbling a cherry tart as she hung on her husband's arm. Christopher spotted the doctor standing alone at the edge of the clearing and made his way over to bid him welcome.

'Pleased to see you, Emerson. What's happened to Coralie this evening?'

Beverley tutted and sighed. 'She's in London, dear. Her poor Mama is ill. I did tell you.'

'Did you?' he queried vaguely.

'Several times. You never listen, Christopher, that's the trouble. You're always so preoccupied...'

'Quite a crowd, eh?' he cut in hurriedly, turning to Mark. 'Ember Night is always a big event. The tenants look forward to it all year round and we are gratified to know they enjoy it so.'

At that point, three of the local men launched into a bouncy tune on the fiddle, squeezebox and tambour, and many of the more energetic immediately skipped into a country dance, their feet patting lightly on the hard earth.

'I see what you mean. I understand there's some sort of ritual involved?'

'Oh, that.' Christopher chuckled. 'Yes, it's really a game for impatient young ladies—but one that's taken half seriously. There's an element of match-making involved and I suspect the forecasts often fulfil themselves simply because the girls believe in them.'

'It sounds intriguing. What exactly happens?'

'Do you see the old lady over there?'

Christopher indicated the weathered little figure sitting on a tree stump a few yards away. In one hand she clutched a cider flagon, in the other a hunk of game pie, and for some reason a long-handled shovel was driven upright into the ground at her side.

'There sits the most important member of this assembly. Her name's Gaddy Scanes and she will be officiating at the 'ceremony' later on. Gaddy's quite an influential person hereabouts. Most of the people seem to believe quite firmly that she has mysterious gifts— second sight and so on. The truth is, she's a

wily old fraud. There is one in every genera-
tion, of course, though I rather think Gaddy
may be the last round here. Science will sweep
away people like her. She has already lost some
of her following because of you.'

Emerson glanced at the old girl, who
stamped her feet in time to the music as it
swung from jig to reel and ever more couples
joined the dance.

'I'm sorry. I hope she doesn't resent me too
much.'

Christopher dismissed that with a shrug.
'Oh, don't worry, she still has other areas of
influence. After all, you can't tell the future,
can you, Doctor? And that is what Caddy is
here for tonight. You see, she practises a form
of pyromancy, and when the fire burns low,
all the unmarried girls will come up to hear who
their husband may be. Gaddy is very clever,
of course. She never gives names, only hints
and descriptions, but she knows who favours
whom and she has an instinct for suitable pair-
ing. What she's really giving is advice dressed
up as prophecy. But the girls—and the lads,
too, I suspect—have so much faith in her that
these "predictions" often lead to a wedding.'

'It may sound a peculiar custom, but most
of the marriages prove to be happy ones.'
Tabitha's tone was a quiet purr as she appeared

at Emerson's side.

'Hmph. I don't think it's Christian,' sniffed Beverley.

'No indeed,' said Tabitha. 'Good match-making requires common sense, and religion offers little of that.'

'What a terrible thing to say!'

'But true nonetheless. The faithful are often dogmatic, irrational and dangerous into the bargain. Wouldn't you agree, Christopher? Remember Kepler and Galileo.'

'And anyone else who showed signs of intelligence,' added Emerson.

'I'm not at all surprised to hear impious sentiments from the pair of you,' snorted Beverley.

Christopher saw a sharp exchange in the making and there was nothing he hated more than a quarrel.

'Come along, dearest, I'll get you another glass of punch. We don't want you to get upset and start feeling faint, do we?' He smiled and nodded to the doctor, steering his wife away. 'Be sure to enjoy yourself, Mark. You'd best hurry up and have some supper. The food seems to be disappearing fast.'

Left alone with Tabitha, Emerson said: 'So you, too, are out of favour? She tells me I'm insensitive.'

'While I, apparently, am selfish.'

In the flickering light of the fire, Tabitha's air of dark humour seemed even more pronounced. Her dress was pale green cotton and a white lace shawl was thrown around her shoulders. She had pinned back her hair with a simple ivory comb and, once again, looked almost like a village girl.

'Anyway, since we have so much in common, we had better stay together, don't you think? Your wife has insisted that I take care of you this evening. As you can see, William has no need of my company.'

She nodded in the direction of her husband, who stood joking with two of his farmers as they helped themselves to brandy punch. Emerson guessed that this was by no means William's first drink, judging by his noisy laughter and high colour.

'So it seems. And how do you propose to entertain me?'

'Can you dance, Mark?'

'After a fashion, but I'm not familiar with this kind of thing.'

'Then you must let me teach you.'

She slipped a hand firmly into his and led him out among the dancers, many of whom already knew and recognised him. To others the whisper went round that this was the new doctor, all the way from London, and Gaddy

Scanes was seen to snort and turn her back.

He followed Tabitha hesitantly through the first steps amid grins and shouts of encouragement, then found himself dropping easily into the rhythm as the music frisked and capered on. They were frolicking dances, breathlessly energetic, and he noted, without surprise, that Beverley did not join in.

Between glasses of ale and helpings of food, he took turns for a reel with some of the local girls as the evening wore on, while Tabitha went off to perform the mingling and supervising duties of a squire's wife. She was much too wise to neglect these obligations, but every now and again, usually when the music slowed, she returned to dance with him.

At first he could not tell if it was just the effect of drink which made him fancy that she sometimes pressed too close, that her hands lingered and stroked a fraction longer than the turnings and linkings of the dance required. Almost everyone around them seemed drunk to some degree. Everyone, he noticed, except Tabitha. He had not seen her take even the smallest glass of wine. Three hours had passed for him in a whirl of alcohol and music, while she grew wittier and more provocative, and he realised that he had not spared a thought for Coralie since the party began.

What was more, he had a growing inclination to go with Tabitha into the dark of the wood, for he had reached that pleasant state where ale impairs conscience but not performance, and he was truly in a mood to take advantage of the fact.

What, after all, would it matter? A single, meaningless lapse—brief, casual and never to be repeated...

The music stopped quite abruptly, breaking his train of thought and replacing it with a faint embarrassment, for Tabitha was grinning at him in a knowing way.

'I think it's time,' she whispered. 'Do you want to see the ceremony, or would you rather find some quiet place in which to—relax?'

He hesitated a long moment. Principle finally shaped his answer, but it was touch-and-go.

'Of course I want to watch it,' he said with certainty that was far from genuine. 'After all, the whole point of the evening...'

'...is to find new partners,' agreed Tabitha. 'Come then.'

The fire had burned down to a mound of glowing embers. Now that he looked about him, he noticed that the gathering had thinned out, for young children had been taken home early and old people had quietly left for the comfort of their beds. One ancient, however, remained. Pleasantly inebriated but still steady on her feet, Gaddy Scanes stepped forward, shovel in hand, while a hopeful semicircle of adolescent girls formed respectfully around her.

Gaddy cleared her throat importantly, gave a thoughtful tug at one earlobe and then scratched her chin.

'Sarey Blewett? Come here girl, and listen well.'

A small ginger-haired girl hurried forward as the old woman plunged the shovel into the embers, turned them over once, then again, scooped a few off the top and scattered them wide across a patch of bare earth. She scuttled around at them, turning and cocking her head to gauge the way they lay.

'He's fair,' she announced suddenly, as the glowing fragments began to burn out. 'Honey fair, he is. Not a big lad, but strong for all that. Take him, Sarey, and you'll never be short of a solid roof.'

Sarey's eyes turned thoughtfully towards the thatcher's ruddy-faced son. The boy shuffled his feet and grinned, bashfully pleased.

'Tilly Dawes?'

Gaddy performed her little act again, this time for a dark and hefty dairymaid.

' 'Tis a big lanky man and a fine hand with

202

horses. Well travelled, he is. You'll be happy with him, so long as you don't bring flowers in the house.'

Tilly's gaze slid hungrily toward one of Roskarnon's stable hands, the one who had been all the way to Plymouth and had hay fever. He winked at her and puffed out his chest.

'Can you see how the old fraud does it?' whispered Tabitha.

'I think so. But what does she get from it?'

'Oh, she commands a good deal of respect, thanks to her strange "gifts", plus considerations from shy lads who need a little help in their courting. There will be presents on her doorstep tomorrow morning.'

Emerson chuckled. 'I would say she is more enterprising than superstitious.'

'Oh, Gaddy has many eccentric beliefs, but the ember ceremony is just a performance. She has a healthy regard for compromise,' Tabitha said as they watched the old woman tossing embers for the next girl, 'and so do I. I also believe in grasping opportunities, don't you?'

'Some. There are others which are best left alone.'

'Quite—and the important thing is to know which are which. I can always tell, just as I always know when a friendship is worth

203

cultivating.' She raised an eyebrow and smiled broadly. 'Are you sure you want to watch any more of this?'

It was another invitation, another chance.

And why not accept? instinct whispered slyly. Where's the harm? She's a luscious little creature—and what is it, anyway, but a few minutes' pleasure? Hardly a capital sin. Certain women have unusual needs and talents. It seems almost churlish to refuse her. I was far from celibate before I married, and frustration does a man no good. Perhaps this once...

He had almost talked himself into it when William suddenly appeared beside them, much the worse for brandy.

'Are you having a good time, Mark? It's not much like London life, I know, but merry enough in its way. Will you have another glass of ale?'

Emerson got quickly to his feet and confusion was writ large on his face.

'Thank you, but... Well, I think I'll be on my way home now. It's been a long day and I don't normally drink so much. It was a grand party, William. I'm sorry my wife had to miss it.' He turned and nodded briefly to Tabitha. 'Goodnight, Tabitha.'

'Goodnight, Mark.' Amusement coloured her voice as he turned and hastened back to where he had left the gig.

Away from the warmth of the fire the air was chill, and Emerson found his head clearing a little as he drove home.

His marriage was little more than a year old, he thought, flinching with shame, and he had nearly, very nearly, been tempted into betraying Coralie. As soon as her back was turned he had found himself drawn to Tabitha Kirkwood, and the feeling of guilt was grim to say the least. He was thankful for William's interruption and he resolved to keep away from her in future.

Tabitha, however, did not intend to stay away from him—or to let the evening end in disappointment.

CHAPTER 17

It was a little past one o'clock and William had been alseep for over an hour; the impenetrable sleep of a normally temperate man who had, for once, overstepped his own limit. Beside him, the bed was empty. He had not felt the small movements as his wife got up, nor did he stir and wake to see her standing at the window.

The moon was just three nights from full, silvering the countryside beneath. Its light flooded across the old garden and laid a pearl-grey sheen upon the quiet water of the creek, but all Tabitha's thoughts were bent upon the narrow path that stretched away into the shadows under the trees. Down there, just a little walk away, was the lodge.

She knew how close she had come, that only William's interruption, only a wavering sense of honour or loyalty to his wife, had stopped Emerson from taking what she offered. Only the lack of the proper time, place, circumstances.

The knowledge excited, intrigued her. She knew that the way to win him was to give his conscience no chance for debate, and now, tonight, as he slept alone, was the time for daring. It almost seemed that the little pathway was waiting, patiently expecting her. She had never in any previous affair attempted quite such a brazen move. Those cheerful afternoon assignations had never required it. But Emerson was different, something of a challenge, for he had principles to be overcome and that was surely the essence of seduction. Tabitha quite understood why this was a time-honoured sport.

As she pulled on a light dressing-gown and

slippers, William sighed once and turned over. Tabitha smiled as she padded out onto the landing and softly closed the bedroom door. She would be back in good time to commiserate over his headache at breakfast.

The night air was fresh and still as she crept out through the french windows from the music room, hurried over the terrace and down across the grass, almost skipping with exhilaration at what she was doing.

A short while later she halted breathlessly beneath the trees and a smile twitched at the corners of her mouth as she glimpsed a spark of light ahead—the lantern which Mark always left burning in the porch to show the way for those who might need him in the night. It was most considerate of him, thought Tabitha. And as she drew near to Curlew Quay she saw with a thrill of exquisite mischief that she would not even have to knock at the door.

In all but frosty weather, Mark had always slept with the window open. He knew all the light, fresh smells that drifted in with the night air; grass and herbs and newly turned earth, the sharp tang of brine from the creek.

But tonight there was something more.

With the drowsy perception of one close to sleep, he caught a scent reminiscent of pinewood and almonds, oddly familiar and yet out of place here, in this room. A woman's perfume—he knew it quite well from somewhere—and it grew more powerful as someone slid into bed beside him, someone quietly insistent who wound herself about him like ivy round a tree.

He murmured and began to turn over, half-consciously seeking his wife. And then, like a splash of cold water, came a sudden lucid thought.

Coralie was in London. She always wore lavender. And above all she was far too shy to climb into bed stark naked.

'Who...? In heaven's name...!'

He was suddenly wide awake, half-certain, even before he heard the husky female chuckle, who the trespasser was. Rolling to his side he searched for the lamp, lit it, and turned an incredulous stare on his visitor.

'I'm sorry, I didn't mean to alarm you. I'm in urgent need of a private consultation, but I saw no call to drag you from your bed.'

She was lying on her side, head propped casually on one hand, and the fall of coiling chestnut hair twined about her like a glossy dark creeper.

For a moment he was too stunned to answer, trying to digest the reality of finding this engaging little baggage in his bed. Swiftly, however, there grew a guilty sense of admiration for the pure effrontery that had put her there, and for the neatly sculpted body of which she was clearly and justly proud.

'Yes,' he said at last. 'I follow your logic, Tabitha, in view of the kind of therapy you obviously want.'

Tabitha grinned, smoothing an approving hand over his shoulder and combing delicate fingernails down through the light growth of hair on his chest.

'Mine is a most persistent and bothersome ailment, sir, one that keeps me awake at night. It requires a specialist and I believe you're well able to—treat me.'

'I take it your husband is not?'

'William, I fear, is indisposed, and when I have a problem I believe in taking it to an expert. You needn't worry, Mark. I'm extremely careful. Discretion, after all, is in the interests of us both.'

'By God, madam, I must give you credit for audacity.'

He could not keep the amusement from his voice, any more than he could bring himself to toss her out of his bed. It was already too late for that. She was too compelling, too invitingly wicked to refuse, no matter what the consequences might be. He would have her now, regardless of all else.

And suffer for it in the morning, when the image of Coralie's face would rise before him with reproachful clarity? Yes, that, too. If it cost him a year of guilt and remorse, still he wanted William's wife. And why? What made it so worthwhile? Just the delicious badness of her, the sheer nerve and blithe immorality. There was something so refreshing about it.

He saw no danger—for himself—of confusing lust with love, and he could not imagine that such a thing might happen to Tabitha, for that would be entirely out of character. No, it could do no harm. This was something quite different from the cosy affection he felt for Coralie. Just a little dalliance, he told himself. And who would be the worse for it in the long run? He meant it to go no further than a single night.

'I trust you'll give me more than credit, Mark. You'll find me a most rewarding case and well worthy of your interest. So, I offer myself for study and any—reasonable—experiments you care to make.'

With that, the last trace of hesitation left him.

'I believe you're right, Tabitha. I can already tell that you're quite unusual. Close examination could easily reveal horns and a tail.'

Tabitha chuckled as he pulled her down beneath the covers with him.

'It seems to me,' she purred, 'that you're well equipped to cope, no matter what you find.'

* * * *

The night was almost gone, shredding from black into grey, when Tabitha made her way homeward through the dew-soaked grass. She had left Mark still sleeping as she rose and padded quietly from the house. If she had woken him, Tabitha knew she would have stayed far too long.

She had not expected anything so intense from him, was unprepared for so much heat and force and skill. Nowhere else had she encountered quite such a mixture of fervour and finesse. It gave him a certain disquieting power which set her at a disadvantage. She had never before regarded any of her partners with quite the same admiration.

The feeling was disconcerting in a pleasurable sort of way, but alongside it there rose the shadow of something else, equally unfamiliar and very, very sour.

Jealousy.

This was a new and bitter-tasting thing. In none of her past affairs had she ever felt any ill-will toward the man's wife. In fact she knew most of those women socially, took tea with them and exchanged amiable chatter whenever she met one in town.

But Coralie? All of a sudden Tabitha had begun to resent her.

In the space of that night she had lost a measure of the old detachment which had always kept her liaisons on a carefully organised even keel. This time she was close to something more hazardous, the kind of involvement where caution and restraint seem to matter rather less and consequences are brushed aside. Tabitha, however, was dwelling on the night's enjoyment as she walked home, not assessing its dangers.

As she reached the point where the path emerged from the trees, a sharp, echoing sound, the crack of a gunshot, intruded on her thoughts. Tabitha stopped, listening intently, trying to place the direction from whence it came. For half a minute she heard nothing more, standing silently in the low-lying mist that writhed about her feet and whirled away across the lawns.

And then came a second shot, from somewhere to the east, she decided, not more than half a mile away.

The poacher again. Like most estates, Roskarnon had its share and the gamekeepers had been on the watch for this one for over a week. He was said to be more enterprising than most—so much so that William had twice mentioned him at dinner.

Tabitha began to feel an odd affinity with the man. Like her, he was becoming more daring. This was the first time she had heard him so close to the house. There were many kinds of thieving, she supposed. Both of them had been at work last night, and each would pay a heavy price if caught.

She shivered, suddeny very cold, wrapped her flimsy garments close about her, and ran the last few hundred yards across the garden and round to the music room windows.

CHAPTER 18

It was early afternoon two days later when the balmy warmth of May weather prompted Mark to take a walk along the shingle beach below the lodge. He had not meant to go far or stay out for long. But somehow, when the time came to turn back home, his steps carried him on towards Roskarnon, just as his thoughts kept stubbornly returning to Tabitha, and the truthful side of him knew that he was hopeful of a 'chance' meeting.

Perhaps it was her custom to sit out in the garden on warm spring days, or maybe she had been half expecting him. Whichever the case, he found her in the grass among the laurel bushes, sitting at Pan's cloven feet and reading the works of Swinburne. No shabby clothes this time, he noticed. Pink silk and cream laced instead. Tabitha glanced up as his shadow fell across the book, and a look of eager pleasure lit her face. She smiled and stretched up a hand to him.

'Mark, I'm so happy to see you. Come and sit with me.'

He was briefly tempted not to. Caution and common sense advised him to bid her good day, go back the way he had come—but he paid no heed to these dull suggestions.

As if nothing had happened two nights ago? It was not possible, of course—churlish, to say the least— and she did look very fetching in that dress.

'Please,' she pressed, 'I can hardly see you with the sun at your back.'

At that, he dropped his jacket onto the ground, then sat down cross-legged beside her.

'I suppose it's very obvious that I've come looking for you?'

'As plain as the fact that I've been sitting here hoping you would.' She closed the book and put it to one side. 'I wanted to see you yesterday; I was disappointed that you didn't call. And then I feared that I must have shocked you after all.'

'You'll agree, then, that it's a startling experience for a man to wake and find someone else's wife in his bed—uninvited.'

'I wanted you,' said Tabitha simply. 'Would you have me play coy little games? I always took you for a very forthright man. And while we're discussing honesty, you must admit that you didn't exactly fling me out and send me home.'

She raised questioning brows beneath the brim of her sun hat.

'Oh, Tabitha...' He laughed and shook his head. 'You know enough about men to realise I was past doing that. Shock tactics, I suspect, were the whole point of the exercise.'

'You make me sound so calculating,' she said reproachfully. 'I was simply acting on impulse. You know how we women are—tossed hither and thither by emotions.'

'They must have been pretty stormy to send you on a midnight excursion to the lodge, with all the risk entailed.'

She shrugged and gave a small nod of agreement.

'You should take it as a compliment, Mark. Believe me, I don't regret it.'

'Are you sure you mean that? I'm enormously flattered, but I wonder if you truly realise how much you stand to lose? What if you had been caught? What if William had woken and missed you in the night?'

'Danger is exciting, don't you think?' twinkled Tabitha. 'But I knew he wouldn't wake after his spree on the brandy punch. As a matter of fact, he was quite unwell yesterday morning. I was so concerned that I thought of fetching you, but I didn't want to trouble a tired man.'

More than tired, he recalled. Physically exhausted and mentally plagued with a mixture of guilt and gnawing, restless desire to see her again.

'I admit you're a rousing woman, Tabitha. You could easily become a bad habit.'

'What a lovely idea,' she murmured, eyeing him thoughtfully. 'We must try and establish it firmly. Why don't you walk with me for a while down by the river? It's much too pleasant a day to spend indoors.'

Ah yes, down by the river, where there was grass on which to lie instead of his own marital bed, surrounded by trees and wild flowers in place of Coralie's belongings. He had passed the previous day in a ferment of self-rebuke,

216

but always it was overlaid with a kind of dark excitement and now, at Tabitha's first beckoning, he was ready to do the same thing again.

Somewhere neutral, with no reminders that this was betrayal, no accusing photographs or fear of guilty clues left behind. One lapse, or two—what difference could it make? Tabitha was such a luxury, pretty and soft and perfumed—such a special treat for one who led a plain and humdrum life, with little money or amusement. She was glamorous, beguiling, a secret indulgence. Of course, he loved—genuinely loved—Coralie, but this was something quite separate. This was merely diversion and he would not lose sight of the difference.

A refusal would be unbearable, Tabitha was thinking. It would matter very much, for here, she believed, was someone exceptional. She recalled with amazement the indifference with which she had first looked upon him in London. Tabitha perceived him quite differently now. He was strong and solid, gold and brown, like wheat and cider and new-baked bread. His was bright, treasure colouring and her hands itched to touch him, covetously longing to keep and consume.

His hesitation was tantalising and, at last, as she thought he was wavering, she sought to tip the balance, forgetting the windows of the house close by. So intensely did she want him that she gave no thought to who might see.

Upstairs in the turret room, Christopher had laid aside the writings of Galileo. He glanced around him at the diagrams and charts of the heavens which covered the walls, then absently rubbed his eyes and thought that he would like some tea.

He got up and went to the window, where his telescopes were tilted skywards on their stands. As was his habit, Christopher shaded his eyes to gaze up for a while at the long streaks of cirrus cloud. And then looked down.

There in the garden, some way off and just visible beyond a thick screen of laurels, was his sister, and she was not alone. She had just risen to her feet, and with her stood the tawny-headed figure of the doctor. As Christopher watched, he saw her reach up to encircle the man's neck, drawing down his head into the shade beneath the wide brim of her straw hat. It was no innocent peck on the cheek, Christopher observed, frowning. It was neither brief nor chaste, and Emerson's response was anything but casual.

'Good God,' muttered Christopher. His glance scanned swiftly across the garden to see if anyone else might have noticed them. Fortunately there was no one around and he realised that this was probably the only room in the house from which they could have been spotted there amongst the shrubbery, the only one high enough. All the same, the incident came as a shock to him—not least because of Tabitha's extreme carelessness. It was just as if she had forgotten where she was, oblivious to everything except Mark Emerson. At last he saw her link an arm with the doctor and set off down a path which led to a track beside the creek; a narrow, quiet way under arches of oak and hazel where the branches dipped almost to touch the water.

Those dells down by the river. Christopher knew them well—lonely places with no sound or movement but the lapping of the water and the curlews' call.

Much disturbed, Christopher shook his head sadly and turned from the window, wondering what—if anything—he should do. It seemed to him a delicate situation in which he would rather not become involved. William would be loath to accept any criticism of his darling and Christopher wanted no ugly confrontations. He also knew what scandal could mean for a man like Emerson, not to mention the misery it would cause Coralie.

Perhaps, he thought vaguely, he should have

a tactful word with Tabitha some time, just to issue a quiet, brotherly warning. That, surely, would be sufficient. After all, it was not his place to interfere in someone else's marriage.

★ ★ ★ ★

'What's the matter? Did you hear something?'

Mark had lifted his head suddenly, distracted, it seemed, by some far-off thought or sound. Beneath him, Tabitha tensed at the lifting of his weight and scanned his face with concern.

'Is there someone about?'

For a moment he did not answer, his mind elsewhere.

'Mark?' She tangled her fingers anxiously in his hair. 'What is it? What are you listening for?'

Not listening, he thought, but remembering—something Coralie has said on their first night at the lodge, side by side in their marriage bed.

'It was nothing. Just a bird.'

A bird, yes. A curlew.

'Ill-omened,' she had said, 'to hear them at night.'

It was the same cry, heard now in broad daylight, like an echo of evil portent.

He rolled away from Tabitha and got up,

walking across to a gap in the screen of bushes to look out over the creek. It was low tide and the shallows were dotted with tummocks of coarse grass and sea pinks. Wading between them was a pair of brown speckled birds, dipping with long, curved bills for morsels of food. Foolish, he thought, to let that cry bother me now, when I've heard it a hundred times before.

Tabitha, lying on her side, watched him with appreciation. He was one of the few men she had met who looked really graceful without his clothes. Not an unsightly inch from head to toe, she thought, and a slow smile crept across her features.

He turned round, saw the way she looked at him, and felt the same hungry admiration for that dainty female figure, so white against the grass.

'You seem apprehensive,' she said as he settled beside her again.

No, he thought. Just allowing a rational mind to be disturbed by old wives' tales.

'In that case, madam, you must find some way to soothe me.'

And he rolled with her, panting and laughing, over and over, almost to the water's edge.

When the curlew called again, he was too happily absorbed to notice it.

CHAPTER 19

The next time Beverley had one of her feverish turns, she found her sister-in-law unusually sympathetic. The servants were reluctant to answer her bell, which tinkled imperiously on and off throughout the day, but Tabitha was solicitous to such a degree that she even volunteered to call the doctor just in case it was something serious.

'It occurs to me that I may have been a little harsh, dear,' she cooed smiling from the foot of the bed. 'I was always so fortunate with my own health, perhaps I lack understanding. I hope you'll forgive me. And from now on we must take better care of you. I've sent someone to fetch Dr Emerson and I'm sure he won't be long.'

'That was very thoughtful, Tabitha, thank you.'

Propped limply against her pillows, Beverley regarded the other woman with puzzlement, pleased and yet suspicious. Why this sudden turnabout, she wondered? Tabitha's friendship would be more than welcome, but still it seemed too good to be true.

'Not at all. After all, you are my brother's wife—my sister.' The green eyes surveyed Beverley steadily across the quilt, bright with calculating humour. At last Tabitha had found a use for the silly creature. She bustled round to plump up the pillows and straighten the covers at Beverley's feet. 'Lunch will be ready soon. I've asked Cook to do your favourite roast lamb, with fruit compôte and cream to follow.'

'It sounds lovely, but I doubt I can eat more than a little.' Beverley sighed tragically. 'Do you think he'll be long? I... Oh, I expect that's him.' She brightened with anticipation as the doorbell sounded in the hall below.

'I'll leave you alone and you can tell him all about it,' Tabitha said, turning to go.

It was altogether a splendid day, Beverley was to reflect later. Everyone was being so kind. Even Emerson displayed exceptional patience. He came and sat down on the side of her bed, took her hand and listened, nodding gravely as she described a new batch of mysterious symptoms. Finally he gave her a pale green potion and a new variety of pill to be taken after meals, and left her to spend the rest of the afternoon in a happy doze.

Beverley sampled the new medicine and found it superbly ill-tasting. She was much in need of something fresh and powerful, being sorely disenchanted with her own concoctions. She had tried every possible permutation, but nothing helped at all. It was just as well, she thought, that the doctor was finally taking her seriously.

The truth, of course, was quite another matter. Mark had known the duplicity of his motives when he answered this summons, realising as he bounded up the steps to Roskarnon with such alacrity that the chance to see Tabitha was uppermost in his mind. All the same, Beverley had provided the excuse and this made him look upon her with uncommon tolerance.

When at last he came out of the room, he was waylaid by a maid bearing an invitation from Tabitha.

'Mrs Kirkwood asks if you'd care to stay to lunch, sir. If you've no urgent business, that is. Mr Kirkwood is out and Mr Summerfield rarely takes a midday meal. She'd be pleased to have your company today.'

He paused to consider, but the decision came quickly.

'Yes, I would like that very much.'

★ ★ ★ ★

Lunch was a quiet charade of casual conver-

224

sation; polite, banal, nothing unfit for servants' ears, not a glance or a gesture out of place. But when the meal was ended, Tabitha called him into the library, ostensibly to inspect a book of particular interest. He knew as he followed her, closing the doors behind him, of the little back staircase to the upper floors—the bedrooms.

Conscience protested less loudly now. It was becoming easier, this treachery. He guessed that for her it had never been otherwise. Deception and infidelity were Tabitha's second nature, her normality. In him they were growing like some progressive illness which he found himself reluctant to fight. Just one final indiscretion. The last time—again. Exception turning into habit and willpower ebbing bit by bit.

Nearly three hours later, in a half-shaded room of the guest wing, he lay awake while Tabitha slept, their limbs interwoven and the covers thrown back, trailing to the floor in company with discarded clothes. The room still whispered of fiercely urgent coupling; hot, hungry and secret.

He shifted a little to stretch his legs, trying quietly to detach Tabitha's hold without waking her, and in so doing he caught sight of them both, reflected in the dressing table mirror.

It was an oval mirror, the frame encrusted

with scallop and cowrie shells, creamy pale like
the guelder roses arranged in the vase beside
it and interlaced with the sharp green leaves of
vervain. He was startled to see the two of them
there, locked in their illicit, naked tangle. They
looked absurdly, almost comically abandoned,
and a tremor of silent laughter shook through
him.

'What do you find so amusing, pray?'

A tapering fingernail trailed down across his
stomach and came to rest, dabbling playfully,
in his navel.

'You and me, madam.' He nodded toward
the mirror. 'If that were a painting it would
fetch a pretty penny in some circles.'

Tabitha closed one eye, lazily studying the
reflection.

'And rightly so. A fine example of erotic art,
unless I'm much mistaken. Moreover, it has
magical properties.'

'Oh?'

'Oh yes. The figures move, you see—winding
one about the other, turning and rolling, over
and over. And the picture has differing moods,
as well. There's slow, delicious languor, then
there's humour—and just a suspicion of vio-
lence now and again. Enchanting, don't you
think? I'm sure there's not another like it
anywhere.'

Emerson chuckled. 'Well it seems, for the time being, to have worn itself out.'

'You think so? Watch the woman's left hand. Do you see it sliding over his thigh and round...?'

He grabbed her hastily by the wrist. 'I believe I know what comes next. Tabitha, I must go. I'm sorry, but it is getting late.'

He pulled away from her, reluctantly bowing to the dictates of caution, and a glance at the clock told her not to argue. In the absence of guests this part of the house was always deserted, the corridors untrodden once the maids had done their brief morning round, but this was by far the greatest chance she had ever taken. To have him here, beneath her own roof, was a fearful risk and getting caught was no fit ending for such a glorious afternoon.

He rose and bent to retrieve his clothes from the floor, slipping quickly into them while Tabitha pulled on petticoats and dress, not bothering with corsets and undergarments. Those she rolled up and carelessly stuffed beneath a pillow.

Emerson scanned the disordered room with some concern.

'Surely the servants will wonder who did this. How...?'

'It's nothing. I'll see to it later.'

'And are you going down to afternoon tea with no drawers on?'

'Why yes,' affirmed Tabitha with a wink and licentious swagger. 'I rather think I will.'

'I hope to God that William isn't home yet.'

'He's gone to Copperhill on business with his father. I don't expect him back until six o'clock.'

Mark experienced an odd flash of almost superstitious unease at the confidence in her voice. She did not believe that anything could ever go wrong for her, too well accustomed to winning. He could not help wondering if Nemesis had heard.

'Nobody's luck holds good for ever, you know.' He raised a sandy eyebrow in warning.

Tabitha sauntered up to him and slid soothing hands beneath the open collar of his shirt, kneading at the muscles of his neck.

'You mustn't worry so. I know William inside out, all his habits, his little ways, even the workings of his mind. And he thinks he knows me just as well. When and where it's necessary, I oil the wheels, smooth the way and steer the course. We have a splendid relationship. I fulfil all his needs and he meets—most—of mine.'

There was something dismissive about the last remark which touched him with annoyance—the way she took for granted the good soul she had married. Why, Mark asked himself resentfully, did she not suffer the same pangs of guilt over William that afflicted him when he remembered Coralie?

'But you don't love the man, do you, Tabitha? You merely find him useful. He loves you; he's good to you in all the best ways. I think he'd even forgive you for this if he found out. And perhaps for all the others, too.'

Her eyes hardened suddenly. Abruptly she stepped away from him, turning her back to hide a disconcerted face.

'It was a good guess, wasn't it?' he said softly.

Fretfully she twisted her fingers together. She had not realised that he suspected previous affairs, or that it would seem so important.

'The little boy, Jonathan. He isn't William's child, is he?'

Tabitha drew a deep breath. All of a sudden she would have given anything to regain some virtue, and she fervently wished there had been no other men.

'No, I thought not,' murmured Mark.

She spun around to face him, anxious and defensive.

'You're different, you know. You're not just another... I mean...' She spread her hands in a helpless gesture. 'Look, I am fond of

William. I recognise his kindness. I appreciate him for it and I would never intentionally hurt him. But he isn't quite all that I need. I thought you understood.' Her mouth tightened for an instant as a little counter-attack sprang to mind. 'Tell me truthfully, Mark, is Coralie all things to you?'

He winced almost visibly at that. 'I don't condemn the inclinations I share with you, Tabitha, but I can't relish deception in the same way. It's not just love-making you enjoy. It's the cleverness of the game as well.'

'Oh don't be so solemn and profound, Mark. It's tiresome. Apart from the fact that it complicates and spoils everything, moralising doesn't suit you.'

'I suppose I deserve that,' he said wryly. 'I admit I'm the last person with a right to pass judgement.'

'We sinners forfeit that,' agreed Tabitha, grinning. 'Hardly a grievous loss. It's a poor privilege at the best of times. I'd exchange it for pleasure any day—wouldn't you?'

Emerson laughed. 'Oh, Tabitha. What a bad influence you are.'

'Why, thank you, sir.'

He reached for his jacket and started for the door.

'Anyway, I'd better go before it gets any

later. Which is the best way out?'

'There's a separate entrance to the side. I'll show you.' She caught his hands in hers and smiled up at him, coaxing again, laying the bait for next time. 'Don't forget to keep a close watch on Beverley, will you? Your patient needs constant attention—and so do I.'

Next time. Oh yes, it was all becoming quite regular. It was frightening to realise how easily a single lapse might grow into something un-controllable. Although his better judgement warned him off, he very much wanted to see her again.

'I'll call in on Friday and—tend—to you both.'

CHAPTER 20

The table had been laid. As he opened the door at Curlew Quay, Mark halted at the sight of cherry cake, bread and butter, place settings for two, while the scent of tea and toasting muffins reached him from the kitchen.

Coralie was home.

Quietly he closed the door, put down his bag and went to find her.

231

She was at the kitchen table, her back turned. A few wispy curls had escaped their pins as she worked and she kept brushing them impatiently away from her face. For a moment he stood unobserved, watching the aproned figure busily setting out dishes of cream and jam. On a cooling rack beside her, obviously fresh from the oven, was a walnut cake—his favourite.

The shame hit him like a clenched fist. He felt mean, sly, unworthy, and he hovered there second by second, delaying the moment when the lies would have to come.

'Why, Coralie! I didn't expect you back yet. You should have telegraphed me to meet you in St Lowen,' he said finally.

She whirled round, her face breaking into a great smile of welcome.

'Oh! I didn't hear you come in. I took a hansom from the station and was home by half past two.' She flung her arms about him in a spirited hug, exuberantly glad to see him. 'Where have you been?'

There was no help for it. He could only hope to make it brief and pray that she would not press for details. Elaborate falsehoods would make it all so much worse.

'Well, let's see,' he said carefully. 'I attended madam Beverley earlier on, you'll be pleased

232

to hear, and she's delighted with her new malady. I stayed to lunch with Tabitha and after that I just made a few calls around the hamlets. Coughs and colic. Nothing very interesting.'

'Never mind. At least your return is nicely timed. The muffins are nearly ready and I've made a cake, with butter cream.'

'So I see.' He gazed down into the plain, adoring face and felt his soul cringe with guilt.

'Are you all right, Mark?' Her eyes searched his features with concern. 'You look—strained. Have you been eating properly this last week?'

Dear God, he thought, is it written all over me?

'Probably not!' he exclaimed, boisterously slapping her rump with both hands. 'Too much of my own charred cooking, no doubt. I concur with your diagnosis. A prompt and heavy dose of walnut cake is indicated. You take the muffins, I'll bring the tea.'

Coralie seemed content with this explanation and happily ferried a few more plates of food into the parlour, but if Mark thought the worst part was over, he found himself mistaken.

Before she sat down, Coralie silently placed a polished wooden box upon the table and bade him to open it. Inside, he found a set of medical books. Six weighty volumes, finely bound and very expensive. He had always wanted these and she had always known it.

'You're not angry, are you?' She stood behind him, her hands on his shoulders with a light, affectionate squeeze. 'I know you used to say they cost too much, and I know how you hate accepting anything from my own family coffers, but I wanted to bring you something special.'

Slowly he shook his head, lifting the first volume from the box, and she could not see the dull misery in his eyes when he opened the cover and read the inscription on the fly-leaf:

For my dearest husband,
with love and gratitude,
Coralie

He had, at times, foreseen discomfort and remorse. Through all his hours with Tabitha he had known there would be a reckoning, but he had never once imagined any feeling as awful as this. And it had to be borne quietly. Confession would be self-indulgent and cruel.

'Angry?' he queried vaguely, his voice unsteady. 'No, I...' He shrugged helplessly. 'They're splendid, Corrie. Bless you, they're wonderful.'

He leafed through the first few pages with

a kind of caressing respect, then turned to look up at her.

'They're much too good for a fool like me— and so are you.'

She bent to kiss his cheek. 'What nonsense. But I'm glad you like them. Now let's have some tea.'

'How was Amelia, anyway?' he asked as they settled down to eat. 'Obviously she was not dying after all.'

'No,' conceded Coralie, 'but she did have the most dreadful wheezing cough and a very painful ulcer on her leg. I really felt sorry for her, although illness doesn't seem to mellow her temper or weaken her will. She hasn't lost the habit of command.'

'I'd guessed as much. And what will you do next time?'

'I don't know, Mark. Let's think about that when it happens.'

'Coralie, I don't want you to go again. This was just one of her dictatorial little games and...' He coloured sheepishly at the lie which came so readily. '...anyway, I missed you,' he ended lamely.

'Oh, come, now,' objected Coralie. 'You can't have been lonely. You're always too busy to mope. Oh—and what about Ember Night? What was it like?'

'Very picturesque. I learned a lot about the local people and their ways.'

She missed the note of irony in his voice. 'I do wish I could have been there,' she said, handing him a chunk of walnut cake. 'It was such bad luck to miss it.'

Guilt ridden, Mark took a bite of the cake so lovingly made that very afternoon, appalled to think of his wife stirring and beating the mixture while he twisted and tossed with Tabitha Kirkwood. He was further shocked to find that his loins continued to stir at that salacious memory even as his tastebuds rejoiced in the butter cream.

'Yes,' he murmured uncomfortably, 'I desperately wish that you had been there.'

Very much later, as he lay in bed with Coralie's sleeping form cuddled close beside him, he was still thinking about Tabitha, trying to endow their relationship with some redeeming trace of value. But cold scrutiny revealed only this: they had little in common beyond that sexual affinity, no shared attitudes, nothing much about which to talk. In many ways he did not even like her, and love was simply out of the question. There would be no long, thoughtful conversations with Tabitha like those he enjoyed with his wife, and she certainly took no interest in his work. Indeed, in one careless

moment she had nearly admitted to a preference for the methods of Gaddy Scanes. A most
peculiar thing, he had thought at the time.

The betrayals, above all, were more than he
could accept, the cynical use of trusting souls
like William—and especially Coralie. He had
found in her more humour, affection and companionship than anyone could have guessed. A
woman for lifelong contentment, lovable in a
score of little ways. He had thought to put an
end to cruelty when he married her, to rescue
her from Amelia's carping criticism, from
undeserved loneliness and pitied spinsterhood.
It would be a contemptible thing if he were to
deal her the worst blow of all.

Those afternoons with Tabitha, however im-
passioned at the time, could never be worth the
risk. It would have to stop.

CHAPTER 21

'Father used to set spring guns for them,'
Christopher said, pushing aside his half-eaten
breakfast. 'I always thought it such a vicious
reprisal for taking a few pigeons or whatever.
I suspect that the old man looked upon the

poachers themselves as a kind of big game animal.'

'Barbarous attitude,' agreed William, 'and all too common at one time. Devices like that are illegal now, thank God. All the same, we seem to be dealing with an especially brazen character in this case. I don't begrudge a man the odd pheasant or a couple of hares, but this fellow's taken to stealing domestic stock as well. One of my farmers has lost a goose and a pair of piglets, and several lambs have gone, too. The man has exceptional nerve, and yet there are ways in which he shows a lack of the skills and knowledge basic to the poacher's trade. He's about on nights when the moon and the weather don't favour him, when the temperature or the wind is wrong. And it's on those nights, I'm told, that he's taken farm stock rather than go home empty-handed. The man's an audacious thief. I'd guess he's well practised in flouting and eluding authority, but he doesn't have the habits of any experienced poacher. To be honest, I'm not at all sure what to make of him.'

'Has anyone actually seen him?'

'Once or twice, at a distance. Never close enough to get a clear look, though. It seems he has a dog with him, Sinewy, grey brute, some sort of cross-breed.'

238

'How about his traps? Have you found any of those?'

'One or two gins, that's all. The keepers have often heard gunshots, yet they never seem to catch up with him, The trouble is that so much of this estate is wooded. It's a huge area for four men to search and watch; I'm afraid he runs rings around them.'

'Yes, and he probably gets a certain pleasure out of it,' observed Tabitha. 'I expect his supper seems all the more savoury and tender when pilfered at such enormous peril.'

'The stolen apple principle, eh?' Christopher's glance turned toward his sister with the merest hint of accusation.

'What extraordinary insight, Tabitha.'

Wide-eyed, she returned his stare. 'I should have thought it was perfectly obvious and not a bit strange.'

'Well I find it all most distressing,' pouted Beverley. 'I shall be frightened to walk in the garden until he's caught. Christopher, you'll have to escort me down to the lodge later on. I don't intend to go alone.'

'The lodge? What for! Are you unwell again?' asked Tabitha. 'There's no need to walk all that way. I'll be happy to send for the doctor.'

'Mrs Emerson is back,' explained Christopher quietly. 'Beverley wants to see her, that's all.'

Just perceptibly, the muscles of Tabitha's throat seemed to tighten and he saw her mouth twitch into lines of displeasure.

'Didn't you know? She returned yesterday afternoon. I happened to see the carriage coming through the gate.'

'Oh,' she muttered, dabbing briskly at her mouth with a napkin. 'I see. So it was just a short trip after all.'

'You didn't expect her so soon?' he questioned casually, stirring some sugar into his tea.

'Well—no.' A quick and guarded smile sprang to Tabitha's aid. 'I had understood her Mama's illness to be quite grave. Coralie might easily have been detained in London for some months. However, it apparently was less serious then we thought.'

'And we must be thankful for that, must we not?' remarked Christopher drily.

'Good heavens, yes!' exclaimed Beverley. 'It's been less than a fortnight, but I've missed her so dreadfully.'

'I'm glad she's back in time for the big celebration at Copperhill,' added William. 'As you know, next month will be Mother's and Father's thirty-fifth anniversary. They're planning one of their lavish parties and I think they would be disappointed if Coralie were not there.'

240

'Well, well. It appears most fortunate for everyone that she is with us once more,' murmured Christopher.

'Will you excuse me, please?' Abruptly, Tabitha pushed back her chair and got up. Her face and tone were calmly pleasant, but a writhing knot of discomfort was growing fast beneath her composure. 'I have so many letters to write, most of them long neglected. I must make a start this morning.'

So Coralie was back. The knowledge slowed Tabitha's footsteps as she went upstairs. The spring had left her walk and she found herself gnawing at the whitened knuckles of a clenched fist as her thoughts ran into channels of anger and resentment.

These feelings were becoming unpleasantly familiar and this was by far the worst attack she had suffered. Wanting to possess a man to the exclusion of all other women was a new experience for Tabitha, and now that his wife had returned the jealousy began in earnest to take its corrosive toll. That Coralie should even touch him was an affront. That she could sleep beside him night after night was almost unbearable. The images it conjured up were enough to fill Tabitha with a white-hot indignation.

The prospect of sharing him was painful

enough, but that was the very worst she had envisaged. Certainly, Tabitha was not prepared for the possibility that he might reject her altogether. It was to be several weeks before this awful fact struck home.

★ ★ ★ ★

Anyone who walked right down to the estuary and then turned northwards along the cliffs which formed Roskarnon's seaward border would discover a series of lonely beaches.

They were not small coves, but broad, level stretches of fine sand, close-packed and hard when wet. Banks of breakers cresting and rolling offshore subsided into gentle ripples as they reached the tideline, leaving behind them no debris save the odd shiny pebble or razor-fish shell. They were clean, uncluttered beaches, swept with an almost ceaseless wind.

Tabitha's solitary walks seldom took her this far, but today, while her mind dwelt on problems emotional, she had wandered on and on until she found herself on the clifftop path. Careful descent of a rough natural stairway led her down amongst a scattering of boulders at the base of the cliff, each one sporting a crowded colony of mussels. She seated herself in the shade of one such rock, pulled off her shoes, and stared despondently out to sea.

The shells were sharp and hard against her back. Moist sand dampened the seat of her skirt and the breeze was far from warm. Tabitha did not greatly care. The conditions matched her mood, for she was miserable.

Five weeks had passed and Mark had made no attempt to see her since his wife had come home. He had also evaded all Tabitha's efforts to speak with him alone, always employing a slight formality to keep her at arm's length. She had never before been shunned by anyone, least of all a man she so palpably desired. It was bewildering, infuriating, and vanity was mocked still further by the knowledge that her rival was an exceedingly plain woman. To lose to such a creature was beyond belief or understanding.

Absently she picked and pulled at the mussels, digging and flicking at the sand with her toes. She was gloomy, restless, and had been so for some weeks past, eating little, sleeping only fitfully. William, inevitably, had noticed it. He kept asking her what was wrong and sometimes received a sharp retort for his trouble. Her behaviour puzzled and worried him. Tabitha knew it was not prudent to show such temper, but still she failed to keep it in check. Sometimes she felt the obsession was wearing

243

away at her wits.

At last she rose and walked out toward the water's edge, a small, dejected figure leaving a trail of shallow footprints across the empty beach. And that was how Mark chanced to see her from the clifftop as he made his way home from a call in St Lowen.

He stopped the gig and peered down at the tiny figure, already nearly certain who it was. Even at a distance there was no mistaking that billowing fall of untethered hair and the old blue cotton dress she wore for walking.

Beverley had said once or twice of late that Tabitha was most sorely out of temper, growing quite listless and thin, as if something were very much amiss. Was it mere conceit, he wondered, to suppose that this had something to do with him? The guilt, as he was painfully aware, was not exclusively hers, and perhaps it was unfeeling—not to say unmannerly—to leave her wondering where she stood. No affair, however short-lived, could have a clean and civilised ending without explanation, apology and acceptance on both sides. After a brief hesitation, he pulled the gig back off the road, got out and went down to make his peace.

In the roar and hiss of wind and surf she did not hear him calling, and by the time he caught up with her he was badly short of breath.

Tabitha gasped and whirled in alarm as a hand seized at her shoulder and pulled her round.

'I'm sorry. I couldn't make you hear me.' He gave a panting laugh. 'I'd prided myself on being a fitter man. For a while I thought I'd never catch you.'

Tabitha's fright gave way to immediate pleasure and excitement. He wondered, as a radiantly happy smile broke upon her face, if he had acted unwisely after all.

'How did you know I was here? If I had realised that you were looking for me...'

It would be a bad start if he allowed her to believe that.

'No, no—I just happened to see you as I was driving by. As a matter of fact, I was on my way home. I often take the cliff road.'

'Oh.' Quietly, half-disappointed, she added: 'Then why exert yourself for my company to-day, when you've managed without it for so many weeks?'

He paused and faced her with a troubled sigh. 'Tabitha, that is why I want to talk to you. I realise that I may have been somewhat less than courteous in my recent behaviour, but you'll agree that our relationship is not of the genteel sort.'

'On the contrary, I would say you've been excessively courteous, my friend. Pompously

245

formal, in fact. I'm aware that you have to be a little more careful now that Coralie is home, but there is no call to be quite so distant. It's difficult and hazardous, I know, but we can still arrange to meet whenever...'

'Please listen, Tabitha, just listen. There are things I must say to you and they are not easy for me.'

Tabitha, mistaking his intent, began softly to laugh. 'Oh Mark, there's no need to struggle for words. I know only too well how painful these weeks have been.' She slid possessive arms about his waist, her face alight with expectation. 'I could hardly bear the waiting and it must have been the same for you. I'm right, aren't I? You have missed me, haven't you? I've thought of you constantly, reliving everything we did. I wouldn't let William touch me, because I wanted you. He doesn't know how to make love. He's so awkward, so ashamed...'

Oh, dear Lord, he thought, I should never have come down here.

'Tabitha, he would be mortified to hear you talk about him this way, wounded and humiliated beyond measure. William is a good man and I won't listen to these things.'

'All right, I don't want to discuss him anyway. We've little enough time to enjoy and none at all to waste.' The arms crept up about his neck. 'This is such a lonely place, Mark—always deserted. People so rarely come this way. We can walk up to the dunes this very minute and find a sheltered place where no one will disturb us...'

Abruptly he pushed her off and stepped back.

'In God's name, Tabitha, why must you persist? I was hoping you would understand and that I wouldn't have to spell it out, but it seems, after all, that I must. I came here to put an end to this ill-considered affair, not to carry on with it. Enough is enough.'

She stared at him, incredulous and impatient.

'A week or so? Three occasions? A handful of hours? It's hardly begun.'

'Please, Tabitha, I've no wish to quarrel with you. It was, I admit, a fleeting but rapturous episode. We had a few exciting days and I enjoyed them very much, but it cannot continue.'

'Because your wife has returned?' Her manner swiftly turned sullen. 'I don't see why that should make so much difference. You are called away from home at all hours of the day and night. The nature of your work is such that she can hardly hope to keep watch on your whereabouts. Surely you can steal a few hours here and there? That's all I ask. I don't expect you to abandon her, much as it pains me to share you.'

'Coralie does not deserve the kind of sly deception you are proposing. I owe her better treatment than that.'

'Dear God, what noble claptrap!' spat Tabitha suddenly. 'You've done her the favour of marrying her. Isn't that balm enough for your conscience? No doubt she is grateful just to be somebody's wife. Generosity can be taken to excess, you know. Must you embellish it with total fidelity?'

Her eyes glistened with a kind of feverish contempt as she spoke of Coralie, and Emerson had to fight down an angry urge to call her vain, spoilt and worthless.

'It so happens that I love my wife. She means far more to me than you do.'

'I cannot imagine why,' hissed Tabitha.

'No, I don't suppose you can. If you understood the real nature of affection, you would have more regard for your husband.'

'Oh, harken unto the righteous! I do wish you could hear yourself preach. There is nothing more sickening than watching some reformed sinner parading his new-found virtue. Perhaps you've mistaken your vocation, Mark. You should have gone into the Church.'

'Doctor or parson, I should still be too poor

for your liking, shouldn't I, Tabitha? You grandly claim that you don't expect me to abandon Coralie. Well, of course not. You prefer your paramours safely married, don't you, my sweet? These little intrigues are all very amusing, but we can't have them threatening your life of opulence, can we? Let us bear in mind that William can and does give you everything you want. I could never do that, could I? How would you feel about living at the lodge, on my income? Nothing quenches passion faster than poverty, and as far as you're concerned anything less than luxury is hardship. No, you wouldn't wish to leave William, any more than you'd have me desert Coralie. You just want to carry on duping them both.'

'That is not so! I really...'

'Are you sure? Ponder it carefully.'

'For God's sake, can't you see that I'm thinking of your good name? Scandal is no help to a man in your profession. Of course we have to be circumspect, but we can still make the best of things.'

Emerson grinned despite himself. 'Neatly twisted, Tabitha, but I'm not convinced. It would grieve you more to endanger your profitable marriage than to see my reputation tarnished.'

'But I cannot bear to think of you living with

her,' she fumed.

'Then you'd best occupy your mind some other way because I have no intention of leaving her. What would you have me do, Tabitha? Throw her out of the house? Send her back to London while I remain at the lodge to play stallion for you? And that's how it would be. That is the sort of arrangement you like, one that allows you the best of both worlds.'

'Damn you, Mark! You create such obstacles with your high-flown notions of loyalty. I just don't understand you. Yes, why not have the best of everything when it's there to be enjoyed? We could both be so happy if it weren't for your cursed conscience.' She groaned with exasperation and threw up her hands in a gesture of despair. 'Oh, for pity's sake, why have you come down here, anyway? What is the point?'

'I thought we might end this business gracefully. William is a good friend and Coralie loves living at Roskarnon, so I've no wish to move away. I wanted to clear the air, so to speak, and make my peace with you, so that none of our lives suffers lasting harm.'

Tabitha turned her back on him and walked away a few paces, her shoulders slumped with dejection. Watching her, Emerson fervently wished he had never become involved, for despite her hard-bitten nature it was evident that she was genuinely upset.

She paused for a moment or two, looking out to sea, then her gaze dropped to the sand and she began, slowly, with the tip of a toe, to draw the outline of a flower. Emerson could not see her face and its baleful expression, or he might have perceived the beginnings of some ominous train of thought, for it was then that she first entertained the idea of destroying her rival.

When she turned round at last, her look spoke only of resignation and repentance.

'All right, Mark,' she said sadly. 'I know that what you say is sensible and I apologise for my spiteful remarks about Coralie. I didn't want to lose you, that was all. It's in my nature to put up a fight, you see.'

Mark's face brightened with relief. She was going to be rational and civilised after all.

'Thank you, Tabitha. I hope we may continue as friends? We need not let this situation decline into one of abiding ill-will.'

'Very well, then.' She sighed and produced her most winsome smile. 'We'll call it a closed chapter, shall we?'

'I think we should.'

'But that needn't prevent you from driving me home, I hope? I'm really very tired.'

'It will be a pleasure, Tabitha.'

CHAPTER 22

Some days later there came a spell of oppressive, thundery weather that lasted for more than a week. Dull and sticky, it rendered everyone weary and short-tempered. The nights were stuffy and it was on the Sunday, just after one o'clock in the morning, that Mark was called to attend a woman whose first child had chosen this time to be born.

He had answered many a similar summons in the past and Coralie accepted these disturbances without complaint. She had never been frightened to stay alone at night and normally went straight back to sleep as soon as he had gone.

That night, however, she lay awake until just before three o'clock, for the room was too hot to allow any rest. First she had thrown off her single blanket and then at last the sheet. Even the thin cotton nightdress seemed to smother the pores of her skin, and the air appeared to grow even thicker despite the open window. For nearly two hours she lay in sweltering discomfort, thinking with pity of the labourer's wife enduring childbirth in such conditions.

When she finally drifted into a light sleep, it was only to last for about half an hour. Half-dozing but half-aware, her attention suddenly seized upon a small, insistent noise which jerked her back to wakefulness. Lying totally still, she listened intently and at first there was nothing but the night's silence. Several minutes passed and she almost laughed at herself.

And then it came again.

Scrabbling. Scuffling. It was quite distinct. The sound of an animal's claws rasping on wood.

Her eyes widened in staring fright, flicking swiftly round the room, searching for movement in the dim light. A few feet away the window stood half open, just as she had left it.

The scratching sounds grew louder and now she could tell where they came from. Her bedroom door was standing ajar; beyond that lay a short passageway ending at the back door—where the creature was trying to get in.

Very slowly she sat up and swung her feet to the floor. As she did so, the bed creaked a little and suddenly the scuffling stopped. For a moment she perched motionless on the edge of her mattress, wondering if the animal had heard. A few seconds later she knew that it had.

From beneath her window came a resonant,

rumbling growl, a menacing murmur building to a snarl that seemed to fill the room. There was a click of canine claws against her window-sill. From the corner of her eye she saw the brutish outline of a long-muzzled head, with pointed ears and a coat so smooth it looked almost wet in the moonlight. The front paws rested on the ledge, while the dog watched her and sniffed as if it scented food.

She moved a little, turning very slowly to face it, and the dog's top lip quivered up and back to show his curving, pitchfork teeth. The ears flattened down as a wet, rasping growl bubbled up from his chest.

He was no more than ten feet away. She sat there quite still, knowing that the animal could move far more quickly than she could. Several minutes passed in paralysing fright—until approaching footsteps and a long, low whistle broke the spell.

The dog turned its head in response, then dropped down from the sill and loped off across the clearing. A second later she heard it yelp with pain, and then came the murmur of a man's voice, cursing.

Grasping her chance, she rushed across to close the window, slamming and barring it. As she did so she saw, in the light of the porch lantern, the slouching figure of a large man who carried what looked like a military rifle. As the window banged shut, he turned, startled at the sound, and swung the rifle up to his shoulder, aiming it straight at the white-clad figure behind the glass.

Coralie almost screamed, but the sound never quite came. There were two or three dreadful seconds as he focused upon her—and then seemed to realise that only a frightened woman stood there.

Slowly he lowered the gun and for a fleeting moment she saw his features quite clearly. He looked to be about thirty-five, with skin that seemed an oily brown beneath a forest of bristles. The lower part of his face had a bulky, ill-tempered cast and his hair was softly greasy as it hung in clumps about his ears and neck. Everything he wore was shabby, heavily stained.

For a brief space the poacher stared back at her, seeming almost as shaken as she. Then, abruptly, he turned away and hurried off into the trees with the dog slinking abjectly at his heels.

Backing away from the window, Coralie sank down on the bed, her eyes fixed warily upon the spot where the poacher had disappeared into the woods. She was still sitting there when Mark came home, a little before five.

She had meant to tell him straight away, but he looked so tired, his hair clinging to his forehead with sweat, that she saved it for the morning. He had seen enough trouble for one day, and such a tale would worry him for what remained of the night.

'Why are you sitting there like that?'

'I just couldn't sleep. I was thinking about that poor woman. Did she have a very bad time?'

'It was appalling,' he said as he sat down and wearily pulled off his shoes. 'One of the worst labours I've ever seen.'

'But she will be all right?'

'Oh yes, I think so. And she has a brand new son with whom she's delighted—though he may grow up an only child. All the way through it she kept swearing she would never let her husband touch her again.'

Coralie smiled. 'That sounds like a hollow threat to me. All women want babies, and one is seldom enough.'

'Beverley would not agree.'

'Oh, well...' Coralie shrugged. '...she's an exception in every way. I'm quite sure that Tabitha is extremely proud of Jonathan and Miranda. I expect she would love to have some more.'

Emerson did not answer that, but carried on

256

silently undressing, disturbed at this unwitting reminder that Tabitha might so easily have had one by him.

'Anyway, I'm looking forward very much to having a child,' continued Coralie softly. 'I can hardly wait.'

'Well I'm afraid I can't do anything about it tonight,' he said, yawning as he flopped into bed. 'Exhaustion takes its toll, you understand. You'll have to carry on borrowing Jonathan and Miranda for a while. They're very fond of you, you know. Tabitha doesn't worship them as much as you seem to think.'

'Oh Mark, I'm sure she does!'

'Then why are they always so thrilled to see. 'Aunt Corrie' every Tuesday? I don't think Tabitha bothers to play with them at all. They wait all the week round for you and your basket of goodies, make no mistake.'

Coralie always went to tea at Roskarnon on Tuesday afternoons, usually arriving around four and staying until Miranda and Jonathan were put to bed. It was the nursemaid's afternoon off and one of the high spots in the children's week.

Auntie Corrie knew such a lot of good games and stories. She always brought brandy-snaps and home-made toffees, and permitted terrific rompings in the nursery at bedtime. These

257

occasions were equally delightful for Coralie, affording her the chance to have the little ones all to herself for a few hours. William would join them for tea on those rare days when he was not busy, but Tabitha always took the opportunity to make herself scarce and Beverley avoided such boisterous affairs.

Coralie smiled as she began drifting off to sleep. 'Hmm. I must remember to take along some gingerbread men one day, Miranda simply loves them.'

★ ★ ★ ★

Thus it was that Coralie's frightening encounter with the poacher was not mentioned until breakfast time, and in the atmosphere of a sunny morning she was inclined to make a joke of it.

Mark, however, took it less lightly.

'William will have to be told,' he said. 'I want something done about this. I will not tolerate having you scared out of your wits. Anyway, the man sounds like a danger to all and sundry.'

'William is already doing all he can, Mark, you know that. Besides, no real harm was done and I'm sure it won't happen again.'

'There's no guarantee of that. I'm not going

to let this matter pass, Coralie. I think it's important that he should know.'

So it was that the subject was raised the following evening at Ruth and Ambrose Kirkwood's anniversary ball. And that was where Tabitha learned of it.

CHAPTER 23

On the night of the anniversary, William went up to their bedroom to find out what was taking his wife so long, for he had been ready for the past half-hour and the carriage was waiting to leave.

Tabitha, he discovered, had dressed with particular care that evening and was still putting the finishing touches to a superb outfit (hitherto a secret shared only with Peggy and Mrs Carkett).

He found her standing before the cheval-mirror, resplendent in silk and lace. The soft lilac fabric flowed snugly over flourishing curves, outlining the contours of bosom, waist and hips. It skimmed wide across the shoulders, leaving them almost bare, and dipped low over the small neat breasts. The skirt, swept tightly back, was caught at each hip with tiny white rosettes. At the back it sloped in tiers of ruffles to end in a short train. Here and there among the folds nestled more rosettes, sprigs of violets with flashes of green, and bows of deep purple ribbon. Her hair had been dressed in curls and sweeps, drawn up and fastened with purple flowers and falling in glowing chestnut waves behind.

Beyond doubt, she was a stunning sight, a spectacle to command the admiration of every man, the envy of every woman. She bestowed upon William her most enchanting smile, allowing him a moment of silent appraisal, and he never guessed that this display was not for him, that in truth she was dressed for combat of a subtle but serious kind, going forth to vanquish a rival.

Mark would be forced to compare, to recognise that no amount of artifice or money could make of his own wife anything so splendid.

'Well, dearest,' she said brightly, 'am I presentable?'

William sighed happily, his face shining with pride. 'You're lovely, Tabitha. Exquisite. I hardly feel grand enough to escort you.'

She picked up her carved ivory fan and surveyed him with wifely approval. 'Nonsense. You look very handsome and important.'

'Come along, then.' He offered his arm. 'Let's make a grand entrance.'

Copperhill was brightly lit from end to end as they turned in through the gates, and rows of coloured glass lanterns were strung from trees that lined the drive. Little fountains sparkled on the terraces, every balcony was hung with garlands and each bedroom prepared for visitors, since many of Ruth's guests would be staying overnight.

'Mother's really excelled herself this time,' remarked William as they went up the steps. 'We'll have to stew a great many hops to pay for it.'

The gathering inside was colourful indeed, and the great hall was a whirl of music and light. A hundred and eighty people had donned their finest feathers for this very special occasion. The men were stiffly splendid in tails and snowy shirts. Hair was sternly parted, moustaches waxed and sideburns trimmed. They were all on show, from the lusty young to the jolly and gouty and white-whiskered. Their womenfolk rustled amongst them in bright billows of satin and moiré, displaying elegant, tight-laced figures, each one confident of her own superior charm—until Tabitha arrived.

Heads turned in appreciation and curiosity

as William and his wife moved among the throngs of guests, exchanging pleasantries with acquaintances. Female stares followed Tabitha, many of them hard and sour as husbands and lovers were too affable in their greetings, too free with their compliments.

At first she could not see Mark Emerson and wondered if his tiresome wife with her fear of social events had persuaded him not to come. But at last she spotted Beverely, in fussy clouds of lemon silk with brown accordion pleating, and beside her stood Christopher with the Emersons.

Tabitha noted with annoyance that Coralie had a new gown of buff satin with coffee-coloured lace. The style was flattering and Coralie's bearing was somewhat less timid than Tabitha might have hoped. In fact she seemed quite merry.

'Tabitha, what a beautiful gown! You look altogether wonderful—does she not, Mark?'

'Splendid,' he agreed civilly.

Coralie's compliment came with honesty. It was never in her nature to insert a sting in the tail. She would not have known how.

'Why, thank you, dear,' Tabitha cooed smilingly. 'I was about to admire your lovely satin. It would seem we share much in common...' As she spoke, her gaze turned smoothly to settle on Mark. '...in terms of taste.'

The moment the words were out she knew she had already made a mistake. There was a defensive closing off, a kind of withdrawal behind the tawny eyes that warned of his annoyance. He had no wish to play hinting games in the very presence of his wife and of William Kirkwood. Warily, he averted the danger with a change of subject.

'William, I don't want to spoil the evening before it even starts, but while we have the chance I must talk to you about that poacher.'

'Indeed? Have you seen him? I can't say we're having much luck in catching the wretch.'

'He was prowling around the lodge the night before last. As it happened, I had gone to attend a patient, so Coralie was alone—and there was quite a nasty incident.'

'Mark, you're making it sound much worse than it was.'

'Am I? The damned dog is obviously vicious —and how would you take it, William, if someone aimed a loaded gun at your wife?'

At that, Tabitha's eyes widened with interest and turned curiously upon Coralie.

'Good God,' said William, 'did he?'

'For a moment, yes.'

'We don't know that it was loaded,' objected Coralie.

'We have to assume so. I don't suppose he knew who lived in the lodge and it sounded to me like a purely defensive gesture—probably just a nervous reflex—but that, if anything, makes him more of a danger. A momentary slip and he might have killed her.'

Yes indeed, thought Tabitha wistfully.

'If your keepers can't cope with this, William, I suggest you call in the police.'

'This isn't London, Mark,' Tabitha said. 'The local police force comprises three constables in St Lowen. I don't see what they could do that a gamekeeper cannot.'

William looked worried. 'That's true enough and we normally deal with such matters ourselves. Poaching is a part of country life—a mere annoyance and not much more. It's the first time I've heard of anything like this. I'm very sorry, Coralie. I feel responsible...'

'Nonsense.'

'How ghastly!' Beverley exclaimed. 'I know I should have fainted.'

'Did you get a look at him?' asked Christopher.

'Yes, I saw him quite clearly,' Coralie said. 'A big, brutal sort of man with a squarish face. I don't think he's local. In fact I'm almost sure of it. I believe I know all the tenants and villagers by sight and he wasn't one of them.'

'That's worth knowing. And what kind of gun was it?'

'I'm afraid I know little of such matters—but it looked like a soldier's rifle. It was certainly different from the guns the keepers carry. This was longer, lighter.'

'You must have been terrified! Just imagine, if you hadn't woken he might have come through the window, discovered you asleep in bed and…Well, poor dear, it's too dreadful to contemplate.' Beverley pressed a hand to her mouth and her nose gave an agitated twitch at these appalling possibilities.

'I don't think that was very likely, dear,' soothed Coralie. 'I doubt he knew that I was alone. The man's just a thief and I don't suppose I would ever have seen or heard him at all if it weren't for the dog.'

'All the same,' insisted Mark, 'there will certainly be other nights when I'll have to go out, and I shall feel uneasy about it so long as he's at large.'

'I'll hire more men to seek him out,' promised William, 'and I'll make it worth their while. He's certainly more cause for concern than any common breed of poacher.'

'And who's to say that's all he is? He could

be some kind of fugitive—a convict, a lunatic, a murderer...' Beverley's eyes grew rounder and her voice more shrill as imagination produced all manner of horrors, like rabbits from a hat.

'For God's sake, Beverley,' muttered her husband, 'all those silly novels you read...'

'If you spent more time with me and less with your telescopes, I shouldn't have to seek entertainment in books.'

'Does it amuse you to frighten yourself?'

'It's better than being bored,' came the petulant retort.

'Well, anyway...' William cleared his throat. 'I'll see that efforts are stepped up in dealing with this. Meanwhile, let's not allow it to mar the evening, eh? Perhaps, Coralie, you'll be kind enough to grant me the next dance?'

A few seconds can seem like a very long time when they form what is known as an awkward pause. Such a pause occurred as William led his cousin on to the dance floor and Tabitha waited for Mark to extend a similar invitation to her. It took a monumental effort of will to maintain a look of unconcern when she heard him ask Beverley instead. Despite valiant attempts to keep it in place, her smile began to wilt. As she felt it droop at the corners, Tabitha snapped open the ivory fan and briskly covered her disappointment before turning to her brother.

'Christopher, we really must offer our congratulations to Ruth and Ambrose. I don't think I've ever attended such a sumptuous event. It makes our little parties at Roskarnon seem quite dull. And what an interesting selection of guests. The notorious, the noble, the fashionable and the fatly prosperous—even a man of science, I see, to entertain you. So many new faces. Come along, we must ask Ruth to make some introductions.'

It was a very old manoeuvre, handed down unchanged through the generations. Mark was to see her dance and chatter and flirt, enchanting the handsome and the titled with her wit and her beauty. He would realise the favour she had granted him, the privilege which any of these men would hasten to accept. It would fuel both his jealousy and his pride. It would bring him back.

So Tabitha believed, in the beginning, and at first she danced with a very light step. But as the hours rolled on, she perceived with growing anguish that he was still avoiding her and in the end it was she alone who suffered the jealousy. For every man who wished to dance with Tabitha, there was a woman equally keen to monopolise Mark for a while, but never did he leave Coralie for long. He chatted and bantered with various ladies while the music swirled and romped, and Tabitha granted dance after dance to a dozen different partners, but he made no bid to be one of them.

Once, between waltzes, as she sipped a glass of punch, absently trading small-talk with an elderly bishop, she stood within touching distance of Mark but he seemed too absorbed in his wife to even notice Tabitha's presence. She almost fancied she could feel the body warmth coming from him and her fingertips recalled the touch of his back, hips and shoulders when bare and heaving in a shaded room.

The punch cup suddenly slipped from her hand to crack in half on the polished floor.

'Oh! How clumsy of me! I'm so...' She shook her head in confusion as the old gentleman bent to retrieve the pieces. 'Forgive me, I'm not feeling quite well, I...'

'Tabitha? Are you all right, my dear?'

Coralie, solicitous and all the more detested for it, laid a hand upon her arm.

'Mark, she does look rather wan.'

'Where's William, Tabitha? Perhaps he ought to take you home.'

He was still, she noticed, keeping a cautious distance.

'It's nothing. I'm just tired.'

'Take her outside for some air, Mark. There are seats on the terrace. Stay and see that she's all right.'

Still he hesitated and Tabitha's hand clenched around the folded ivory fan.

'Yes, I'd like that,' she said steadily.

'That's right. Go along now,' Coralie fussed.

Reluctantly, Emerson escorted Tabitha outside.

'I'm sorry to be a nuisance,' she said stiffly as they settled on the white cane chairs.

'Not at all. Is there anything I can get you?'

'I don't think so, thank you. I just felt giddy for a moment. It's really quite unusual for me.'

'Tight stays and too much dancing, I expect.'

There followed a moment's uneasy silence and Tabitha remembered the optimism with which she had dressed for this occasion; the assurance that was now ebbing second by second.

Finally she asked: 'Has Coralie enjoyed herself tonight?'

Emerson smiled. 'Yes, I rather think she has. As you know, she normally tries to avoid such events, but this one has been quite a treat for her.'

'Well, of course, you've been very protective. You've hardly left her side all evening.'

'I wouldn't say that.'

'Then let's say you didn't stray far enough to dance with me.'

'Stray,' he said slowly, 'is an excellent choice of word in this case. I've given up "straying", as we agreed.'

'Dear God, I'm speaking of a mere waltz, not a public copulation on the ballroom floor,' said Tabitha tartly. Then, on a sudden suspicion, she added quietly: 'Or is your resolve so feeble that it cannot withstand even a dance?'

Mark took a moment to answer that.

'I think it would be courting trouble,' he admitted finally. 'I've never said that I don't want you. I wouldn't be normal if I didn't, but there's no question of taking up where we left off. You know all the reasons, Tabitha, and they still hold good. I have Coralie to consider above everything else.'

But of course. Coralie. The chief obstacle as always. He could stifle his conscience where William was concerned, but his wife would always command this tiresome loyalty. Tabitha looked upon her own marriage as an amicable business arrangement and not much more. His, however, was hallowed ground where she had trespassed, thieving, and now he was putting up fences to keep her out.

'Naturally. I understand. My own evening

270

has been quite spoilt—but no matter. My feelings are unimportant and we must on no account upset your wife. That would be unforgivable.'

'Yes, madam, it would.'

There was ice in his tone and Tabitha knew it would be foolish to push the argument any further. She sighed and stood up.

'I'm sorry, Mark. I'm being difficult again, aren't I? Perhaps we'd best go back now. I'm feeling better and it must be nearly time to leave.'

He glanced at his pocket watch. 'Ten minutes to the witching hour, and none too warm either. I agree. Let's go inside.'

Christopher saw them come in together from the terrace. He thought that his sister was looking strained and very pale. And later, as carriages pulled away from the front door amid clattering hooves and cries of farewell, he noticed something else.

As the Emersons climbed into their modest little conveyance, bidding goodnight to Ruth and Ambrose, he spotted Tabitha standing alone in the porch while she waited for William. She was ready to leave, a dark violet cloak wrapped close about her against the night air, and her eyes were fixed intently upon Coralie.

There is something of peculiar malevolence

271

about a pretty face when its owner is nursing some hellish emotion, a kind of baleful beauty which is somehow more chilling than ugliness. That look disturbed Christopher very much. Though he had known her all his life, he had never seen the like of it before. He could only have described it as murderous.

CHAPTER 24

It was almost a week later that the idea came into being, a week of resentful brooding and helpless anger. How painful it was to have fallen from favour, to have been discarded. Sometimes Tabitha recalled that she had once been casual in matters amorous, and very much the controlling party—a different, level-headed person who never fell victim to turmoil such as this. A practical Tabitha, seldom short of solutions. Now she found herself too confused and miserable to think clearly at all—until the idea arrived.

It came because she chanced to see the poacher.

She had walked down to the estuary again, meaning to sit for an hour on the clifftop, but a piercing easterly wind drove her homewards long before that. As she was starting back, there came a rumble of wheels from behind her and she was overtaken by a battered wooden caravan. The vehicle was almost upon her before she heard it and hopped hastily to the side of the track. Turning, she caught a quick glimpse of the driver as it passed, and instantly recalled Coralie's description of the night-time intruder at the lodge.

He was a bony, surly-looking man, heavy-jawed and unshaven. Beside him, nursing an infant, sat a pale young woman. And, as they rattled by, Tabitha spotted a large grey dog sprawled in the back with lolling tongue, its paws hanging over the tailboard.

Coralie had been right. He was not a local man, but a gypsy, and one for whom Roskarnon had become most unfriendly of late. Tabitha then remembered that group of Irish gypsies and the attack upon the head game-keeper just before Ember Night. It had formed a topic for brief, indignant comment at the time, as William recounted the keeper's report over dinner. The gist of it now returned to her.

Going north, they had said. Home to Ireland.

Was this a straggler heading the same way, Tabitha wondered? The caravan was obviously leaving the estate by the northbound road. She guessed that the man had made his camp somewhere among the miles of dunes behind these lonely beaches. Since William had offered some healthy cash incentives, the local people had warmed up their efforts to catch him and the poacher evidently felt it prudent to move on.

He gave hardly a glance to the small figure in the old cotton dress as Tabitha stepped back out of his way. With her hair snarled and face stung red by the wind, she looked no more impressive than his own shabby wife, who sat crooning to the baby some lilting song in a husky patois.

Irish tinkers. Oh yes, Tabitha had little doubt of that. She stood for a while, watching the swaying, clanking old wagon disappearing down the track, her mouth twisted slightly at the corner. William would be pleased to know that the man had cleared off. Perhaps now he would stop worrying about his wretched cousin.

Such a fuss, thought Tabitha. Such a hullabaloo, with everyone clucking over the tiresome Coralie. William, Mark, Christopher—all so foolishly concerned about her. Tabitha glared resentfully at the caravan as it vanished round a bend in the road. Why could he not have pulled the trigger, she wondered bitterly?

Why had fortune let her down? A moment's panic or a nervous slip would have solved everything. It would have been a perfect solution, but now the chance was gone.

Or was it?

Perfection, perhaps, was too much to ask, but one could still make use of circumstances and a good example.

Dear heaven, the answer was so simple, so obvious.

Why should she tell William the poacher had gone? Why, if no one else had seen him on this lonely road, should everyone not assume the man was still around? Was there not a means of using this prowling thief who had already given Coralie such a fright?

Tabitha could think of an excellent way.

★ ★ ★ ★

That afternoon found her rummaging by candlelight through one of Roskarnon's attics, searching among the items cast out during those early months of her marriage, that had been spent in refurbishing the house. Many of Edgar's possessions had been given away at the time—but not the one she now sought. No, she knew it was here somewhere, waiting providentially through all these years for a time of need.

And eventually she found it, propped up in a corner. Uncle Marsden Summerfield's rifle and the box of cartridges to go with it.

Tabitha remembered quite clearly the last time she had seen the gun—that day when she stood in Edgar's study with Aunt Clementina, her mind upon nothing more weighty than carpets and curtains. She had been a different person then, and all had been right with the world.

Well, it would be so again. Better than ever before, in fact. All could be arranged. She had only to settle the details.

★ ★ ★ ★

Every so often, Roskarnon would lose an old and valued employee. Most of the tenants were born on the estate, lived out their spans within its borders and finally died there, handing on jobs and tied cottages to their offspring down through the generations. Such a man—one of the gardeners—had ended his days that very July. However, having no children, he left behind him an empty cottage. It was very small and stood no more than a mile from Curlew Quay.

Tabitha, plotting as she lay in the dark beside
276

her husband that night, remembered the cottage and thought it well suited to her purposes. Too excited to sleep, she occupied her mind with the practicalities of scheming and, as the hours wore on, her busy brain worked upon the details till finally there emerged a plan of action. Always pleased with her own daring and cleverness, Tabitha thought it nothing short of brilliant. The flaws, when perceived at all, were impatiently dismissed and whispers of misgiving were instantly suppressed. She would not be stopped by doubt and trivialities, for she wanted desperately to believe in her plan and feel that it would work. Her pursuit of the doctor had become characterised by the kind of zealous commitment that drove soldiers to foolhardy exploits of war, and religious martyrs to the stake in centuries past.

When she rose next morning she was bright as a kitten and just as frisky, despite the lack of sleep, singing as she dressed and chattering merrily across the breakfast table. Hope had returned and Tabitha smiled upon the world in her optimism. Later that day she went to the nursery and bestowed upon her children an especially fond hug and kiss—which quite surprised the little creatures.

'What are you doing?' she asked, for upon the table there stood a shaky cardboard construction and the floor was littered with cut-out paper figures, coloured crayons, wire and paste and scraps of material.

They were making a theatre, they explained earnestly. Aunt Corrie had shown them how to do it.

'But darlings, Papa would buy you a lovely theatre with real puppets if only you asked him. Wouldn't you rather have that?'

No, they said. The whole idea was to make their own, and it had to be ready by Tuesday because they were going to put on a play and surprise Aunt Corrie.

'Well!' exclaimed Tabitha, beaming. 'I think that's a splendid idea. And I know that Aunt Corrie is going to get the biggest surprise of her life.'

CHAPTER 25

Tabitha was up at dawn on Tuesday morning.

Just before five o'clock there came the first suspicion of light. She had been lying there, and now it seemed that black was giving way to grey in the sky. Time to be up and moving if she were to finish this preparatory errand before the maids rose to start work at six.

She remembered, sliding softly out of bed, the last time she had left her sleeping husband in this way. For a moment she wondered if there might be some process, like the reversal of a spell, whereby she might elect to climb back between the covers at this point and become her old self again, erasing the events of the past few months as if the whole anguished affair had never been.

Ah, but there were no magical antidotes— or none that she believed in. She had dipped a playful toe in these waters, then waded deeper till caught by the current. There was nothing to do now but go with it.

Quickly she dressed and slipped out onto the landing, up three flights to the top floor which comprised the servants' quarters. She was pleased to note that snores issued from some of their rooms, notably that of the cook. They slept heavily, these hardworking souls, as Tabitha padded past their doors and up the spiral stairway to the attics.

She came down again within five minutes, bearing a bundle of some length and considerable weight. By the time she reached the ground floor and emerged into the garden through the music room doors, the sky was brightening with the promise of a fine day.

Twenty minutes later she opened the door to the gardener's cottage and stepped inside, laying her bundle on the scrub-top table in the centre of the room. The place was spartan to say the least, comprising one room upstairs and one down, with a lean-to shed against the back wall, in which were stored shovels, rakes and so on. There was, in addition, a tiny earth closet some ten yards away among the trees. The windows were veiled with spider's webs, and the ashes of the old man's last fire still lay in the hearth. Aside from the trestle bench and wooden settle, the only other funiture was a heavy oak dresser and a mesh-fronted food cabinet. The walls were of the same rough stone as the fireplace and the floor was clay dirt, overlaid with irregular flagstones.

There were two doors to the base of the oak dresser. Inside it, Tabitha found shelving running right across. It was easily long enough to accommodate the bundle, which she laid in the very bottom and then closed the doors again.

So far, so good. The first small but important step in the venture and all had gone well. She straightened up and drew a deep breath. All she could do now was go home and wait. The time, she guessed, was nearing six. The servants would be stirring by now, but it was still far too early for breakfast, so she loitered for an hour on the way back, picking a large bunch of pink roses as she passed through the garden.

William, evidently, had missed her. When finally she came in at a quarter past seven, he was just sitting down to an early breakfast. He looked worried and also, she fancied, slightly annoyed.

'Tabitha, where on earth have you been?'

She sighed. 'I didn't sleep at all well, William. I've been awake since about three o'clock. I always feel so stale and heavy after a bad night, so I went out for some air.' She sniffed at the damp, dewy, roses. 'Look at these, aren't they lovely? I think we'll have them in the drawing-room.' She handed the flowers to a waiting maid. 'See to it, will you, please?'

'I hope you haven't been far, Tabitha.' William looked reproachful. 'We have still not found that poacher.'

Tabitha laughed, dismissive and sounding deliberately vague as she surveyed the choice of dishes on the table. 'Oh, William, really! We've heard nothing of him for several days now. I expect you've scared him away.' Her hand hovered over a pot of damson jam. 'Let me see, I think I'll just have...'

'Never make rash assumptions, Tabitha,'

retorted William, much concerned and close to severity. 'I will not have you taking risks by wandering off alone, especially at odd hours.'

'Surely I may walk in my own garden without permission?' Tabitha contrived to look affronted.

'For the time being, no.'

'This is most unlike you, William.' She sounded peevish and slightly hurt.

William looked uncomfortable, but he held his ground.

'I am your husband and though it is not my nature to be repressive, I must take thought for your welfare.'

'You're being silly,' said Tabitha, a trifle sharply.

'I think not. A man must protect his wife.'

Tabitha smiled. 'Well, I say it's all thoroughly stupid.'

She frowned at him across the table and William stared sadly back at her.

'Tabitha, we're not going to quarrel, are we? We have always been happy together and we seldom disagree, but I cannot give way to you on this issue. I'm sorry, my dear, but you know the circumstances and must take them seriously.'

'I simply find it outrageous that I should be denied the freedom of my own property on account of some—ruffian.' Tabitha sounded exasperated.

'That is understandable, but it cannot be helped. Come along, dearest, have some breakfast.'

'I've no appetite now.' She tossed her napkin to one side and got up. 'I think I'll go and see Cook about the luncheon menu. I believe she is planning to serve gammon and I fear there will be a fuss. Beverley always complains that the tougher types of meat upset her stomach.'

She started for the door, then paused briefly and returned to deliver a wifely peck to William's cheek.

'I'm sorry if I was ill-tempered, dearest, but it all seems such a storm in a teacup to me.'

★ ★ ★ ★

'Peggy,' said Tabitha later that day, 'where's my old blue dress? I'm going for walk.'

The maid looked doubtful. 'Didn't Mr Kirkwood say that you shouldn't...?'

'Oh, it's all a lot of nonsense,' scoffed Tabitha, 'and I shall prove it to him. My husband is a dear, kind man, Peggy, but he worries too much.'

'I don't know. With respect, madam, I think he's right—and what will he say if he finds out that you went walking after all? Won't there be an uproar and a dreadful to-do?'

'Tabitha, prepared for an uproar of the first order, was hardly to be frightened by something as mild as William's displeasure.

'I don't care. I will not be confined to the house on such a lovely afternoon. Come along, help me dress. I'm sure a walk will improve my temper. It's been a trying day altogether—one argument at breakfast and then a second over lunch.'

'What was wrong with lunch, madam?'

'Oh...' Tabitha shrugged impatiently. '...I had the gammon taken off the menu and asked Cook to serve lamb instead. I thought it would better please Mrs Summerfield. But no, quite the contrary, it seems she would have liked the gammon after all. So now she has gone to her room without eating a thing.'

Peggy laughed as she finished fastening the dress.

'I believe the Reverend Devoy is right, madam, when he says these things are sent to try us.'

'I suppose so.' Tabitha picked up a light shawl. 'I'd better take this, I think. It's a fine day, but cool. I shan't be long.'

'And I hope you'll be careful,' ventured Peggy.

'I am surrounded by worriers,' sighed Tabitha, smiling, 'But I know you mean well.'

★ ★ ★ ★

A short while later, in the musty silence of the gardener's cottage, she rescued the bundle from the bottom of the dresser, laying it upon the wooden table. Wrapped in sacking, bound around with string, it contained a few items of clothing—male clothing—together with Uncle Marsden's rifle and cartridges.

The waistcoat, shirt and trousers made for Christopher when he was fourteen were now a passable fit on his sister. She tucked in the shirt-tails and peered curiously at the dim reflection of herself in the glass-fronted top of the dresser, deciding that breeches suited her very well. How comfortable, too, and how simple, a far cry from corsets, bustles and binding skirts. She was less enthusiastic about Christopher's boots. They were wearable, but hard, heavy and over-large.

The last item of the outfit was a dark brown corduroy cap. Tabitha pulled it on carefully, so as not to disturb her neatly dressed hair. The curls, waves and hairpins vanished from sight, and with them went all trace of the lady. This odd little figure had tasks to perform which were neither delicate nor decorous, beginning with some hard manual work and followed by something dirtier still.

Outside, in the lean-to, she searched among the old man's gardening tools and pounced upon a square-bladed shovel. The next chore was to move the oak dresser some four feet out from the wall—which took her several minutes, accomplished with much puffing and a little swearing. Having managed this, Tabitha stared thoughtfully at the roughly rectangular flag-stone, across part of which the dresser had stood. Lines of brownish dirt marked the edges of the flags, forming a dull jigsaw pattern right across the floor. With the blade of her shovel, Tabitha prodded tentatively along the cracks outlining that particular stone—until she found a spot where it fitted only loosely with its neighbour. The blade sank down, far enough to give leverage, and she drove it farther with her foot as she had seen the gardeners do so many times. A sharp downward jerk on the spade handle and the edge of the flagstone lifted two or three inches—enough to give a hand-hold. Slowly she heaved it from its bed of earth, pushing it upright till it stood on its edge, lean-ing squarely against the back of the dresser.

Tabitha was perspiring a little by now. Just for an instant, common sense enquired whether

Emerson was really worth it all, infatuation firmly insisted that he was.

Grimly she set about the next task—to dig a trench, some two feet deep and one foot wide, into the patch of bare earth where the flagstone had lain. Tabitha found to her annoyance that it was not quite long enough to accommodate the rifle barrel, and she was obliged to dig for some inches beneath an adjacent stone—which meant getting down on her knees and using a trowel. By the time she had finished, Tabitha was dirty and foul-tempered, but undeterred.

At last she stood up and surveyed her handiwork. Along the sides of the trench lay two neat mounds of soil, ready to be pushed back in when the time came. The flagstone had only to be dropped into place and the dresser returned to its old position. All, it seemed, was going well.

Tabitha slipped two cartridges into the waistcoat pocket, then placed the box containing the rest at the bottom of the trench. Finally she picked up the rifle, knowing it must be nearly three o'clock and time to go.

★ ★ ★ ★

Beverley, pouting in her room after lunch, was thinking about gammon. Contrary as always, she had formed a fancy for gammon on hearing that Tabitha had removed it from the menu.

'How many times have I heard you say that it's tough and indigestible?' Tabitha had been snappish, Beverley petulant.

'I could have managed just a little.'

'Well, it's not important, is it?'

'Yes. I'm disappointed.'

'Then we'll have gammon this evening.'

'I may not want it by then.'

At that point, Tabitha had risen to her feet and stalked from the dining-room. Already fraught with tension, she was past enduring caprice from Beverley.

Horrid, as usual, Beverley thought. The superficial pleasantness between them had evaporated in no time at all. Tabitha, in fact, had been growing steadily more waspish for some weeks past, and it was merciful that Coralie had returned so soon from London—for where else would Beverley find a sympathetic soul to listen and soothe? A comforting chat was always helpful in times of distress, as to-day. Coralie, of course, was due to call at four o'clock, but Beverley could never endure those noisy tea-parties with the children.

She glanced from her window to assess the weather. The day had begun mildly with broken clouds and spells of sunshine. Certainly there was no sign of rain and it was not yet two o'clock. Time enough to stroll down to Curlew Quay and spend an hour or so with Coralie. It was, after all, only half a mile by the carriage track and she thought they could return together at four.

By the time Beverley arrived at Curlew Quay, Tabitha's excavations were already well under way, and while one toiled in the dirt of the gardener's cottage, the other spent a happy hour pouring out her latest complaints to Coralie Emerson. Thus distracted, it was some time before any of them noticed the change in the weather.

★ ★ ★ ★

Just after three, a light drizzle began to blow in from the creek, laying a wet film against the parlour windows at the lodge, growing silently thicker as the clouds closed and darkened overhead.

'My, you have been busy,' Beverley was saying as she watched Coralie loading her basket with tins full of brandysnaps, home-made peppermints and fudge. 'Young Jonathan is getting tubby, you know. He seems inclined to acquire fat, which is an odd thing when William and Tabitha are both so slender.'

'I expect he's like his Grandpapa. I believe Ambrose has always been corpulent. Mark maintains that chubby children are less healthy, but I do so love to see their little faces when I bring out the goodies.'

'I don't follow his reasoning,' Beverley sniffed. 'Solid, sturdy people are so much stronger and less likely to succumb to every passing illness, don't you agree? I do wish I had a healthy appetite. Sometimes I feel so insubstantial—rather like the angel hair which appears at a seance.'

Her eyes acquired a faraway, soulful look to emphasize her belief that she had been little more than ectoplasm all her life.

'Good heavens, what a dreary thing to say! You really must keep your mind off gloom and graveyards, dear. It's all so silly and bound to be bad for you.'

'I'll try,' said Beverley weakly. 'Christopher says that I...Oh! Oh dear! It's raining quite heavily and I haven't a coat.'

Coralie peered through the curtains. 'Well, I wouldn't call it heavy rain, not yet anyway.'

Beyond the glass, a cold grey blur of drizzle clouded the air.

'Just like a shroud,' observed Beverley wistfully.

'Still, I'm afraid it's going to get worse,' muttered Coralie. 'There's a bank of black cloud building up over the far side of the creek. You'd best hurry home before it starts to pour. It's a pity Mark is not here to drive you back, but at least I've a warm, hooded cloak to lend you.'

'What about you? Aren't you coming? It's twenty to four already.'

'I'm afraid I'll be a little late today. I've a tray of gingerbread men in the oven, but I let the fire burn low while we were talking. They will need another quarter of an hour, so I'll follow in a while. Perhaps you would be kind enough to tell the children I'm on my way.'

'You'll be drenched if there's a downpour,' objected Beverley, as Mrs Emerson fetched a brown woollen cloak from the cupboard.

'I don't mind a shower of rain, and Miranda so loves gingerbread.'

'Oh, just as you please.' Beverley fastened the cloak and pulled up the hood. 'I detest damp weather. It always goes straight to my chest. Ah well, here I go.'

And with that she scurried off down the path, clutching the cloak about her as if it meant her very life.

★ ★ ★ ★

A few hundred yards away, where the track took a series of sharp bends through thick woods and undergrowth, Tabitha was growing wet, cold and very impatient. The trees had sheltered her at first, but by now a fine mist was filtering down through the canopy, the leaves had begun to drip and a spattering of heavier droplets was falling. Like Beverley, she had not expected it, and she huddled uncomfortably against the trunk of a tree while raindrops plopped annoyingly down her neck and off the peak of the corduroy cap.

She was almost sick with tension. Expectation and some degree of fear registered themselves in a tight little frown, her mouth pressed into a stubborn line of determination.

It would work, she told herself doggedly. And it was worth it. Worth anything. Think of the prize. Just think of him. All the more valued for costing so dear.

He would be upset, of course, for a while. And she would comfort him. He would need that, wouldn't he? Until he saw sense and realised his good fortune. She knew whom he really wanted. Loyalty had clouded his thinking, concluded Tabitha with all the clarity and wisdom of infatuation.

Never mind. She was about to rectify everything.

Clutching Marsden's rifle, she watched the path and waited, while the rain gathered into a hissing rush.

First came the light bumpety-bump of running footsteps and then, through the trees, weaving with the track, a little brown-cloaked figure.

Tabitha knew that cloak very well. Coralie wore it all the time. Like the rest of her clothes, it performed long, hard service.

They can bury her in it, too, thought Tabitha savagely as she lifted the rifle to her shoulder.

It was uncomfortably heavy. Her arms began to ache within seconds and the shining length of the barrel swayed before her eyes, since she lacked the strength to steady it for long. Cursing inwardly, she lowered it for an instant, took two deep breaths, then heaved it back to her shoulder. On several past occasions she had tried her luck at weekend shooting parties, always with William's help and guidance, his hands beneath the stock to take the weight. She had never hit anything, and all the men consoled and chuckled wisely about little ladies and great big guns, while the game made its escape.

This time, thought Tabitha grimly, she would not miss. Coralie, after all, was a large target at close range. Stumbling through the rain, head down, passing within twenty feet, she could hardly be easier to hit.

Tabitha's features knitted in a frown of concentration as she squinted along the barrel and remembered William's patient voice telling her not to jerk at the trigger. All it needed was a firm and gradual—squeeze.

There came a heart-stopping noise, accompanied by a slight jolt as the butt recoiled against her shoulder and...

The running figure crumpled and collapsed with a dull thud on the path, all the bright blonde hair spilling out on the wet earth as the hood fell back. Very pale, fine babylike hair. Beverley had always been proud of it.

Tabitha, who had never fainted in her life, felt for a moment that she would surely do so now. The world and her stomach heaved together, and her mouth sagged stupidly open in blank dismay as she dropped the rifle.

She should have realised, of course—the woman was not carrying a basket. Coralie always, always brought a basket of treats for the children. She had never been known to come empty-handed.

Beverley lay without moving. Where her cloak had fallen aside, a patch of sticky red could be seen at the centre of her bodice. Tabitha could not see the face, which was turned away from her, but she shrank from approaching her victim's body and using the second cartridge to ensure death, as she would have done had Coralie been lying there. Whether Beverley was dead or not, the plan was lost in confusion and Tabitha's nerve had gone.

She pressed a hand to her mouth and stared for a moment; then, her wits returning, she snatched up the gun and plunged headlong into the woods, running for dear life back to the little cottage as the rain kept pouring down.

★ ★ ★ ★

Once inside, she slammed the door closed and leaned against it, panting, for several minutes. The rain, torrential now, drummed upon the roof and whirled in gusts against the window panes. Raining failure and disaster, chaos both outside and in. Tabitha, her head spinning, closed her eyes and shed a few frustrated, frightened tears.

This, however, was no time for dawdling. Feverishly she began pulling off her wet clothing, till she stood at last in only her camisole and drawers, her feet bare upon the stone floor. She must she knew, look a fine shivering sight as she fitted the rifle hurriedly into the bottom of the trench and stuffed the trousers, shirt and waistcoat, together with the cap and boots, down beside it.

Tabitha paused and looked around her. That was everything—wasn't it? Gun, clothing, cartridges...Oh yes, the sacking and string. She snatched those from the table and threw them in on top.

It took no more than five minutes to shovel the dirt into the trench and drop the flagstone neatly back in its place. Despite the care she had taken, there were traces of freshly-dug earth visible around the edges, and several more minutes were spent in removing these. The spade and trowel were returned to the lean-to shed after a thorough rinse in the rain-butt, and when at last she replaced the dresser, Tabitha was satisfied no signs of disturbance remained.

Finally she struggled back into her own clothes—petticoats, dress, stockings, button boots. Her hair was damp despite the cap, and a few wisps had escaped from their pins, but this was hardly strange for a lady caught in a rainshower. She tucked and tidied them, then smoothed her dress. It, too, was faintly damp by now, as moisture seeped outward from her sodden underclothes. The effect, she thought, was helpful—as if she had spent a few minutes in the rain, instead of nearly an hour.

Outside, the cloudburst continued, so Tabitha

sat down, her heart still thumping, to start thinking up some lies.

She had not planned on such panic, counting on more time, not expecting rain, tricks of fate or simple misjudgement. She was thankful at least for the modicum of foresight which had prompted her to dig that hole before, and not after, the event.

She would have to say, of course, that she had been in the cottage since the rain became heavy and had seen no one. Perhaps then, please God, they would not bother to search it, or at least not thoroughly. The word of an important lady was a weighty thing—she hoped —though at that moment her soical position felt like scant protection. For the first time in her life, Tabitha was truly terrified.

CHAPTER 26

Only Christopher was at home when a sobbing Coralie arrived, breathlessly pounding on the door at Roskarnon, some twenty minutes after four o'clock. His shock and confusion were dreadful to see when he was abruptly fetched from the peace of his studies to hear that Mrs

Emerson had found his wife dead upon the path from Curleew Quay.

Pandemonium followed. William was out on business. No one knew where Mark might be found. And Mrs Kirkwood had gone for one of her walks, twittered Peggy. Alone and unprotected, with a lunatic at large.

A stable-boy was despatched to look for her. Another was sent to fetch the constable while Coralie, dripping wet and still crying, was consigned to the housekeeper's care.

Christopher took two manservants and followed Coralie's directions to the spot where he found the pathetic, soaking bundle lying under the trees.

He had never been passionately fond of Beverley, and after marriage the first gentle flush of affection had quickly subsided into kindly tolerance, nothing more. Conscience reproached him now. He should have tried harder, he thought, as he turned her over and looked on the sad, muddied face with a groan of guilt and pity. Remorse, as he already knew, was a dismal companion. It would shadow him for years to come.

★ ★ ★ ★

It was nearly five o'clock when Tabitha heard

running footsteps approaching the cottage. The rain had been easing for some little while and she was just summoning the courage to venture forth and face whatever was happening at Roskarnon. Much more composed by now, she had rehearsed her act most carefully.

Even so, she jumped when the door burst open and a breathless youth appeared.

'Good heavens, Albert, you're like a hurricane yourself! There is no need to...'

'Oh, Mrs Kirkwood, ma'am...' The boy had to stop, gulp for air, then start again. 'Thank the Lord I've found you. I've been looking everywhere...Something terrible's happened.'

'What do you mean—something terrible? For mercy's sake, calm down.'

'I'm to bring you home straight away.'

'It's still raining,' objected Tabitha, somewhat impatiently. 'Now, what is the matter?'

'I don't know how to tell you, ma'am, since it's one of your own. The poor little lady...'

Tabitha's face registered the appropriate anxiety.

'One of my own? Is someone ill? Stop dithering and tell me at once!'

'Somebody's killed her,' blurted the boy. 'Soaked in blood, Mrs Emerson says.'

Tabitha went white to hear it so announced.

'Are you talking about my daughter? My Miranda?'

As horrified whispers go, it was very good indeed.

'Oh no, no.' The boy shook his head emphatically. ' 'Tis Mrs Summerfield, the poor little soul.'

'Albert, surely there is a mistake?'

'No, ma'am, I'm afraid not.'

'But why should anyone wish to hurt Mrs Summerfield?'

'Some people,' said the stable-boy sagely, 'are just plain wicked. You've led a sheltered life among gentlefolk, ma'am, so you wouldn't know, but 'tis true for all that. I'm only glad I've found you safe and well.' He took off his old woollen jacket and offered it gallantly to Tabitha. 'Shall we be going then? They're all worried about you up at the house.'

★ ★ ★ ★

Tabitha found her brother in the drawing-room, nursing a brandy. He had just deposited Beverley upstairs upon the bed where she had spent so much time in life. Finding her there in the mud had been a double shock, since he had always expected her to die in her favourite place.

300

He perceived that Albert had told Tabitha the news. She looked waxen and was plainly most upset, agitation writ large upon her face.

'Oh, Christopher! What a dreadful, dreadful thing! I can hardly believe it.'

'Nor can I.' His shoulders slumped as he wearily topped up the brandy. 'Thank God you're safely home, at any rate.'

'Yes, well, I didn't get much chance to walk far, thanks to the weather. I took shelter in the little cottage when it started to rain, and that's where Albert found me. How did it come about, Christopher? Was it one of the keepers? I don't understand how it could happen. I've never known them take careless pot-shots, especially so close to the house.'

'You know who is responsible as well as I do. It's not a shotgun wound and our keepers don't carry rifles.'

He eyed her accusingly and for a moment Tabitha felt her insides turn over.

'I hear that William told you not to go out alone. You were warned this very morning, but you went anyway. There are times, Tabitha, when it's a good idea to listen to your husband and obey him.'

Tabitha, with vast relief, allowed herself to look as guilty as she felt.

'I thought he was just being silly.'

'Obviously he was not. Had it not been for the rain, sister, you might have encountered that character yourself. William has good cause to be very angry with you.'

'We've always had poachers on the estate,' said Tabitha defensively. 'And this is all speculation anyway. One should never draw hasty conclusions, no matter how things look.'

'None of the local people have firearms, and in view of Coralie's recent experience, I'd prefer to call it a reasonable assumption. Let's face the facts, we don't know who the man is or where he came from. It looks as though Beverley was right about him and not so silly after all. The Lord only knows what he may have done in the past.'

'But he didn't actually harm Coralie.'

'His reaction when she startled him was to turn that gun on her. Perhaps she was simply lucky—and poor Beverley just a little less so. Anyway, I've sent for the police, which is what we should have done long before now. We'll see what they have to say.'

Tabitha shivered uncomfortably, poured a dose of brandy for herself and sat down beside her brother.

'How are you feeling, Christopher? I wish there was something I could say to console you, but nothing ever seems adequate at such times.'

He gulped back his brandy and began slowly shaking his head. 'Guilty, Tabitha, that's how I feel. It seems almost like a judgement. I never had time for her, I didn't want to be bothered, so now she has been—taken. If I had been a little more attentive she wouldn't have gone running to Coralie for companionship at every opportunity. She might not have gone out today.'

'Christopher, you mustn't blame yourself. It wasn't your fault, merely a dreadful trick of chance. The victim could as easily have been anyone anywhere on the estate. You've just said that I'm lucky it wasn't me. It happened to be Beverley, but that doesn't mean you're being punished for neglect. You were never unkind to her.'

'No? I tired of her, though, didn't I? I married her on impulse and then lost all interest. I never took care of her in the way that William takes care of you. He's a good husband Tabitha. Appreciate him, be grateful.'

'I do, Christopher, and I am. I merely thought that he was being, well, worrisome.' She took a sip of her brandy and added: 'By the way, is anyone looking after Coralie?'

'She's been given some laudanum and put to bed.'

Tabitha, glancing from the window, spotted

a pair of constabulary gentlemen coming up the drive and fervently wished that someone would do the same for her. She was beginning to feel quite ill herself.

* * * *

The aftermath was a nightmare. Questions and statements and more questions, policemen with dogs combing the estate—indeed the whole county. Condolences poured in, along with visits from the morbidly curious. Numerous reports appeared in the local newspaper, mixing lurid descriptions of the murder with the pathos of Beverley's frailty. No one could talk of anything else and tenants in lonely cottages became very nervous indeed.

Nobody, however, was more frightened than Tabitha. Somehow she could not recapture the equanimity with which she had handled Edgar's demise. That particular venture, of course, had been an unqualified success. No doubt she could have borne all this uproar more stolidly, had she but killed the right person.

The funeral was held on the Saturday morning, with the Reverend Devoy officiating as Beverley had always said he would. Christopher hardly listened to the service. He was still chiding himself for having neglected her so. Far from finding solace in his hobby, he had begun to look upon it with loathing, repenting the devotion he had given it. Closing his ears to the clergyman's drone, Christopher scanned the circle of faces around him and saw that he was not suffering alone.

Coralie's eyes were red and swollen from crying, and William looked as if he, too, had shed a few quiet tears. Beside him, seeming more embarrassed than bereaved, was the balding, bespectacled man who was Beverley's father. There was Emerson, with the composure of one who so often saw death. And Tabitha, her features shadowed behind a black lace veil.

Christopher knew that his sister had never been at all fond of Beverley, and yet he gained the impression that the tragedy had affected her quite deeply. It was strange, somehow, and it bothered him. His glance slanted curiously at her across the open grave and suddenly, like a slide in a magic lantern show, there came a vivid recollection of Tabitha's face that night at Copperhill—and with it there stirred a dreadful idea. For a moment he suffered a certain disquiet at the knowledge that Beverley had been wearing that brown cloak—Coralie's cloak.

No. He pushed the thought away. The notion was preposterous and the implications for

305

his own negligence too much to contemplate. If such a thing were true, it would raise too many other questions. It could mean that he had given protection to a calculating menace from the day that Father died.

No, he repeated inwardly, one should never let a wild imagination get the upper hand. The facts were simple and spoke for themselves. Sooner or later the man would be caught and all would be well.

Some time later, as they were leaving the churchyard, Tabitha turned her foot against the kerb of a grave and sustained a badly twisted ankle. In considerable pain, she had to be carried back to the brougham by her husband and was confined to bed for several days afterwards.

To Tabitha, the injury was more than welcome. It removed her from the midst of the enquiries, gave her solitude in which to think, and allowed her to drop all the wearisome pretence.

It also meant visits from Mark.

She would watch him silently as he examined the puffy, bruised ankle, trying to absorb the feel of his hands, to be remembered later, imagined and lived on for a while. He always kept his head bent with determined interest over the injury, carefully strapping it up, his manner kind but slightly impersonal. Often she tried to engage him in chat, just to prolong his stay for a few more minutes, but he was always busy, always brief. Once, as the door closed behind him, she found tears of frustration rolling down her face. Tabitha had risked so much for the touch of those hands. She imagined how different things would have been if the ambush had only succeeded, and her soul writhed to think of the chance she had lost.

★ ★ ★ ★

As the weeks wore on, Tabitha became inclined to blame the wretched Beverley for the whole fiasco. If only she had not been such a tedious, complaining weakling. It was just as well, thought Tabitha sourly, that she had put her out of her misery once and for all, since Beverley always maintained that life was a burden.

Roskarnon's everyday routine had regained as much normality as might be expected in the circumstances, but the episode had naturally forced a few changes. Christopher abandoned his beloved astronomy and started to show a belated interest in local affairs. Tabitha, for some weeks, declined to go anywhere without William. He was always a comfort in times of trouble, and the fear from which she clung to him was perfectly genuine. Mark was more than glad to see Tabitha cleaving at last to her husband. He wished he could spend as much time with Coralie, but such was not possible, so he installed a vigilant Alsatian dog at the lodge to protect her whenever he was out.

Gradually, police and public attention were decreasing. Three men were arrested and then released again in the months leading up to Christmas, but the gypsy, to Tabitha's relief, was never found. She had viewed the prospect of his capture with awful trepidation. Coralie, after all, would know him on sight and confirm that he was indeed the poacher. To have the man hanged in her stead would test even Tabitha's nerve.

And there was yet a worse possibility—that the gypsy could prove his presence elsewhere that afternoon. Furthermore, there were rifles and rifles, she realised. That which the poacher carried was not necessarily of the same type as Uncle Marsden's. It might fire an entirely different type of bullet. If the man were found and such questions arose where she wondered, would suspicion turn then? Thus far, no distrustful eye had been cast upon the esteemed Kirkwood and Summerfield families, leading lights of the county, especially since none of them had any good reason for despatching a silly little woman like Beverley. But if the supposed culprit were suddenly vindicated, there would be much fresh interest and speculation. Tabitha did not care for that idea at all, so she fervently wished the gypsy Godspeed. In the cold aftermath of failure, without the comfort of blind optimism, she recognised how very poor her planning had been.

Attempts to find the man continued, and were destined to do so in lethargic fasion for some years to come. But after the initial fervour and the drawing of many blanks, the search became spasmodic. The investigation lapsed and was soon half forgotten, as old news and lost causes so often are. By the following spring it lay in limbo, and popular interest around this time was diverted to two new and much juicier crimes. The first was the sensational horror of Kate Webster and the boiled employer, the second a local rape—treats a-plenty for the ghoulish and the prurient.

Tabitha was mightily pleased to see the matter fall dormant, but she knew she could never consider it quite dead and therefore resolved to do nothing that might stir it up again.

In the end, of course, she was left with the same old problem—Coralie Emerson. As soon as the fright subsided, the obsession came sweeping back with renewed force and hardened determination. One could hardly give up after daring so much.

Mark was still the secret pivot of her life. He seemed to grow more golden each time she saw him, especially when Coralie was there, hanging on his arm, watching him with proud eyes. It gave him the lustre of a prize desperately sought, worth any dishonour in the winning.

Tabitha had not consoled herself with other men through these trying months. No one seemed adequate any more. There was just the affectionate William making a hopeful bid for another child now and then. It was not very often, for she used the excuse that Beverley's death had distressed her most terribly, that her nerves were upset by too many demands. William, true to form, did not press the matter.

The need for Emerson therefore became voracious as spring passed into summer. At dusk, dawn and all through the day she thought of nothing else. And at last, in August, there came news which propelled her into a new, though equally perilous, course of action.

CHAPTER 27

Tabitha encountered Mark Emerson in St Lowen one morning. She had just emerged from the milliner's and he from the chemist's shop. It was always the same when she met him unexpectedly, a nervous jolt to her insides and a rising of hope that this might be the start of some renewal.

He stopped to talk, always friendly now, for the awkwardness between them had lessened since Beverley's death, swept aside by the larger drama. He was no longer wary or distant, for he believed she had given up. A civilised friendship could be safely resumed, he thought. She was always amusing, and lovely to look at, a pleasure to admire at arm's length.

'Tabitha! How are you?'

'Well enough, thank you.' She dimpled and smiled up at him as they stood there on the pavement amid bustling shoppers. 'I see you've been buying supplies. Is Coralie in town today, or did you come alone? It occurs to me that I've not seen her for a while.'

'That's because she has been sick these last

few days. Happily sick, I might add—every morning this week.'

Tabitha's smiled sagged.

'Do you mean to say that she is expecting a child?'

'Yes, at long last. You know how she loves children. Naturally, she's overjoyed.'

Polite congratulations were all that Tabitha could manage.

'Of course. How exciting for her. You must be very proud, Mark. Do you think you will enjoy fatherhood? William does, as you know. He's such a sentimental old thing.'

They were flat, unsmiling remarks, expressing mere civility. There was no pleasure in them, but nor was there indifference and he could tell that his news was unwelcome.

'I confess that I'm quite looking forward to it,' he agreed cautiously. 'I see a great many children in the course of my work, so I've never felt deprived, but I suppose one's own offspring are bound to be special. It's Coralie, though, for whom I'm most pleased. She has everything she wants now.'

Everything—including you. It's not right, thought Tabitha miserably. Why should that drab little creature be happier than I?

Emerson saw with growing dismay that she was taking it badly, although he did not

312

altogether understand why. He had thought she accepted that the affair was decidely finished, baby or no baby. There was no reason why Coralie's pregnancy should make a difference. He could not know how forcibly it underlined the galling fact that his wife was alive and fruitfully healthy when she should have been long dead.

'Quite. Please be sure to pass on my congratulations. William will be delighted when I tell him. He and Christopher have both been so disconsolate, you know, since poor Beverley died.'

'So has Coralie. She used to brood about it all the time. There was a period when she kept dreaming about it and woke up crying night after night. Thank God that's over, anyway. The baby's taken her mind off everything else.'

'Naturally. No doubt it will create a cleansing wave of cheer in every quarter. Very timely, Mark. Well done.'

He could hear it now, the rancour, the bitterness, and it saddened him.

'I imagine you'll be thinking of getting a maid at last,' she went on, turning stiffly to matters practical. 'I've always wondered how Coralie managed alone, and children mean such a lot of extra work.'

'A maid, yes—and probably a larger house

before long. We've been happy at the lodge, but it's really only big enough for the two of us. We'll have to look around for something else.'

How disturbing to hear about his plans when they did not include her. This was not what Tabitha wanted at all. He was meant to be there always, just down that wooded pathway, alone and available as he had been on Ember Night. She did not want him to move, to change in any way, to become a family man with servants and perhaps new friends of his own. He was her lover and nothing else, to be isolated in a little circle of secrecy and passion which would never admit any other person. This notion of exclusive possession did not seem at all unreasonable to Tabitha, which indicated just how far she had fallen into fantasy.

'I'll have a word with William,' she said. 'There are one or two other houses on the estate which might be suitable. I'm sure there's no need for you to move into St Lowen. William's whole idea was to have you near at hand.'

It's time to be honest, he thought wearily. Why, oh why can she not just admit defeat?

'William's idea at the outset, but yours now.'

Tabitha flushed and stared back at him in silent confirmation.

'I thought we had dealt with all this,' he went

314

on quietly. 'I thought we had reached agreement. It doesn't matter where I live, Tabitha, because our little adventure has long been at an end. It would still be so if Coralie and I lived out the rest of our lives without children. The baby makes no difference, so it's pointless to resent it. It's not a matter of children cementing the union or any of that rubbish. Our marriage has always been a happy and secure one.'

'Outwardly, perhaps,' said Tabitha tartly, 'but you were quick enough to suspend loyalty when Coralie's back was turned. I saw the symptoms of discontent and I still...'

'No, Tabitha, you imagined them because it suited you to do so, and you seem to forget who initiated our liaison. I did not pursue you, madam. You were not coaxed down to the lodge that night, or cajoled into my bed.'

'Nor was I pushed out and sent home.'

'As you undoubtedly should have been,' he said evenly. 'Of course I took the opportunity, as any man would, but I've since been greatly sorry that I didn't have the willpower to throw you out.'

'As drunkards and gamblers are sorry each time, but sooner or later they always do the same again.'

'Not always, Tabitha. Furthermore, it's conceited of you to term yourself an addiction.'

'You, sir, are as weak-willed as any, given the right circumstances, and clearly you hate to be reminded of it.'

'If you are trying to goad me into a fight, Tabitha, you've chosen the wrong place for it. I'm not going to dispute with you here in the main street.'

All around them, people went about their business, never suspecting the content of that quiet conversation between two well known and respected persons outside the chemist's shop. Tabitha broke off and glanced up with an automatic smile and greeting for a passing gentleman who raised his hat, before turning to Mark with a counter-attack.

'I'm sure we can find somewhere more private,' she suggested sweetly, in the knowledge that a blazing quarrel could easily slide into something more physical, ending in bed or on the floor or anywhere else that would serve. She was not averse to exchanging a few slaps if such were needed to provoke him. It was a grand old game, the rougher the better, and she knew how well he would respond once the process began.

He knew it, too.

'Oh no, Tabitha. I learn from my mistakes.'

Exasperated, she was tempted to hit him anyway, there on the pavement, regardless of everyone—for was he not admitting that he still wanted her, did he not trust himself alone with her? Damn his conscience and his principles and his homely, pregnant wife. He was like a small boy staring covetously at a cake-stall but refusing to steal. It tried her patience beyond words. Tabitha, who had never denied herself anything, did not understand guilt. She could not imagine how wretched it felt.

'I don't know why I waste my time with you.' Her voice was edged with petulance.

'Nor do I, my dear. You'd best go home and spend it with your children instead.'

'You're a prig!'

'If you say so. Good day, Mrs Kirkwood.'

Seething at his sheer stubbornness, she watched for a few seconds as he walked off down the street. It was no longer simply a matter of infatuation. It was a contest now.

CHAPTER 28

Late afternoon found Tabitha seeking out a few old friends in the pages of *Wilmott's British Flora*. Here they all were: purple foxglove and golden rain, blue rocket and black bryony, henbane and thorn-apple, belladonna and hemlock. Death in all colours, with pretty flowers and bright berries to entice the unwary. Strange, too, how one would often counteract another, and how some could save life as well as take it. Poisons a-plenty, there for the picking and the digging. One did not have to sign a chemist's book for these.

But now, when she needed them once more, Tabitha dared not use them. Not after Beverley's demise. This time, circumstances did not conspire to help her. The police enquiries had set her nerves on edge and another strange death would be most untimely.

And yet she could not wait, could not stand by and let Emerson become locked ever more firmly into Coralie's ownership. He had to be retrieved somehow, by whatever coercion Tabitha might devise. It came to her suddenly that she had lost all pride over this entanglement. Desperation and lack of dignity were the hallmarks of a weak, besotted female, that breed upon whom she had always looked with such scorn. Now she recognised them in herself and knew that they had her quite firmly in their grip, that she was not immune after all, nor so very different from the rest of her sex.

Sighing, Tabitha closed the book, tucked it back in its place and scanned the shelves for something else, a fresh idea, anything to trigger a brainwave. It seemed to her that some of the mental agility she once possessed had disappeared. There had been a time when she could view a situation as a chess player sees the board; weighing the capabilities of each piece against every other and from all possible angles; summing up potential loss or gain, areas of weakness, opportunity and threat. She had seen these patterns clearly in all their dimensions, like the criss-crossed threads of a cat's cradle.

There was now a degree of confusion, a loss of concentration and clarity which often refused her any inspiration at all and reduced her powers of judgement in a most alarming way.

Moving on from shelf to shelf, Tabitha came upon some of her mother's old books. Mama's favourite novels—romances every one. Tales of love and loneliness, betrayal and retribution, severance and reunion. Fantasies, all of them, melting with sentimentality. Here she had taken refuge from the reality of Edgar and an awful marriage.

The old Tabitha, tough and worldly adolescent that she was, had flipped with scornful amusement through these pages and wondered how Mama could be so foolish.

The new Tabitha, desperate in the misery of rejection, glanced hesitantly over the rows of emotive titles and entertained the notion of reading one of these silly books. She examined three or four of them without much interest— and then her attention fixed upon one particular title.

The Poppied Sleep.

It was a phrase from one of Swinburne's poems. She recognised it instantly and lifted the book down from the shelf.

'I am changed by tribulation,' the narrative began, 'but stronger for it, too, and all has been restored to me at last.'

Tabitha turned a few more pages, faintly curious despite the overtones of melodrama which would normally annoy her. The book was quite short and written mostly in dialogue with only the briefest of paragraphs, so as not to tax the gentle reader's patience. Tabitha supposed it would help to pass the hours until dinner; perhaps a little diversion, however fanciful, would serve to refresh a tired mind. So she took the book upstairs to her bedroom, seated herself at the window and began to read.

★ ★ ★ ★

She had skipped over many pages, but not from boredom so much as impatience, a desire to know the outcome of the tale. There had come a point, quite early on, where it seized upon her mind, if only because of the growing emotional tumult so strongly resembling her own.

When Peggy came knocking at the door just on seven o'clock, ready to help Tabitha dress for dinner, she found her mistress staring absently out of the window and plainly deep in thought.

Tabitha had finished the book some ten minutes before and was musing with excitement on the manner in which the story was resolved. Alternately spurned and pursued by a somewhat capricious lover, the heroine had finally won his devotion by nearly dying of consumption. Repentant at the bedside, and vowing never again to abuse or take her for granted, he had come to heel in a manner most pleasing.

Tabitha thought it a very satisfactory ending. More than that, she saw a principle there with practical applications for her own dilemma. Since attacks upon his wife were now inadvisable, perhaps there was another way to reclaim Mark's attention.

What he needed, she decided, was a damned good shock.

Supposing she were to make a gesture of despair? A calculated bid to kill herself? Mark was the doctor, after all. He would be called to attend her, would he not? Just in time. She would arrange it so.

William need never know the truth of it. To him she could pass it off as a foolish accident. It would upset him, to be sure, but not nearly as badly as she meant to frighten Mark Emerson when she gave him the blame for her action, claiming he had made her wish to die. For a moment she fondly pictured his remorse, his consternation at seeing her lying limp and wan and close to death, all for his sake and thanks to his cruelty. The scene was so heart-rendering that it brought her close to tears and she made a mental note to order a special new nightgown for the occasion.

Of course, whispered that cold and hard-bitten corner of her mind where the old Tabitha still lived, it was possible that he might not respond in the manner desired. He had already proven himself obstinate and difficult to manage, but the beauty of this ploy was the fact that it could be repeated, with certain extra pressures added on.

If he did not repent and renew the affair, she could always threaten to do it again, promising a suicide note full of ruthlessly candid confessions. God help his marriage and his reputation then. At the very least it would cost him his peace of mind. If Tabitha had to be miserable, she would see that he was not happy either.

Self-destruction, or the threat of it, was, as she knew, a time-honoured ruse. Skilfully employed, it could be a most efficient means of control. Indeed, Tabitha was personally acquainted with a certain lady in St Lowen who brandished her imminent death like a loaded gun whenever husband or children showed signs of being difficult. The woman, as Tabitha had often remarked, was a hysteric, but her strategy worked and that was all that mattered —apart from the fact that there was nothing else left to try.

Mark, of course, would not be an easy man to fool, conditioned by his very profession to spot the malingerer, the seeker for sympathy and attention, knowing nearly as much of human nature as human anatomy. It was vital that he should be made to take her seriously and no half-hearted gesture would accomplish that. The attempt would have to be grave enough to convince him that she meant business, otherwise he would probably call Tabitha's bluff and leave her looking really very foolish.

Dangerous? Most certainly. A venture not to be undertaken without prior research and careful calculation. And so, next morning, Tabitha went back to the library, this time to study *The Modern Pharmacopoeia* and *The Evolution of Patent Medicines.*

★ ★ ★ ★

It was William who inadvertently set the date. He wanted to give a dinner party, in tacit celebration of Coralie's condition. Just a modest family occasion, a jolly little get-together for everyone to enjoy.

'Such a long time since the Emersons came to dinner,' he said. 'Wonderful to see new life and happiness after so much tragedy.'

Delightful, thought Tabitha, but this was going to be her night and Coralie would not be the centre of attention for long.

She gave no thought to her husband or her children when she sat down at the dressing-table that afternoon, preparing for the great gamble. She meant to look her sweet, alluring best, as all dying heroines should—especially when the hero is scheduled to snatch them from the reaper's clutches in the very nick of time.

She had bathed at two o'clock and then retired to her room—for a nap, she told her maid. She wished to be fresh for the evening's festivities. Well, there was nothing unusual in that.

Alone in the bedroom, she stripped and sat

down before the mirror, trimming the oval, shell-pink nails, dabbing her face with rose-water and reflecting with pride that her body was still firm and neat despite the bearing of two children. She wondered derisively if Coralie would fare as well after her confinement.

Tabitha unpinned the coiling, waist-length hair and brushed it till it shone. Then, going to the chest of drawers, she brought out a nightdress of plain white silk with a mere trimming of lace.

It was most appealing, she thought, studying herself in the glass. Very virginal. She would make a touching sight.

Carefully she arranged the kiss curls around her temples and smoothed the little peaks of her eyebrows with a steady finger. Tabitha was twenty-four years old and full of life; life which she did not mean to throw away.

Dinner was planned for eight o'clock and the maid would come at seven to help her dress. This was part of the household routine, regular as dawn and dusk. She needed no special arrangements to ensure that she was found in time. The trick, as she knew, lay in measuring the dose. It would have to be judged to a nicety.

With a kind of apprehensive thrill, she opened the top drawer of her dressing-table and took out a brown fluted glass bottle. It bore a label depicting a smiling young woman, clutching a bunch of poppies in one hand and a glass of the wonderful potion in the other. The wording promised sound sleep and serenity.

Tabitha next took a goblet and poured in a measure of port wine, filling it to just over one third. Tilting the brown bottle cautiously over the rim of the glass, she allowed a single drop of dark liquid to fall into the wine—then another, and another. Slowly, deliberately, she began to count as the little shining beads of fluid picked up a regular rhythm, second by second, one by one, plopping and dissolving into the wine.

She paused as she reached fifteen—the maximum safe dose. From here on they would cease to be benign, turning against her, each one stealing another little portion of life. But not all of it, of course, thought Tabitha confidently. Nothing she could not regain when the doctor came. All would be restored, her life and his attentions.

Stolidly she continued, watching the droplets roll slowly from the neck of the bottle, each suspended for an instant, forming a little ball, then plunging into the ever more potent mixture below. Twenty, twenty one, twenty two... On she went, and on, lost in concentration. It would never do to miscount.

At last she stopped. There—that was it. She had gone to the limit. Too dangerous by far to add any more. Tabitha gently swirled the mixture in the glass. It was now three-quarters full.

Getting up, she took the brown fluted bottle and placed it prominently on the table by the bed. It was most important that Emerson should know what she had taken.

She looked at the clock and it said twenty-five past three. The time appeared to be right.

Quietly she unlocked the door to ensure that the maid could get in. The house was silent, peaceful as always in the afternoons, and she smiled to think of the panic she would cause later on.

Picking up the goblet, she climbed into bed and sat for a moment, propped against her pillows, waiting for the last nervous shreds of hesitation to leave her. She hoped the port was sweet enough to obscure any other taste. Tabitha had always disliked conventional and patent medicines, avoiding them whenever possible. She had never found much use for them until now.

Suddenly, with swift decision, she lifted the glass and swallowed back the contents in three determined gulps. There was a faintly unpleasant flavour and the port brought a momentary heat to her stomach, but that was all. The slightly chemical after-taste soon disappeared and she lay down, arranging her pillows comfortably, to wait.

The drowsiness came very fast, closing out the afternoon sunlight and the pretty, pale blue walls, the crisp lace curtains and green summer garden beyond. For a while her fingertips still felt the cool satin of the bedspread and she distantly caught the ticking of the clock. But soon even these sensations were gone, and that was when the dreams came.

They were such lovely dreams; vivid with detail, brilliant with colour, bringing what she wanted most. As bright and warm and loving as a drugged imagination could make him. It was better than reality. There were no such people as William and Coralie here. For as long as it lasted, the fantasy was perfectly fulfulled.

The sunlight was turning to the darker gold of early evening by the time she slid from bliss into limbo and from there into death.

★ ★ ★ ★

The maid, as it happened, came before seven, for Mark and Coralie were already downstairs and William had sent her to hurry his wife in her dressing. But Emerson's early arrival made not the slighest difference. By the time she was found, Tabitha had already been dead for forty minutes.

Once again she had miscalculated, and yet again the blunder involved her sister-in-law.

If there were truly some other plane from which the dead watch the living, Beverley would have laughed to see Tabitha take the brown glass bottle from Christopher's room. Another of Beverley's experiments, that bottle contained quite a powerful cocktail of drugs which belied its simple label, making nonsense of Tabitha's careful study and calculations. It was the only one of Beverley's concoctions ever to prove itself effective, although not in any curative capacity. Indeed, Beverley had sampled the brew herself and was disappointed as ever, but even she would never have contemplated taking such a very large dose, or for such a purpose.

CHAPTER 29

A tragic mishap or a wicked gesture? Christopher wondered afterwards. It was difficult to be sure. He expressed no doubt to anyone else, however, taking thought for the feelings of those who were left.

Yes, of course it was an accident, he maintained stolidly. Why on earth should Tabitha want to kill herself? Had she left a farewell note? No, nothing. Was she not in a cheerful frame of mind that afternoon and looking forward to the dinner party? Peggy confirmed that she was. Did she not have everything a woman could want—youth, health, money, beauty, a husband who adored her? Indeed she did.

Yes, he said, it was Beverley's medicine. He had meant to get rid of it all months ago, but somehow he had not yet found the heart to go through her belongings and clear them out. His wife had been a hypochondriac, of course, and God only knew what other elixirs and patent rubbish she had hoarded over the years, poring over her bottles and pill-boxes day by day like some wistful alchemist.

That was what he said—to the grieving William to ease his sorrow; to the now familiar constables to satisfy the interest of the law; to the horrified Emerson to spare him self-reproach and avert any agonised confessions to Coralie.

In his own mind, however, there could be no certainty. He was left with a grim conundrum that would puzzle him all his life.

He had guessed from the night of the Copperhill ball that his sister nursed a singular dislike for Coralie Emerson. In view of the relationship between Mark and Tabitha, it was easy enough to imagine why. He had seen a dreadful malice on her face that night and he sometimes entertained the notion that Coralie's brown cloak had made a target of poor Beverley that Tuesday afternoon.

But always, in the end, he pushed the idea away from him, because the simple, obvious explanation of the poacher was so much more palatable. All the same, there persisted a stubborn doubt which would never allow him to accept it wholeheartedly.

Sometimes, as he turned the matter over in his head, he would find himself repeatedly coming back to the question of guns, as if something important were trying to surface. And then, one Saturday morning some two months after Tabitha's death, he realised what it was.

Uncle Marsden's rifle. He had not thought of it in years, since guns were a matter of no interest to him, but as his thoughts dwelt upon the subject he suddenly noticed its absence.

Where was it, he wondered? Did it not once hang above the fireplace in Father's old study, in the days before Tabitha rearranged the house?

That afternoon, Christopher went through all the attics, seeking the long-forgotten weapon. He then searched the house from top to bottom, every cellar and outbuilding, but nothing came to light. He enquired of William, in a round-about way, if Tabitha had ever sold or given away any of Edgar's old belongings. Kirkwood quite truthfully replied that he did not know, and there Christopher reached a dead end.

It was missing. That was all he knew for sure, and its absence proved absolutely nothing. It simply left another question mark over Tabitha's life and death, and Christopher chose to preserve that comforting element of doubt.

These, then, were the two conflicting stories with which he learned to live. For his peace of mind he chose the simpler one more often than not. A necessary illusion, it would always rush to his aid whenever he was threatened by that other, darker version.

The publishers hope that this book has given you enjoyable reading. Large Print Books are especially designed to be as easy to see and hold as possible. If you wish a complete list of our books, please ask at your local library or write directly to: Magna Print Books, Long Preston, North Yorkshire, BD23 4ND England.